——The world is all yours.——

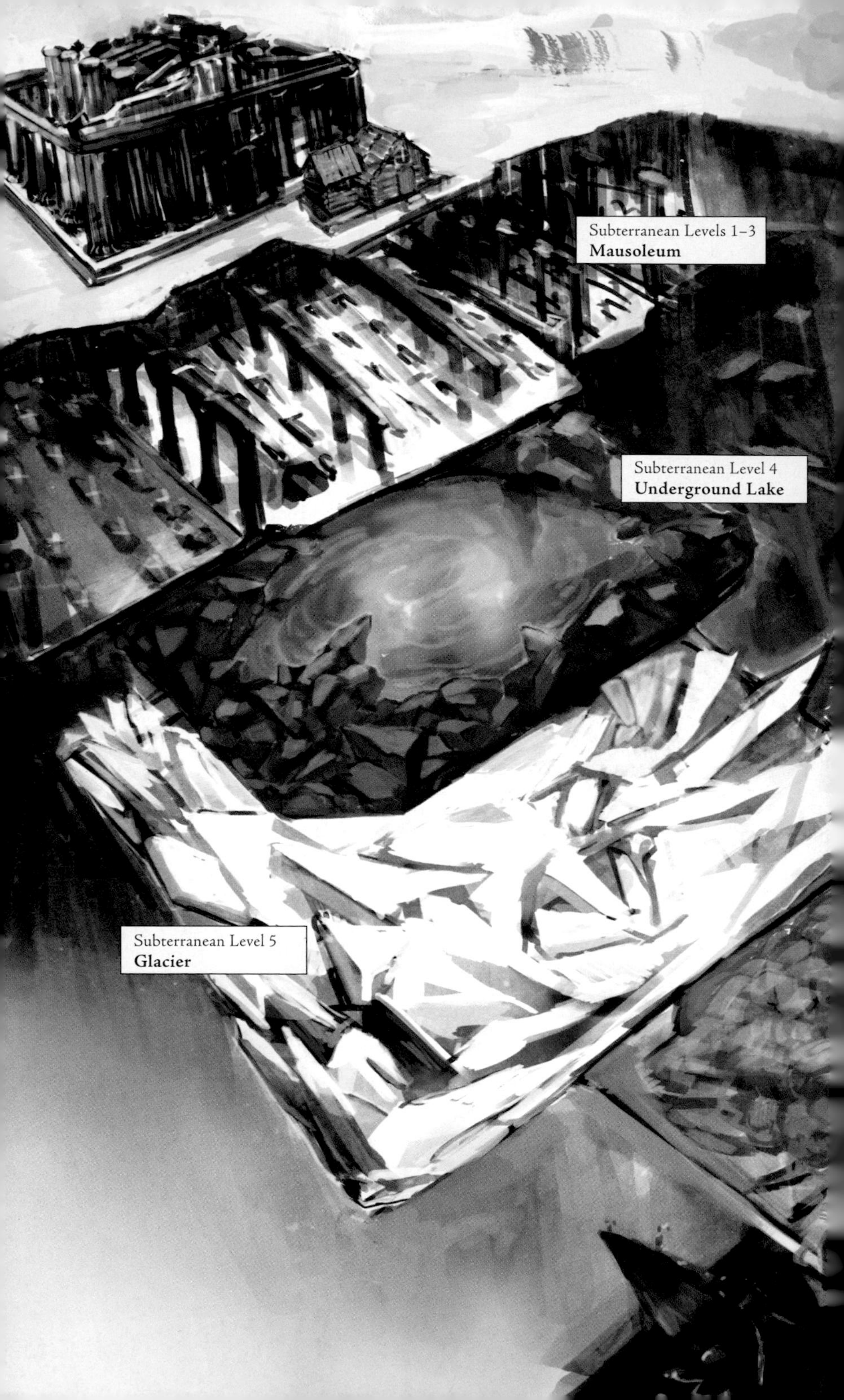
Subterranean Levels 1–3
Mausoleum
Subterranean Level 4
Underground Lake
Subterranean Level 5
Glacier

OVERLORD

Volume 1: The Undead King

Kugane Maruyama | Illustration by so-bin

NEW YORK

OVERLORD

VOLUME 1

KUGANE MARUYAMA

Translation by Emily Balistrieri

First published in Japan in 2012 by KADOKAWA CORPORATION ENTERBRAIN. English translation rights arranged with KADOKAWA CORPORATION ENTERBRAIN, through Tuttle-Mori Agency, Inc., Tokyo.

Yen On
1290 Avenue of the Americas
New York, NY 10104
www.yenpress.com

Yen On is an imprint of Yen Press, LLC.
The Yen On name and logo are trademarks of Yen Press, LLC.

First Yen On Edition: May 2016

Library of Congress Cataloging-in-Publication Data

Names: Maruyama, Kugane, author. | so-bin, illustrator. | Balistrieri, Emily, translator.
Title: Overlord / Kugane Maruyama ; illustration by so-bin ; translation by Emily Balistrieri.
Other titles: Ōbārōdo. English
Description: First Yen On edition. | New York, NY : Yen On, 2016-
Identifiers: LCCN 2016000142 | ISBN 9780316272247 (v. 1 : hardback)
Subjects: LCSH: Alternate reality games—Fiction. | Internet games—Fiction. | Science fiction. |
BISAC: FICTION / Science Fiction / Adventure.
Classification: LCC PL873.A37 O2313 2016 | DDC 895.63/6—dc23 LC record available at
http://lccn.loc.gov/2016000142

13

LSC-C

Printed in the United States of America

Contents

Prologue — 001

Chapter 1 — The End and the Beginning — 007

Chapter 2 — The Floor Guardians — 049

Chapter 3 — The Battle of Carne Village — 107

Chapter 4 — A Duel — 159

Chapter 5 — The Ruler of Death — 203

Epilogue — 229

Character Profiles — 239

Afterword — 245

OVERLORD

Prologue

Before one girl and another even younger one stood a figure in full plate armor brandishing a sword.

The blade swung, sparkling in the sunlight as if to say that taking their lives in a single stroke would be an act of mercy.

The girl shut her eyes. She didn't want to be biting her lower lip. She just had no choice but to accept what was about to happen. If she had even a little power, she probably would have been able to shove the figure away and escape...

But she was powerless.

And so there was only one ending.

She would die.

The blade came down—

...The pain still hadn't come.

She unscrunched her eyes.

The first thing she saw was the sword, stopped mid-swing.

The next was the figure holding the sword. The knight was practically frozen, looking at something off to her side. His unprotected stance manifested his internal shock.

The girl turned to follow his line of sight...

* * *

...and saw despair.

It was darkness.

A patch of raven black, ultrathin but so deep it seemed as if it went on forever. It was an oval rising up out of the ground, its bottom half cut off. It was a curious sight, but at the same time, it made her feel indescribably uneasy.

A door? was what came to mind when she looked at it.

A heartbeat later, she would be proven correct.

Something glided out of the darkness. And when she saw what it was—"Eegh!"—a dry shriek escaped her lips.

A human would have no chance against this being.

Hazy red light flickered flame-like in the vacant orbs of a bleached-white skull. The gaze was trained unfeelingly on the girls as if they were live prey. Skinless, fleshless hands, both sublime and terrible, clutched a staff so gorgeous it seemed to be the concentration of all the world's beauty.

It was as if Death had donned an intricately ornamented raven-black robe and been born into this world from another along with the darkness.

The air instantly froze.

At the entrance of the Absolute even time seemed to stop.

As though her soul had been taken, the girl forgot to breathe.

With no sense of time, inhaling was difficult, and she nauseously gulped for air.

A messenger from beyond has come to lure us away. But that didn't seem right. The knight behind them had frozen as well.

"Ngah..." She heard an exhalation that could not even be called a scream, but whether it had been her, her trembling little sister, or the knight with the sword before them, she didn't know.

Death's fingers—of which only the bones, picked clean, were left—stretched out slowly and then violently snatched at, not the girls, but the knight.

She wanted to look away, but she was too scared. She had the feeling that if she looked away, the monster would transform into something even more horrible.

"Grasp Heart."

Death incarnate made a clenching motion, and metal clanged noisily next to the girl.

She was scared to take her eyes off Death, but she lost to the tiny bit of curiosity still dwelling inside her and looked at the knight lying facedown on the ground. He wasn't moving.

He was dead.

Yes, dead.

The danger threatening to take her life had evaporated in a laughably simple way, but she couldn't celebrate. Death had only assumed a more concentrated form.

Sensing the fear in her gaze with its entire body, Death moved toward her.

The darkness that had been contained within her field of vision began to expand.

It's going to swallow us up.

She hugged her sister close.

The idea of running away didn't even occur to her anymore.

If her opponent had been a human, she might have been able to act on the faint hope of "maybe," but the being before her dashed that hope as if it were nothing.

Please let it not hurt, at least...

That was the most she could hope for now.

Her little sister clung to her waist, shaking with fear. She wanted to save her, but she couldn't. All she could do was apologize for her powerlessness and pray that they would die together so she wouldn't be lonely.

And then...

Chapter 1 The End and the Beginning

Chapter 1 | The End and the Beginning

1

In the year 2138, there exists something called a "DMMO-RPG."

This stands for "Dive Massively Multiplayer Online Role-Playing Game." While connected via an intracranial nanocomputer network called a "neuro-nano interface," which combines the best of cyber- and nanotechnology, players experience physical sensations as if they were really inhabiting an imaginary world.

In other words, you play as if you're actually in the world of the game.

And among all the various DMMO-RPGs that had been developed, one stood above the rest.

Yggdrasil.

It had been released twelve years earlier, in 2126, by a Japanese developer who had been waiting for just the right moment.

Compared to other DMMO-RPGs at the time, *Yggdrasil* gave players an incredible amount of freedom.

For example, consider the class system, a fundamental element of character customization. Counting the advanced classes as well as the base ones, there were well over two thousand. Since each class had only 15 levels, players could have seven or more classes by the time they hit the overall level cap of 100. As long as they met the basic requirements, they could dabble as they pleased. Though it would be inefficient, a player could acquire one hundred classes at level 1 if they wanted to. In other words, the system was such that, unless they were deliberately created that way, no two characters would ever be the same.

Then, by using the creator's tool kit—sold separately—players could edit the appearance of their weapons and armor, as well as the advanced settings of their in-game residences.

The environment awaiting players who ventured into this world was enormous. In fact, there were nine worlds: Asgard, Alfheim, Vanaheim, Nidavellir, Midgard, Jotunheim, Niflheim, Helheim, and Muspelheim.

A vast world, a staggering number of classes, and graphics that could be tweaked to one's heart's content—it was precisely the amount of customization that poured nitroglycerin onto the Japanese creative spirit and led to the game's explosive popularity. It got to the point where in Japan the word *DMMO-RPG* was practically synonymous with *Yggdrasil*.

But that was all in the past now…

•

In the center of the room, a gigantic circular table shone with an obsidian gleam. Around it were forty-one magnificent seats.

Most of them, however, were empty.

Once, all the seats had been filled, but now only two figures remained.

One wore an extravagant raven-black academic robe with purple and gold trim. The collar was perhaps a bit overembellished, but strangely, it suited the wearer.

The bare head of the figure in question had neither skin nor flesh—just bone. Reddish-black flames burned in his gaping eye sockets, and something like a black halo shone behind him.

The other one wasn't human, either. More of an amorphous black blob, almost like coal tar. His constantly shifting surface meant that he had no fixed shape.

The former was an elder lich—an undead being that was what remained of a caster who had pursued magic ability to its extreme—and the most elite type: an overlord. The latter was an elder black ooze, which was a slime race that had some of the most powerful acid abilities in the game.

Both races occasionally appeared as monsters in the most difficult dungeons. The various types of overlords used the highest-level evil magic while the elder black ooze had the ability to corrode weapons and armor, so both were famously hated.

But these two weren't monsters.

They were players.

The races players could choose from in *Yggdrasil* were split into three main categories: basic humanoid races (humans, dwarves, elves, and so on); subhuman races, who weren't pretty but performed better than humanoids (goblins, orcs, ogres, etc.); and grotesques, who had monster powers and got more ability points than other races but were penalized in other ways. Including all the elite races, there was a total of seven hundred at the users' disposal.

Naturally, overlords and elder black oozes were two of the elite grotesque races that players could become.

The overlord spoke without moving his mouth. Even for what had once been the pinnacle of DMMO-RPGs, it had still been impossible to animate expressions to align with conversation.

"It's been a really long time, HeroHero. Even though it's the last day *Yggdrasil*'s servers are open, I didn't think you would actually come."

"For real—long time no see, Momonga," another adult male voice answered, but compared to the first, it sounded pretty lifeless.

"It's been since you changed jobs IRL, so…how long ago was that? Two years?"

"Mm, yeah, about that. Geez, it's been that long.…Damn. My sense of time is messed up from working so much overtime."

"Sounds rough. Are you doing okay?"

"My health? It's pretty much in tatters. Not doctor-visit level, but pretty close. Ugh. I really wanna just run away from it all. But I gotta eat, so I'm working my ass off and getting whipped like a slave."

"Yikes..." The overlord Momonga leaned back to exaggerate his wince—this conversation was kind of killing the mood.

"It's seriously awful."

Momonga was already put off, but HeroHero's follow-up sounded exactly as awful as he said things were.

Their gripes about their jobs in reality gathered steam: how their subordinates had no communication skills, how the spec documents were liable to change from one day to the next, how their bosses would grill them if they didn't meet their quotas, how they could barely ever go home because there was too much work, their abnormal weight gain caused by the crazy hours they kept, the increasing number of pills they took.

At some point, it was like a dam broke inside HeroHero, and Momonga shifted to a listening role as the complaints flooded out.

Talking about one's real life in a fantasy world was frowned on by many. "Please keep your reality out of my daydream" was certainly an understandable sentiment, but these two didn't feel that way.

There were two requirements that all the members of their guild, Ainz Ooal Gown, had to meet. One was that members had to be working adults, and the other was that they had to play grotesques.

Since that's the type of guild it was, real-life work woes were a common topic of discussion, which was fine with the members. The conversation these two were having was an everyday occurrence in Ainz Ooal Gown.

Enough time had passed that HeroHero's muddy flood of grievances had calmed to a clear stream. "Sorry, I don't mean to just whine. But I can't really talk about this stuff IRL, you know?" A part of him that must have been his head wiggled.

Momonga took it as a bow of apology and said, "Don't worry about it, HeroHero. You accepted my invitation to come tonight even though you're exhausted, so listening to some complaints is the least I can do—I'll take as many as you've got."

HeroHero seemed a bit livelier than before and gave a weak chuckle. "Really, though, thank you, Momonga. I'm glad I was able to log in today and see you after so long."

"It makes *me* glad to hear you say that!"

"But I should probably get going soon..." HeroHero's tentacles began moving in midair. He'd opened his menu. "Yeah, it's getting late. Sorry, Momonga..."

Momonga paused for a breath so as not to betray his emotions. "Ah, that's too bad. Time really does fly when you're having fun..."

"I really wanted to stay till the end, but I'm just too tired..."

"Yeah, I can imagine. Log out and rest up."

"I'm really sorry... Momonga—err, no—Guild Master, what are your plans?"

"I'll think I'll hang around until the forced log out when the servers shut down. There's still some time left, so there's a chance someone else might show up."

"I see... Honestly, I was surprised this place still even existed!"

Times like this, Momonga was truly grateful that their expressions were fixed. Otherwise, his grimace would have been immediately apparent. In any case, his emotions would have been evident in his voice, so he had to keep his mouth shut to suppress them.

Hearing something like that from a guildmate after having worked so hard to maintain their base precisely *because* it was a place they had all built together elicited feelings in Momonga too mixed to explain. But those feelings vanished when he heard what HeroHero said next.

"As the guild master, you kept it going so we could come back anytime, didn't you? I really appreciate that."

"Well, we all built it together, you know? Making sure members can come back anytime is the guild master's job!"

"I think having you as our guild master was what made this game so fun for us. I hope to see you again...in *Yggdrasil II*!"

"I haven't heard any rumors about a sequel...but yeah, I hope so, too."

"If it happens, let's definitely play together! Anyhow, I'm falling asleep here, so I'm gonna log off. I'm glad I got to see you at the end like this. It's been great playing with you."

"..." Momonga choked up for just a moment. Then he managed his final good-bye. "I'm glad I got to see you, too. Nice playing with you."

Ba-ding! A smiley emoticon appeared over HeroHero's head. In *Yggdrasil,* expressions didn't change, so players used emoticons when they wanted to convey emotions.

Momonga opened his menu and picked the same emoticon.

HeroHero got the last word in. "See you again somewhere."

With that, the last of the three other guild members who had made the farewell gathering disappeared.

Silence returned to the room, a silence so deep it was hard to imagine anyone had been there. No echoes, no vestiges of anyone's presence.

Looking at the chair where HeroHero had been sitting until a moment before, Momonga murmured the words he'd suppressed. "I know you're tired, but it's the last day—the servers are shutting down. Won't you stay until the end?"

Of course, there was no reply. HeroHero was already back in the real world.

Momonga heaved a sigh from the bottom of his heart.

There was no way he could have said that.

It had been evident from their short conversation and the tone of HeroHero's voice how extremely tired he'd been. A guy that exhausted had read the e-mail Momonga had sent and came out for the last day. That was more than enough to be thankful for. Any further requests would have overstepped the bounds of nostalgia and just made Momonga into a nuisance.

Momonga stared at HeroHero's empty chair and then shifted his gaze. There were thirty-nine other chairs. The places where his guildmates used to sit. He looked around at all of them before coming back to HeroHero's seat.

"'See you again somewhere'...?"

See you again sometime.

See you later.

He'd heard those words many times. But they almost never came true. Nobody ever returned to *Yggdrasil*.

"Where and when exactly are we going to meet, huh?" Momonga's shoulders shuddered violently, and the true feelings that had been building up all this time suddenly gushed out. "Don't fuck with me!" he roared, pounding the table with both fists.

The game's system registered his motion as an attack and began computing countless parameters, such as his unarmed attack strength and the table's defense stats. The result appeared above the place where his hands had struck: "0."

"This is the Great Tomb of Nazarick! We built it together! How can you all abandon it so easily?" After the intense anger came loneliness. "No…I know that's not right. I know it wasn't easy at all. They were just forced to choose between reality and a daydream. It's not something they could help. No one betrayed us at all. It was a hard decision for everybody…," Momonga muttered to himself as he stood up. In the direction he faced, a staff hung on the wall.

It was based on the god Hermes's staff, caduceus, and consisted of seven intertwined snakes. Each writhing snake held a different-colored jewel in its mouth. The grip was made of a transparent crystalline material that gave off a pale glow. Anyone who saw it would know it was a top-tier item—it was a Guild Weapon, so named because each guild could have only one. This staff was the symbol of Ainz Ooal Gown.

It was meant to be wielded by the guild master, so why was it on display here?

Precisely *because* it was the symbol of the guild.

If the Guild Weapon were destroyed, it would mean the collapse of the guild. So, in most cases, a Guild Weapon was stored in a safe place, its mighty powers untested. Even the weapon of a top guild like Ainz Ooal Gown was no exception.

That was why even though the staff was made for Momonga, he had never once held it.

He reached his hand out and then stopped himself. Did he really want to taint the glorious memory of all they had built together now, at this moment before the servers shut down?

He recalled the days when the guild members had gone questing together to craft the Guild Weapon. They had split into teams and competed to see who could collect the most resources, argued about what the design should be, summarized the opinions each member brought to the table, and built it up piece by piece.

Those were the glory days of Ainz Ooal Gown.

There were people who were tired from work but forced themselves to show up anyway. There were people who slacked on their family obligations and got into huge fights with their wives. There were people who laughed and said they took a sick day.

Sometimes they'd wasted the whole day just chatting. They'd get so excited about the silliest things. They'd plan quests and hunt for treasure like there was no tomorrow. Once they mounted a sneak attack on a castle that was an enemy guild's base and stormed right in. Once they were nearly annihilated by one of the strongest secret monsters in the game, known as World Enemies. They'd discovered some previously undiscovered resources. They'd positioned all kinds of monsters in their base to take care of any intruders.

But now there was no one left.

Out of forty-one players, thirty-seven had quit. The other three had remained members in name, but Momonga couldn't remember the last time they had come before today.

Momonga opened the menu to access official data and looked at the guild ranking. Now there were slightly fewer than eight hundred guilds. Once they had been ranked ninth, but they had fallen to twenty-ninth. *This is our rank on the last day, huh?* The lowest they'd ever been was forty-eighth.

That they had only slipped that far was not thanks to Momonga's efforts, but to the items left by former guildmates—what remained of the guild's former glory.

It was a wreck now, but it had had its heyday.

And the fruit of that period was their Guild Weapon, the Staff of Ainz Ooal Gown.

Momonga didn't want to tarnish the memories harbored there, but a rebellious feeling also smoldered within him.

Ainz Ooal Gown valued majority rule. Although Momonga's title was guild master, the duties he performed were mostly routine, often communications-type tasks.

Maybe that's why now that no one was left, he thought for the first time that he'd like to try claiming a guild master's rights.

"Well, I can't do it looking like this," he muttered and went into the menu. He would equip himself in a manner befitting the master of a top guild.

The gear in *Yggdrasil* was classified by how much data it contained. The more data, the better the item. Players started off with low-tier gear, then medium-tier, upper-tier, superior-tier, legacy, relic, legend, and finally god-tier, the highest possible.

Nine rings, each with their own power, adorned Momonga's ten finger bones. His necklace, gauntlets, boots, cape, cloak, and circlet were all god-tier. From a monetary point of view, each item was an astonishingly rare and valuable treasure. The splendid robe mentioned previously hung from his shoulders.

A reddish-black aura shimmered up from beneath his feet, giving him an ominous, evil appearance. But he wasn't using a skill—the robe data had room, so he had just plugged in an "ominous aura" effect. It wasn't like anything would happen if someone touched it.

Out of the corner of his eye, Momonga saw various numbers pop up to indicate his stat increases. Having fully equipped himself, he nodded in satisfaction. Now he looked like a guild master. Then, he reached out and grasped the Staff of Ainz Ooal Gown.

The moment it was in his hands it began radiating a shimmering, dark red aura. Anguished human faces would occasionally form, warp, and dissipate, seemingly so real one could almost hear their tortured cries.

"...Maybe we went a little overboard."

Finally, on the last day the servers were running, this elite staff was in the hands of its rightful owner. While confirming the icons indicating his dramatic stat boosts, he still felt lonely.

"Well, symbol of the guild, shall we see what you can do? Or should I say 'symbol of *my* guild.'"

2

Momonga left the room they called the Round Table.

Unless they specified a different location, anyone with a guild member ring would appear there when they logged in. If anyone was coming back today, they would be standing by in that room. But Momonga understood that there was practically no chance of any other guild members making an appearance—that he was the only player left who wanted to spend the final moments of the game in the Great Tomb of Nazarick.

Suppressing the surging waves of his emotions, Momonga walked silently through his palace.

It was a majestic, ornate world reminiscent of Neuschwanstein Castle.

Chandeliers hung at regular intervals, shining warm light from the high ceilings. The polished floor of the wide hallway reflected the light as marble would, gleaming as if it were full of stars. Upon opening any of the doors to the right or left, the grandeur of the furnishings inside would take one's breath away. If any nonmember came here, they'd be amazed—amazed that such luxury could exist in this legendary place, the notorious Great Tomb of Nazarick, where the largest army in the game's history (an alliance of eight guilds, plus other affiliated guilds, mercenary players, mercenary non-player characters (NPCs), and so on, for a total of 1,500 men) had once arrived on a punitive expedition only to be completely wiped out.

The Great Tomb of Nazarick was originally constructed with six levels, but after Ainz Ooal Gown conquered it, it was dramatically transformed.

At present, there were ten underground levels, each with its own [illegible] features. Levels one through three made up the grave. The fourth was an underground lake. Five was a glacier. Six was a jungle. Seven was lava. Eight was wilderness. Nine and ten were a shrine. This was the headquarters of a guild that broke the top ten back in an era when there were thousands, the guild of Ainz Ooal Gown.

What better word for this world than *divine?* Momonga's footsteps echoed throughout the halls accompanied by the hard *clack* of his staff on the floor. After walking a ways down the wide corridor and turning a number of corners, he saw a woman coming toward him from up ahead.

She was gorgeous, with abundant blond hair falling around her shoulders and distinctive facial features. Her clothing was a maid uniform with a broad apron and a long, unobtrusive skirt. She stood about five feet, seven inches tall and had long, delicate limbs. Ample twin swells asserted themselves by straining against the chest of her outfit, but the overall impression she made was one of modesty.

Soon the gap between them had closed; the woman moved into a nook and bowed deeply to Momonga.

He responded with a small wave.

Her expression didn't change. There was such a slight hint of a smile that it was difficult to tell if it was there or not, just as before. In *Yggdrasil,* expressions never changed, but in her case, the implication was a little different.

This maid was an NPC, a "nonplayer character." She was not controlled by a human but moved on her own according to her AI—a program. Basically, she was a walking mannequin. No matter how sophisticated she was or how politely she bowed, it was all just according to her programming.

Momonga's response might have seemed a foolish way to treat a mannequin, but there was a reason he wanted to show some consideration.

The forty-one NPC maids working in the Great Tomb of Nazarick were all based on custom drawings. The artist was a guild member who made his living as an illustrator and who was now serialized in a monthly manga magazine.

Momonga gazed fixedly at the maid. He was looking at the girl certainly but mainly her outfit. It was surprisingly detailed. The meticulous embroidery on the apron was especially impressive. But how could he expect anything less when the artist was a guy who said, "A maid's uniform is a battle-deciding weapon!"? Momonga fondly recalled the graphics producer's screams.

"Ahh, right. Even back then he was all about 'Maid uniforms for great justice!' Actually, even the manga he's doing now has a maid as the heroine. Are you making your assistants cry with all the detail work, WhiteLace?"

HeroHero had designed the AI program, along with five other mates.

In other words, this maid was another former guild members' collaboration, so it would be sad to simply ignore her. Just like the Staff of Ainz Ooal Gown, this maid was a shining memory of the good old days.

As Momonga reminisced, the maid, who had straightened up, cocked her head as if to say, *May I help you?*

Oh, is this the idle pose she would strike if you were near her for a certain amount of time? He searched his memory and was impressed by how detailed HeroHero's program was. He knew there must be other secret poses. He was taken by the urge to see them all, but unfortunately, time was running out.

He checked the semitransparent watch face on his left wrist.

He indeed had no time to waste.

"Thanks for all your hard work," he said to the maid out of sentimentality and then slipped by her. Of course, there was no reply, but he felt like it was the proper thing to do on this last day.

Leaving the maid behind, Momonga continued walking.

It was not long before a grand staircase with its primarily red carpeting came into view. At least ten people could walk abreast down it with their arms outstretched. Momonga slowly descended to the deepest level of the Great Tomb of Nazarick, the tenth level.

The stairs led to an open hall where he found several people.

The first one he saw was an old man superbly dressed in a traditional butler uniform. His hair was completely white, as was his beard, but his back was as straight as the blade of a steel sword. Conspicuous wrinkles in his chiseled Caucasian features gave him an air of kindness, but his penetrating eyes were like those of a hawk targeting its prey.

Behind him, trailing him like his shadows, were six maids. These, however, were equipped completely differently from the one before.

They all wore armor based on manga-style maid uniforms featuring metal vambraces and greaves of silver, gold, black, and other colors, with white lace headpieces instead of helmets. They also each carried a different weapon. Basically, they were maid warriors.

Their hairstyles were varied as well: a chignon, a ponytail, a straight cut, braids, rolled curls, a French twist. The only thing they had in common was how beautiful they were, but even their beauty came in various types: bewitching, wholesome, Japanese…

Naturally, they were also NPCs, but unlike the earlier one who was made pretty much for kicks, these existed to intercept raiders.

In *Yggdrasil*, there were perks for guilds who possessed a base of castle size or larger. One was that there were NPCs who would protect said base. The Great Tomb of Nazarick had undead mobs. They could be up to level 30 and it didn't cost the guild anything if they died—they'd just respawn after a set amount of time. The only thing was that the appearances and AI of these auto-spawning NPCs couldn't be edited, which made them too weak to repel other players.

But then there was another perk: the right to create the guild's own NPCs from scratch. Even a weak guild that occupied a base of at least castle size would get at least seven hundred levels to dole out to custom NPCs as they liked. Since the level cap in *Yggdrasil* was 100, one could, for example, make five level 100s and four level 40s. And for this type of NPC, it was possible to adjust their looks, AI, and gear for those who could equip it. With this system, guilds could station guards far stronger than the auto-spawning mobs at key locations.

Of course, there was nothing forcing people to create NPCs with combat in mind. There was one guild, the Great Cat Kingdom, that made all their NPCs cats or other members of the Felidae family. It wouldn't be mistaken to say that this ability was meant to bring out the personalities of the guilds.

"Hm." Momonga brought a hand to his chin and looked at the butler bowing before him. He didn't come here very often, since he normally used teleportation magic to go from room to room. That must have been why the sight of the butler and maids here made him feel so nostalgic.

He stretched his fingers out for the menu and opened up the members-only guild page. Checking a box there instantly caused the names of all the NPCs in the room to appear over their heads.

"So that's what you're called." He cracked a smile. It was part pained wince for not remembering their names, but also part nostalgic grin, as memories of the dispute over what the names should be surfaced from his fragmented recollection.

Sebas the butler's background said he could perform all the duties of a house steward. The team of combat maids, known as the Pleiades, reported directly to him. Besides them he was also in charge of the male servants and assistant butlers.

There was probably more detailed background info in the text log, but Momonga wasn't interested in reading any more. He didn't have much time left, and there was somewhere he wanted to be sitting when the servers shut down.

Incidentally, the reason all the NPCs, including the maids, had detailed backstories was that Ainz Ooal Gown was full of people who loved to write them. And because there were so many illustrator and programmer members, everyone was really obsessed with getting the graphics right, which in turn spurred on the writers' imaginations.

Sebas and the maids were meant to be the last line of defense against raiders. Not that anyone thought it was possible to repel players who managed to penetrate this far, but at least NPC guards could buy some time. That said, no players had ever gotten to the tenth level, so all the guards had ever done was wait.

They had never received orders from anyone, but just stood by wondering if or when an enemy would arrive.

Momonga tightened his grip on the staff.

It was stupid to feel sorry for NPCs. After all, they were just data. If it seemed like they had emotions, it just meant the human who designed the AI had done a good job.

But…

"A guild master should make his NPCs work!" While teasing himself in his head for sounding so arrogant, he added, "Follow me!"

Sebas and the maids acknowledged the order with a bow.

Momonga's guildmates didn't mean for these NPCs to leave this area, and Ainz Ooal Gown valued majority rule. It was unacceptable for one person to do what he wanted with things that everyone had made together.

But it's the last day. Everyone would surely forgive me on the last day, he thought as he continued on with multiple sets of footsteps sounding behind him.

Presently they arrived at a large domed hall. Crystals in four colors on the ceiling gave off white light. There were seventy-two alcoves dug into the walls, most of which contained a statue. There were sixty-seven in all, each in the form of a demon.

This room was called Lemegeton after the famed grimoire also known as *The Lesser Key of Solomon*. All of the statues, carved out of ultrarare magical metals, were golems based on Solomon's seventy-two demons. The only reason there were sixty-seven instead of seventy-two was that the person making them got bored partway through.

The crystals on the ceiling were monsters. During an enemy raid they could summon the major elementals (earth, wind, fire, and water) and simultaneously bombard the enemy with wide-range area-of-effect magic attacks. If all of them were mobilized, it would be enough power to take out two parties of level-100 players (twelve people) with ease.

This room was the very last line of defense before entering the heart of the Great Tomb of Nazarick.

Momonga took the servants with him as he crossed Lemegeton to stand in front of a large door. It was a huge—probably more than sixteen feet tall—double door with extraordinarily detailed carvings: a goddess on the left and a demon on the right. They looked so real it seemed like they might jump off the door to attack. Despite that, Momonga was fairly sure they didn't move. "If a bunch of heroes manage to get this far, we should welcome them. A lot of people say we're evil and whatnot, so let's lie in wait for them here like final bosses." The suggestion was adopted by majority rule.

"Ulbert..." Ulbert Alain Odle had been the most obsessed with the word *evil* out of anybody in the guild. "That guy just never got through adolescence..."

Momonga took another sentimental look around the grand hall.

"...Okay, you're not going to attack me, right?"

His anxiety was not unwarranted. Even he didn't know how everything in this labyrinth worked. He wouldn't have been surprised if one of the retired members had left a twisted "parting gift," and the guy who made this door was definitely the type to do something like that.

Once, he said he wanted to show Momonga a powerful golem he had just made, but when Momonga booted the golem up, a bug in the combat AI caused it to start throwing punches at him. He still wondered if that had been on purpose.

"Hey, Luci★Fer. If you attack me today of all days, I will be seriously angry."

Momonga touched the massive door with caution, but his worries had been for nothing; it opened automatically but slowly, with appropriate gravity.

The mood changed.

The previous room had already been as tranquil and solemn as a shrine, but the scene here surpassed even that. The new atmosphere exerted a physical pressure; the exquisite workmanship could be felt weighing on one's entire body.

The room was huge—a hundred people could come in and there would still be space left over—and the ceilings so high. The walls were primarily white with ornamentation done mainly in gold. The magnificent chandeliers that hung from the ceiling were made of jewels in a rainbow of colors and cast a dreamy sparkling light. On the walls, hanging from the ceiling to the floor, were large flags, each with a different crest—forty-one in all.

On the far side of this lavish gold-and-silver room was a short flight of ten stairs. At the top was a throne carved out of a giant crystal, its back practically tall enough to reach the heavens. Behind it was a large scarlet tapestry bearing the guild's crest.

This was the most important location in the entire Great Tomb of Nazarick, the Throne Room.

A "wow" escaped Momonga's lips as he admired the overwhelming room. He was sure the workmanship was the best, or maybe second best, in all of *Yggdrasil*. That made it a perfect place to spend the last few minutes of the game.

It was so large, the sound of his footsteps seemed to vanish into the room as he entered. He eyed the female NPC standing next to the throne.

She was gorgeous, wearing a snow-white dress. Her faint smile was like that of a goddess. Her lustrous hair was a black the exact opposite of her dress and reached all the way to her waist. Her golden irises and vertical slit pupils were odd, but they didn't detract one bit from her peerless feminine beauty. She did, however, have thick horns that curled forward out of her temples, like a ram's. But that wasn't all. Black angel wings sprouted out of her back near her hips. Perhaps because of the shadows caused by her horns, her goddess smile seemed like it might be a mask hiding something else. She wore a glittering golden necklace like a spiderweb covering her shoulders and chest. In her delicate silken-gloved hands, she carried a strange wand-like object. It was about eighteen inches long, its end tipped by a black orb that floated there with no supports.

Momonga hadn't forgotten *her* name. How could he have? She was Albedo, captain of the Great Tomb of Nazarick's floor guardians. There were seven floor guardians, and she was the NPC who oversaw them; she was the character at the top of the NPC hierarchy in the Great Tomb of Nazarick. Which was why she was allowed to stand by in that innermost room.

But there was some harshness in the way Momonga looked at her now. "I knew there was one World Item here, but why are there two?"

There were only two hundred of these extraordinary items in *Yggdrasil*. Each World Item contained an absolutely unique power. There were even game-breaking items that allowed their owner to demand the admins to change a part of the game's system. Of course, not all of them were so extravagant. Even so, if a player were able to own one individually, one can imagine how far their reputation would spread.

Ainz Ooal Gown was in possession of eleven World Items. That was more than any other guild—far more, in fact. The guild with the next most had only three. Of Ainz Ooal Gown's, Momonga had gotten permission from the guild to carry one as his own, and the rest were scattered around the Great Tomb of Nazarick, although most of them stayed in the treasury, protected by the Avataras.

There could only be one reason that Albedo had come into possession of one of these secret treasures without his knowledge: The guild member who created her had given it to her.

Ainz Ooal Gown valued majority rule. It was unacceptable to move the treasure everyone collected together around on one's own. Momonga was somewhat offended and felt he should probably take it back. But today was the last day. He decided to take that guildmate's feelings into account and leave the item where it was.

"That's far enough," Momonga said to Sebas and the Pleiades in a dignified tone when they'd reached the steps to the throne.

Then, he started up the stairs, but after he had gone up a couple, he realized he could still hear footsteps behind him and winced (although, of course, the graphics of his skull face didn't move a bit). When it came down to it, NPCs were inflexible programs. They wouldn't take an order unless it was one of their set phrases. Momonga used NPCs so rarely that he had managed to forget that simple fact.

Since the other guild members left, Momonga had been doing all he reasonably could to go treasure hunting and raise the funds necessary to maintain the Great Tomb of Nazarick. He never teamed up with any other players and stealthily avoided the kinds of difficult areas the guild had quested in back when the members were still around. Every day he just threw money into the treasury like it was his job and logged out. He didn't have much occasion to meet NPCs.

"Stand by." The footsteps stopped when he gave the correct command. Then, he climbed the stairs and stood before the throne.

He scrutinized Albedo without reserve. He never really came to this room and couldn't remember ever taking a good look at her. "I wonder what her backstory is..." All he could remember was that she was captain of the floor guardians and the most elite NPC in the Great Tomb of Nazarick. With curiosity fluttering in his chest, he accessed the menu to look up her info.

And there certainly was info—writing flooded his field of vision. Her backstory was the length of an epic poem. If he were to take his time reading it, the servers would shut down before he was done.

If Momonga's expression could move, his face would have been screwed up in disbelief. He felt more or less like he'd stepped on a land mine. How could he have forgotten that the guild member who created Albedo was so obsessed with backstories? He was extremely disappointed in himself.

He was the one who had looked it up, so he resigned himself to browsing the bio. He barely even skimmed it, scrolling in one big swipe to the bottom. The last thing it said caught his attention: "By the way, she's a bitch."

His eyes nearly popped out of his head. "Huh? What the heck?" he yelped in spite of himself. No matter how many times he doubted his eyes and reread, the words didn't change. And no matter how hard he tried, he couldn't think of anything for them to mean besides the first thing that popped into his head. "It's gotta be 'bitch,' the insult..."

All forty-one members of the guild had set up at least one NPC. He wondered if someone would really give the character they created that sort of background. If he took his time and read the whole thing, maybe there was some deeper meaning?

But there *were* some people who came up with the craziest backstories... And the member who had created Albedo, Tabula Smaragdina, was one of those.

"So you're into that unexpected contrast, eh, Tabula? Still..." *Isn't this going a bit too far?* The NPCs the guild members made were like the legacy of the guild. If the one on top of the hierarchy had this in her bio, it seemed pretty...

"Hrm..." Was it okay to mess with someone's original NPC due to personal feelings? Momonga thought for a moment and then gave his answer. "I'm gonna change it."

Now that he was carrying the Guild Weapon, he was guild master in both name and substance. He figured it would be okay to exercise the privileges he'd mostly ignored in the past. Using the fuzzy logic of "If a guild member makes an error, it should be corrected," he broke through his hesitation.

Momonga pointed his staff. Usually one would need the creator's tool kit to edit bios, but he could access them with his guild master privileges. A couple menu inputs later and the sentence about being a "bitch" was gone. "I guess that'll do." Then, he thought for a moment and looked at the space he'd opened up. *Maybe I should put something in there...*

"This is so stupid." Momonga winced at his own idea and input the characters via the menu keyboard. It was a short sentence:

"And she's in love with Momonga."

"Ugh, how embarrassing." He put his hands over his face. He felt he might collapse due to sheer mortification, as if he'd made up his own ideal lover and written a romance about it. He fidgeted. He was so embarrassed he considered changing it again, but he decided it was okay.

It was the last day. This embarrassment would disappear in just a few more minutes. Plus, both sentences had the same amount of words—what perfection. Deleting it and leaving an empty space would be a bit of a waste.

Momonga sat on the throne and distracted himself from his slight satisfaction (and thus multiplied shame). He looked out across the room and noticed Sebas and the maids standing stiffly at the bottom of the stairs. In this room, their rigid postures seemed somehow lacking. *Oh right, I think there was this one command...*

"Genuflect!" Albedo, Sebas, and the six maids all dropped to one knee at once and bowed as if they were his subjects.

That's better.

Momonga lifted his left wrist and checked the time: 23:55:48. *Made it just in time. By now the game masters are probably making announcements nonstop. There are probably fireworks...* But Momonga was cut off from all that, so he didn't really know. He leaned back in the throne and looked up at the ceiling.

He had thought a party might show up to storm them on the last day, since this was the base of the guild that had crushed that punitive expedition. He'd been waiting. As guild master, he was ready to take on the challenge. He'd sent an e-mail to all of his old guildmates, but only a handful replied. He'd been waiting. As guild master, he was excited to welcome his old mates.

"Is this guild just a relic of the past?" he wondered. Now there was no one around, but it sure had been a lot of fun. He moved his eyes to count the flags hanging from the ceiling. Forty-one. A flag for every guild member with their crest. He pointed a phalanx at one of them. "Me." Then, he moved his finger one over. That flag had the crest of Ainz Ooal Gown's—no, the entire game's—best player, the one who originally proposed starting their guild. He was also the one who had united its forerunner, the First Nine.

"Touch Me."

The next one over was the crest of Ainz Ooal Gown's oldest member age-wise, a university professor in the real world: "Death Suzaku."

Momonga's finger sped up as he went. The next was one of the guild's only three women members. "Ankoro Mocchi Mochi."

Momonga continued naming all the guild members according to their crests, with no hesitation. "HeroHero, Peroroncino, BubblingTeapot, Tabula Smaragdina, the Warrior Takemikazuchi, Variable Talisman, Genjiro..." It didn't take very long for him to say all forty of his guildmates' names. They were still burned into his brain.

He slumped down in the throne, somewhat tired. "Yeah, we had fun..."

The game was free to play, but Momonga spent about a third of his monthly salary on microtransactions. It wasn't that he was making so much—he just didn't have any other hobbies, so *Yggdrasil* was all he spent money on.

Once he put so much into a lottery that came with a bonus that he blew straight through the bonus. He went to all that trouble and finally got the rare item he'd been after, but Yamaiko, a guildmate, won it for the price of a single lunch out. Oh, did that suck. He'd writhed around on the floor.

Since Ainz Ooal Gown was made up of working adults, almost everyone was buying stuff in-game, but Momonga was definitely up there in terms of spending. He was probably pretty high up even among everyone on the server.

That's how hooked he'd been. Questing was fun, too. And playing with friends was even more fun. To Momonga, with his parents already gone and no friends in the real world, Ainz Ooal Gown represented the awesome times he'd spent with his friends.

And now he was going to lose it.

How miserable, how awful.

He tightened his grip on the staff. Momonga was a normal office worker. He didn't have the money or connections to do anything. He was just another user whose only choice was to silently accept the end.

In the corner of his field of vision, he saw the time: 23:57. The servers would shut down at midnight.

There was almost no time left. His fantasy world was ending, and soon all his days would be spent in reality.

It's only natural. Humans can't live in a daydream. That's why everyone left. Momonga sighed.

He had to be up at four tomorrow morning. If he didn't go to bed as soon as the servers went down, it would affect his work.

23:59:35, 36, 37…

Momonga counted down along with the numbers.

23:59:48, 49, 50…

He closed his eyes.

* * *

23:59:58, 59—

He counted the moments as they ticked off the clock…to the end of his fantasy… *Here comes the blackout*—

0:00:00… One, two, three…

"…Huh?"

Momonga opened his eyes. He wasn't back in his room. He was still in *Yggdrasil* in the Throne Room.

"…What's going on?"

The time was accurate. He should have been booted by now.

0:00:38…

It was definitely after midnight. The time displayed by the system clock could not possibly be off.

Unsure how to proceed, he looked around for any information.

"Was the shutdown postponed?"

Or is there some kind of loss time?

Countless possibilities crossed his mind, but they were all far from convincing. The most likely was that for some reason, some unfavorable reason, the server shutdown had been postponed. If that were the case, the GMs would probably be making announcements. He rushed to turn the communication channels back on—his hands stopped.

His menu wouldn't come up.

"What the…?"

Feeling slightly uneasy and confused (but surprised by how calm he was), Momonga tried to use some other features: forced system access that bypassed the menu, chat, a GM call, force quit. He couldn't get to any of them. It was like he'd been locked out of the system.

"What is going on?!" His irate voice echoed across the spacious Throne Room and faded away.

This is the last day. It's unthinkable that something like this could happen on the day that is supposed to be the end of it all. Are they teasing us? What came over him now was irritation at not being able to make a beautiful exit at the game's glorious end. It could be felt in each word he spoke and almost sounded like he was taking out his anger on someone, but there shouldn't have been any response. However...

"Is something the matter, Lord Momonga?"

It was a woman's pretty voice, and he was hearing it for the first time.

Dumbfounded, Momonga looked to see where it had come from. When he saw who had spoken, he was absolutely shocked.

It was an NPC who was looking up at him—Albedo.

3

Carne.

It was a small village not far from the Tove Woodlands at the southern edge of the Azerlisia Mountains that formed the border between the empire and the kingdom. The population was about 120. Twenty-five households was not an uncommon size for a village on the frontiers of the Re-Estize Kingdom.

Carne mainly relied on agriculture and the bounty of the forest, and the only visitor apart from an apothecary who came to acquire herbs was the tax collector. The phrase *like time had stopped* was an apt descriptor of the place.

The day started early in the village. Villagers generally awoke at dawn. Unlike the larger cities, they didn't have magically maintained Continual Light, so they rose and slept with the sun.

Enri Emmott's mornings began with fetching water from the well near her house. Fetching water was women's work. Her first chore was done when the large pot in her house was full. By that time her mother would be finished preparing breakfast, and the four members of their family would sit down together to eat.

Breakfast was barley and wheat oatmeal, sautéed vegetables, and on some days, dried fruit.

After that, she would go out to work in the fields with her mother and father. Her younger sister, soon to be ten, would gather wood near where the forest started or help in the fields. The bell in the center of town on the edge of the village square rang at noon. They would take a break from their work and eat lunch.

Lunch was brown bread baked some days earlier and soup with bits of preserved meat in it.

Then, it was back to the fields. When the sky began to redden, they would return home and eat dinner.

Dinner was the same brown bread as lunch and bean soup. If a hunter caught an animal, they would sometimes get a share of the meat. After the meal, they would chat as a family and mend clothes by what light remained in the kitchen.

They usually slept around six PM.

Enri Emmott had lived her whole life, from the moment she was born to her current age of sixteen years, as a member of this village.

She thought her uneventful life would continue on the same way forever.

One day Enri awoke as usual and went to fetch water. She hauled the bucket out of the well and filled her small pot. It took about three trips to fill the large one at home.

"Oof." She rolled up her sleeves. The parts of her skin that weren't tanned were glaringly white. Her arms were slender but well toned from working in the fields—she even had some muscle.

The pot was quite heavy once it was full of water, but she picked it up like usual. *If I had a pot one size bigger, maybe I could reduce my number of trips? Oh, but I probably wouldn't be able to carry it.* Enri was about to head home when she thought she heard something and looked in the direction it came from. Something set the air roiling and her heart frothing.

Off in the distance, she heard the sound of something wooden being crushed. And then—

"A scream?" It was like the cry of a bird having its neck wrung and yet altogether different. Something cold raced down Enri's spine. *No way. It's just my imagination. I misheard.* Words to drown out her anxiety bubbled up, popped, and disappeared.

Panicking, she started to run. The scream had come from the direction of her house. She abandoned her pot. *It's too heavy to run with.* Her feet got tangled in her long skirt and she nearly tripped, but luckily she managed to keep her balance and run on.

More voices.

Enri's heart was pounding.

Human screams. No doubt about it.

Run. Run. Run.

She couldn't remember ever having run this fast. She felt like she was going to trip over her own feet.

Horses whinnying. People screaming. Shouts.

It was all getting louder.

Still quite a ways away, Enri saw an armored figure swinging a sword at a villager. The villager screamed and crumpled to the ground. The sword followed up with a finishing stab.

"Mr. Morger!" There was no one in this small village she didn't know—they were all like family—so of course she knew the man who had been killed. He could be a bit loud at times but was a good-natured person. He certainly didn't deserve to die like that. Enri nearly stopped in her tracks, but she grit her teeth and pushed herself to sprint even faster.

This distance never felt terribly long when she was carrying water, but now it seemed like she would never arrive.

Angry shouts and curses reached her ears on the wind. Finally her house was in sight.

"Mom! Dad! Nemu!" she called out to her family as she opened the door.

Their three familiar faces were frightened but all present, huddled together. As soon as she burst in, their expressions softened into relief.

"Enri! You're safe!" She felt her father's rough farmer hands on her back as he hugged her. And the warm hands of her mother.

"Okay, now that Enri's here, let's get out of here!"

The Emmott family was in a pretty bad position. They didn't want Enri to come home to an empty house, so they'd missed their opportunity to escape. *The danger must already be closing in…*

That fear soon became reality.

As the four of them were just about to make a run for it, a shadow appeared in the front entryway. Standing there with the sun at his back was a knight in full armor, the arms of the Baharuth Empire emblazoned on his breastplate. In his hand was a naked blade—a longsword.

The Baharuth Empire occasionally invaded its neighbor, the Re-Estize Kingdom, but usually the fighting was centered around the fortress city of E-Rantel; the enemy had never made it as far as Carne.

But now the village's peace had been shattered.

From the icy stare coming through the gap in the close helmet, Enri could sense that they were being counted. She hated the feeling of his eyes moving over them.

A squeak from his metal gauntlet announced that he had tightened his grip on the sword. He moved into the house—

"Yaaargh!"

"Urgh!"

Enri's father tackled the knight, and the pair of them tumbled out the front door.

"Go! Hurry!"

"You bastard!"

Her father's face was lightly smeared with blood. He must have cut himself when he rushed the knight. The two of them thrashed around on the ground, her father struggling to keep the knight's dagger at bay, the knight struggling to keep her father's knife at bay.

Seeing a family member's blood right before her eyes made Enri's mind go completely blank. *Should I try to help him or escape?*

"Enri! Nemu!" The shout brought her back to reality. Her mother, though anguished, was shaking her head.

Enri took her sister's hand and started to run. Hesitation and guilt made her reluctant, but she had to just run as fast as she could to the forest.

The whinnies and screams of horses, angry voices, the clanging of metal, and...the smell of something burning. From all over the village, the sensations bombarded her eyes, ears, and nose. *Where is that coming from?* She was frantic to know even as she ran. In open areas, she moved in a half crouch, trying to stay in the shadows of houses.

Fear that made her blood run cold. The exertion of running wasn't the only reason her heart was pounding. The only thing keeping her moving was the little hand clasped in hers.

My sister's life...

Her mother, running a few paces ahead, was just turning a corner when she suddenly stiffened and shrank back. She motioned with a hand behind her back to *run the other way!*

When Enri realized why, she bit her lip to hold back a sob.

She squeezed her sister's hand and ran to get as far away as they could.

She didn't want to see what was going to happen next.

"Is something wrong, Lord Momonga?" Albedo repeated her question.

Momonga wasn't sure how to answer. This series of mysterious events had short-circuited his brain.

"Please excuse me." Momonga gazed at her absentmindedly as she got up and came up close to him. "Is something the matter?" She leaned in with her beautiful face. A faint but wonderful scent tickled Momonga's nostrils. Perhaps kick-started by the fragrance, his thoughts began to return to him.

"No, I'm all right, thank y— It's nothing." He lacked the particular naïveté required to speak too terribly politely toward a mannequin, but as soon as she had spoken to him, he felt compelled to answer. There was something undeniably human about the way she spoke and moved.

The situation he and Albedo were in was way off, but he couldn't quite put his finger on why. He did his utmost to suppress the confusion and amazement that such a vague understanding generated, but he was just a normal guy—it didn't seem possible. Right as he was about to scream, he remembered the words of one of his guildmates: "Panic breeds failure. One must always have a composed, rational state of mind. Calm your heart and broaden your outlook. Don't let your thoughts take you prisoner. Keep your mind quick, Momonga."

With that remembrance, his calm came flooding back to him. He mentally gave his thanks to the man known as the guild's Kongming, Squishy Moe.

"Are you all right?" Albedo asked, awfully close to him. She'd tilted her head adorably and leaned in so far that their breaths were overlapping. With this gorgeous girl in his face, the calm Momonga had just regained threatened to fly straight back out the window.

"The...GM call isn't working." Swallowed up by Albedo's glistening pupils, he found himself consulting with an NPC.

A member of the opposite sex had never approached Momonga with this look in her eyes before, especially with such a lack of propriety. He knew it was just an NPC someone had made, but the flow of her expressions was so natural it was unsettling.

But somehow he noticed those feelings settling down already, as if they were being held back. The lack of wider emotional fluctuation, however, gave him a touch of anxiety. He had thought it was due to his former mate's words, *but is that really it?*

Momonga shook his head. Now wasn't the time.

"...Please forgive me. I am so ignorant I fear I am unable to answer your question regarding this 'GM call' you speak of. Nothing would make me happier than a chance to clear myself of the disgrace of failing your expectations. Your wish is my command..."

...*We're having a conversation. No doubt about it.* The realization assailed his entire body with a petrifying amazement. *Impossible... This can't be happening.*

An NPC was talking. Well, there were macros that allowed them to do that. Players had been passing around data for battle cries and cheers, etc. Still, conversation was impossible. Even just a minute ago, Sebas and the maids wouldn't respond to anything that wasn't a simple command phrase.

So how is this happening? Is Albedo just special?

He motioned for her to step back and glimpsed a flicker of reluctance as he looked away to Sebas and the maids, who still had their heads bowed.

"Sebas! Maids!"

"My lord!" They answered in magnificent unison, raising their heads in a slick motion.

"Come to the foot of the throne."

"Yes, sir." Their voices aligned again, and they sprang to their feet. The group walked together with beautiful posture to the bottom of the steps leading to the throne before each dropping again to one knee and bowing.

From this exchange, Momonga learned two things. First, although he had purposely avoided using command phrases, they could understand his intentions and carry them out. Second, Albedo was not the only one who could talk. *At the very least, something weird is going on with all the NPCs in the Throne Room.*

As he was reflecting on these things, he had the same feeling as before that something was off about both Albedo and himself. Wanting to understand it, he scrutinized her.

"Is everything all right? Have I done something wrong?"

"Agh!" When he recognized the root of the incongruity, a sound that was neither word, gasp, nor choking noise escaped his lips.

It was the changing expressions. Her lips were moving, and he could hear her words.

Flustered, he brought his fingers to his own lips. And spoke. "Im…po…"

My jaw is moving…

In the world of a DMMO-RPG, that went against all common sense. Mouths moving and words coming out?! Expression graphics were fixed; they didn't move. Otherwise why would the developers have made emoticons?

Plus, Momonga's face was a skull—he didn't have a tongue or a throat. Looking down at his hands, there was no flesh and the bones weren't even anatomically correct. Continuing along the same lines, he probably didn't have any internal organs, not to mention lungs. So why could he talk?

"Impossible…" He felt the internal logic he had built up slowly over time begin to crumble away—and an equivalent panic replace it.

He wanted to scream but held it in. As expected, the heat in his chest was abruptly soothed by a wave of calm.

Momonga pounded the throne's armrest. As he thought, the number showing damage didn't pop up.

"What should I do? What makes the most sense…?" He was in an incomprehensible situation, but venting wouldn't get him anywhere. First, he needed information. "Sebas!"

The expression on Sebas's face as he lifted his head was earnestness incarnate. He looked like he was really alive.

I can give him an order, right? I'm not sure what's going on, but I can assume the NPCs in the Tomb are loyal to me, right? Actually, I don't even know if these are our NPCs…

Countless questions, and the anxiety that went with them, arose in his mind, but Momonga tuned it all out. In any case, there was no one better to send out for reconnaissance than Sebas. He did glance momentarily at Albedo, who was waiting off to the side, but he made up his mind to give the order to Sebas.

He imagined what executives at work were like when directing regular employees and tried to act like he was one of them. "Leave the Tomb, and confirm our surroundings within a half-mile radius. If there are any intelligent life-forms, negotiate to bring them here on amicable terms. You can give them practically whatever they request in return. Avoid combat to the extent possible."

"Understood, Lord Momonga. I will leave without delay."

In *Yggdrasil,* it was definitely not possible to take NPCs who were built to protect a base and send them outside, but here it was. *Well, I won't know for sure until he actually makes it outside, but…*

"Take one member of the Pleiades with you. If you're attacked, have her retreat immediately to bring back any information you have." With that, Momonga had made at least one move.

He let go of the Staff of Ainz Ooal Gown. It didn't clatter to the ground, but instead hung in the air as if someone were holding it. It was against the laws of physics, but it was just like the game. In *Yggdrasil,* it wasn't uncommon for items to float in the air when one let go of them.

The staff's aura of anguished faces twisted around his hand as if reluctant to dissipate, but Momonga calmly ignored it. Not that he was…used to it, but that sort of macro wasn't so strange; he shook his wrist to get rid of it.

Crossing his arms, he thought what his next move should be. *I suppose…* "I need to contact the admins." The administration was sure to be the most informed of anyone about this abnormal situation. The problem was how to reach them. Usually a shout or GM call would work, but if they didn't now…

"A message maybe?"

There was one magic spell that was a way to contact people. It could only be used in specific places and situations, but it seemed like it would be effective now. The only problem was that it was usually used to communicate between players; he wasn't sure if it would work to contact a GM. He didn't even have any guarantee that magic in general would work normally in this crisis.

"But…" He had to find out.

Momonga was a level-100 magic user. If he couldn't use magic, his area of operations and information-gathering powers would be severely limited, not to mention his combat strength. Right now he had no idea what the situation was, so he needed to confirm as soon as possible whether or not he could use magic.

In that case, I need to go somewhere I can test it out... He looked out over the Throne Room and shook his head. This was an emergency, but he didn't want to disturb this room's sublime tranquility for magic experiments. *But then where?* he thought and came up with an ideal location.

It was also necessary to test the extent of his influence. He had to see whether he had maintained his authority as guild master. So far everyone he had met was loyal to him, but there were several NPCs in the Great Tomb of Nazarick at his level. He needed to make sure the rest of them were still loyal, too.

But... He looked down at Sebas and the maids who were still on one knee and then at Albedo beside him. *What is it?* her faint smile seemed to say. She was beautiful, but the shadows cast by her horns made it seem like something was hidden behind her smile. It made Momonga nervous.

Is the loyalty they have now inviolable and unchanging? In the real world, a boss who makes stupid moves all the time loses support. Does it work the same way here, or is it once faithful, always faithful?

If I suppose their loyalty could change, how do I maintain it?

By giving them rewards? The treasury contained vast riches. It would pain him to lay a hand on the items his former guildmates had left, but if it was to keep Ainz Ooal Gown going through this crisis, they would forgive him, wouldn't they? Then, of course, he didn't have any idea how much he should pay...

Or displaying the excellence you'd expect of a ruler? What constituted excellence, however, was unclear. He had the feeling things would work out if he just kept maintaining the dungeon.

Or... "Maybe through power?" The Staff of Ainz Ooal Gown flew automatically into his outstretched hand. "Overwhelming power?" The staff's seven jewels began to sparkle, as if appealing for their vast magical power to be used. "Well, I guess I'll think about it later."

He let go of the staff. It swayed in the air for a moment and then clattered to the floor like someone going to bed in a huff.

Anyhow, it seemed like if he acted like he was in charge, he was unlikely to meet hostility anytime soon. It's hard for animals to turn their fangs on one who doesn't show any weaknesses, and the same thing went for humans.

Momonga raised his voice. "Pleiades! All of you besides the one going with Sebas, go up to the ninth level and be on the lookout for any raiders coming down from eight."

"Yes, Lord Momonga." The maids behind Sebas complied.

"Now go immediately."

"Understood, Lord and Master," their voices echoed. Sebas and the combat maids all paid their respects to Momonga, stood at once, and set off.

The huge door opened and then closed after them.

I'm so glad they didn't say no or something. Relieved, he turned to the last remaining NPC—Albedo was still waiting beside him.

"Now, then, Lord Momonga. What may I do for you?" she asked with a gentle smile.

"Oh, uh...right..." Momonga leaned out of the throne to pick up his staff. "Come here."

"Yes, sir!" She sounded overjoyed and sidled right up. Momonga worried about her wand and the black sphere floating on the end of it for just a moment, but decided to forget about it. She was closer than last time, all but clinging to him.

She smells so good—but what am I thinking? The thought popped up again, but he promptly dismissed it. He didn't have time for that sort of nonsense now.

Momonga reached out and touched her hand.

"...Ngh."

"Hm?"

The look on Albedo's face said she was in pain. He whipped his hand away as if he'd been electrocuted.

I wonder what's wrong. Did I creep her out?

Mixed in with the numerous sad memories (like having cashiers drop change into his hand from above to avoid accidentally touching him) flitting across his mind, he found the answer.

"...Ohhhh."

An overlord was a higher rank of elder lich, and one of the special abilities an elder lich could acquire by leveling up was the dealing of damage by touch—normally as an attack. *Maybe that's it?*

But even if that was the case, there were still questions remaining.

In *Yggdrasil,* the system would judge mobs and NPCs within the Great Tomb of Nazarick as belonging to Ainz Ooal Gown. Friendly fire for guild members was always off so allies couldn't harm one another. So did that mean she didn't belong to the guild? Or that friendly fire had been turned on?

The latter is a distinct possibility, Momonga decided and said to Albedo, "Sorry, I forgot to turn off Negative Touch."

"Never you mind, Lord Momonga. That level of damage wasn't even damage. Besides, I would suffer any agony for you… Eek!"

"Oh, uh…huh… I see. But I'm sorry," Momonga stammered, not knowing how to act toward Albedo as she made that cute little shriek and covered her blushing cheeks with her hands.

But it did seem like the issue had been damage from Negative Touch.

Averting his eyes from Albedo, who was going on about a virgin's pain, Momonga tried to think how to temporarily turn off a passive power—and suddenly, it dawned on him: Using any of an overlord's various powers was now as natural an act as breathing. He found himself laughing in spite of himself at what an extraordinary situation he was in. After all the strange things that had happened so far, it didn't even surprise him. *Adaptability is a terrifying thing.*

"I'm going to touch you."

"Oh…!"

After turning off the ability, he reached out and touched her hand. Countless thoughts came up—how delicate it was, how white—but Momonga dismissed any that stemmed from his being male. What he wanted to know was if she had a pulse.

She does.

The beat was a steady *ba-bum, ba-bum.* It would be only natural for a living thing.

Yeah, for a living thing…

Momonga took his hand away and looked at his own wrist. There was no skin, flesh, or anything besides a pure white bone. He had no blood vessels, so of course he had no pulse. That's right, an overlord was undead—a being who had transcended death. Of course he wouldn't have a pulse.

He looked up at Albedo. He could see himself in her glistening pupils. Her cheeks were awfully flushed—her body temperature was probably skyrocketing. Noting these changes in her was enough to shake him up.

"...What's going on?"

This is an NPC—just some data, right? What kind of AI can make data look like it's actually alive? It's practically as if Yggdrasil *has become reality...*

That's impossible.

Momonga shook his head. *It can't be anything as crazy as that.* But once the idea had lodged in his mind, it wouldn't come unstuck so easily. Feeling vaguely uncomfortable about the changes he was noticing in Albedo, he hesitated about what to do next.

His next move would be his last. *If I check this last thing, all of my hunches will turn to convictions. The balance that shows whether this is reality or not will swing one way or the other. So I have to do it! I wouldn't be surprised if she attacked me with that weapon she's holding...but even so...*

"Albedo... Can I touch your ch-chest?"

"Huh?"

The atmosphere froze solid. Albedo blinked, bewildered. The moment he said it, Momonga felt he might die of embarrassment.

Sure, he'd had no choice, but what kind of thing was that to say to a lady? He had the urge to howl that he was the worst person in existence. *I've abused my power in order to sexually harass a woman—I really am the worst.*

But I can't help it. Yeah. It has to be done.

He forcefully talked himself down and regained his mental equilibrium rather quickly, then mustered all of his coercive power as a superior. "You don't meow— Mind, do you?"

Utter failure.

His timid words caused Albedo to beam as if she were the sun making all the flowers bloom. "Of course, Lord Momonga! Please have your way with me." She puffed out her chest and her substantial breasts were thrust into Momonga's face. If he had had the ability to gulp, he would have surely done so several times.

Her breasts were giving her dress great lift, and he was about to touch them.

On the one hand, Momonga was feeling oddly nervous and shaken, but some corner of his brain was being calmly and objectively self-observant. He started to feel incredibly stupid. *Why is* this *the test I thought of, and why am I actually doing it?*

For some reason when he peeked at Albedo, she stuck her chest out even more as if to say, *Go ahead,* her eyes twinkling.

Was Momonga aroused or ashamed? He willed his hand to stop shaking, made up his mind, and reached out.

Under the dress, he felt something a bit rigid, but beneath that he could feel something soft.

"Ahh… Ngh…" Amid Albedo's sticky moaning, Momonga got the information he was after.

Assuming he was still sane, Momonga had two hypotheses for explaining the current situation.

One was the possibility of a new DMMO-RPG. In other words, at the same time *Yggdrasil* had shut down, *Yggdrasil II* had started up. But that didn't seem terribly plausible after what he'd just experienced.

In *Yggdrasil,* doing anything rated R was strictly forbidden. Even PG-13 could be considered out of line in some cases. Violators were dealt with severely: Their names were posted to the list of abusers on the game's website and their accounts were suspended. That's because if a log of it were made public, the operators could find themselves afoul of the adult entertainment business laws. Under normal circumstances, it wouldn't have surprised Momonga if what he'd just done had been against the rules. If he was still in a game world, there should have been some measure in place to prevent it. In the first place, if the GM and admins were monitoring, they would have tried to stop him, but there was no sign of that.

Additionally, the cyber-tech laws that governed DMMO-RPGs viewed forcible, nonconsensual participation in a game as kidnapping for ransom. If someone were forced to be a test player, it would be immediately exposed. The inability to force quit would probably be seen as illegal confinement, too.

If that was what was going on, the game's proprietary console had to keep a week's worth of records by law, so exposing it would be easy enough. When he didn't show up for work, someone would probably come over to check on him, and once the police investigated the console, that would clear things up.

But was there really a company stupid enough to commit a crime so easy to get caught for in an organization-wide way? Of course, if they said, "It's an early demo version of *Yggdrasil II*," or "We just released a patch," there was a gray zone, but he couldn't believe it would be worth it to the developers or admins to take that kind of risk.

So there had to be something at work besides the developers' intentions. In that case, he needed to make a fundamental change in the way he was thinking or he wouldn't get anywhere. The problem was that how he should think was unclear. There was one other possibility...

That the fantasy world had become the real world...

Impossible. He promptly rejected the idea. There was no way something so outrageous—so illogical—could be true. On the other hand, the longer this went on, the more he wondered if it might actually be the case. He remembered the fragrance coming off Albedo earlier.

The senses of taste and smell were altogether banned from fantasy worlds by the cyber-tech laws. *Yggdrasil* had a system for eating and drinking, but anything players consumed only affected their in-game stats. Even touch was regulated to some extent. This was all so that the game couldn't be mistaken for the real world. As a result of all the limitations, fantasy worlds featuring sex hadn't really caught on.

But here he could smell.

The reality of that hit Momonga so hard it completely blew away all his *What about work tomorrow?* and *What if I can't get out of here?* type of worries.

"If this weren't reality... Just in terms of the bandwidth that would be required to run this fantasy, it'd be impossible..."

His mouth was bone-dry, but he swallowed anyway. Even if he couldn't understand it, his mind had already accepted it.

Finally, he let his hand fall limply from Albedo's full chest. He felt he'd been groping her a bit longer than necessary, but he told himself it was something he had to do for confirmation. It certainly wasn't because she was so soft he couldn't take his hand away... *At least, probably not.*

"Sorry, Albedo."

"Ahhh..." She exhaled hotly, and he could feel why her cheeks had turned so red. Then, she said, looking slightly askance, "So here it is, my first time."

"Huh?!" Momonga let out a confused yelp in spite of himself. It took him a moment to understand what she was saying. *"First time"? For what? And what's with that look on her face?!*

"What shall I do with my clothes?"

"...What?"

"Would you like me to take them off myself? Or did you want to do it? If I keep them on, um, they might get dirty... Oh, but if my lord prefers it that way, I have no objections."

Finally her words sank in. Actually, Momonga wondered if he even had any brain left for them to sink into. Once he understood where all this was coming from, it grated on him. "Stop. Stop it, Albedo."

"Hm? Yes, sir."

"Right now we can't... Er, we don't have time to be doing such things."

"M-my humble apologies! I shouldn't have prioritized desire when we're having some sort of emergency." She jumped away from him and went to prostrate herself, but Momonga put out a hand to stop her.

"You're fine. It was my fault. All is forgiven, Albedo. More importantly...I have orders for you."

"Anything you wish, my lord."

"Contact the floor guardians and tell them to gather at the Amphitheatrum in the sixth level one hour from now. I will let Aura and Mare know myself, so there is no need to contact them."

"Understood. To repeat, you would like me to contact all the floor guardians besides those of the sixth level and tell them to meet in the sixth level's Amphitheatrum one hour from now."

"Right. Now go."

"My lord." Albedo turned to leave the Throne Room with slightly quickened steps.

Watching her go, Momonga heaved a tired sigh, and once she had left, he let out an agonized moan. "...What the hell. It was just a stupid joke. If I'd have known this would happen, I wouldn't have done it. Have... Have I defiled the NPC that Tabula created...?" He could think of only one reason Albedo would react to him in that way: the text he'd edited into her bio, "And she's in love with Momonga." It had to be connected to that.

"Ahhh, crap!" he groaned.

Tabula Smaragdina had put his all into filling that blank canvas with Albedo's backstory. Then, Momonga condescendingly painted over it for his own selfish reasons, and now this was the result. He felt like he'd vandalized a masterpiece.

But he had to put that issue aside for now. Still wincing—though it wasn't obvious, given that his face was a skull—he stood up from the throne. He told himself he could figure that problem out after taking care of the more urgent tasks.

Chapter 2 The Floor Guardians

Chapter 2 | The Floor Guardians

1

"Return, demons of Lemegeton!"

At Momonga's command, the ultrarare ore golems returned to their seats and resumed their postures of vigilance on lighter feet than one would expect for their builds.

The first thing Momonga had done upon resigning himself to officially wondering whether his fantasy world had indeed become the real one was to guarantee his safety. The NPCs he had met a moment ago all submitted to him, but that didn't mean the ones he would meet next would. Even if they did prove to be allies, there was no telling what dangers might lie ahead. His survival could very well depend on whether or not the Tomb's facilities, golems, items, magic, etc., all functioned as in the game or not, which made confirmation of those things his most urgent priority.

"That should be good for now," Momonga said to himself out of relief as he surveyed the golems. He'd ordered them not to take commands from anyone else, so in the worst-case scenario of an NPC rebellion, he would at least have one way to protect himself. Satisfied with the robust figures of the golems, he looked down at his own finger bones.

There were nine rings on his ten fingers; the only one that didn't have one was his left ring finger. In *Yggdrasil,* it was normally only possible to wear one ring per hand, but by purchasing an expensive cash store item with a permanent effect, Momonga had gained the ability to wear them on all ten, as well as use all the powers they contained. Not that that made him very special—if a player prioritized being strong, buying that item was a no-brainer.

The ring Momonga was looking at now bore the same crest that was embroidered on the scarlet tapestry hanging behind the throne. It was a Ring of Ainz Ooal Gown, a magic item that every member of the guild possessed; he wore his on his right ring finger.

He could use all the powers of ten rings, but he'd had to choose which ones when he used the item that allowed him to equip that many. It was impossible to swap after the fact. Compared to his other rings (including the one he wasn't wearing, stored in the treasury), this one's power was pretty basic, but he wanted it at the ready, since, in certain circumstances, he used it far more than any of the others.

The Ring of Ainz Ooal Gown let its wearer teleport freely to almost any named room within the Great Tomb of Nazarick. It was even possible to teleport in from outside. The Tomb blocked teleportation magic except for in designated areas, so there was no more useful way to get around. There weren't very many places, save the Throne Room and the members' individual rooms, that couldn't be teleported to. Without this ring, however, there was no way to get to the treasury. So it wasn't something he would want to be without.

Momonga exhaled deeply. He was about to exercise the ring's power, but he wasn't sure what would happen. Would it work as expected? He was anxious but had to know.

He unleashed the power and his vision went dark, like he'd blinked.

The scenery changed—now he was in a dimly lit passage. The end was blocked by a barred gate. White artificial light came in through the gaps.

"Success...," he murmured, relieved that he'd been able to teleport. He set off walking down the broad, high-ceilinged passage toward the gate. The stone floor caused his footsteps to reverberate loudly. Flickering torchlight sent shadows dancing along the walls, making it seem like there was more than one of him.

As he neared the gate, his nostrils, which should have just been holes leading to nowhere, were invaded by scent. He stopped to breathe in and out. A pungent green odor and the scent of earth—this was the smell of deep forest.

Having his nose working again, like it had before with Albedo—even though it should have been impossible in the game's fantasy world—made Momonga feel even more strongly that this place was now reality.

But with no lungs and no respiratory tract, how am I even breathing? He racked his brains, but soon realized trying to reason the problem out was ridiculous and abandoned the idea.

When he got close enough, the gate drew quickly up into the ceiling like a well-timed automatic door. Passing beneath, Momonga saw the Colosseum, with its multiple levels of spectator seating encircling its central arena. It was an oval of 615 by 510 feet, 157 feet high, identical to the Colosseum built in Rome during the imperial period. Continual Light was cast in various locations, throwing enough white light that he could look around the area and see as if it were high noon. There were too many seats to count, and in them, a great many clods of "dirt"—no sign of movement from the golems.

This place was called the Amphitheatrum. The actors were captured raiders, the audience was made up of golems, and in the VIP seating would be the members of Ainz Ooal Gown. What was on the program? A slaughter, of course. With the exception of the 1,500 in that huge raid, every intruder, no matter how strong, had met their end here.

Momonga walked into the center of the arena gazing up at the pitch-black night sky. If there hadn't been any light, he probably would have been able to see the stars.

Of course, this was the sixth level of the Great Tomb of Nazarick. Being underground, the sky hanging overhead was a false one. But it was made with quite a lot of data, so it changed with the passage of time, and there was even an accurately arcing sun that rose and set. Was the reason that even this fake sky could take the weight off Momonga's chest and relax him because under all the graphics he was still human? Maybe also because it was programmed according to the particularities of a former guild member. He wished he could just stay and take it easy, but the situation didn't allow that.

Momonga glanced around. *They're not here. The twins should be managing this place, but...* Just then he felt someone looking at him.

"Yaaa!" At the same time the shout sounded, a figure hopped down from the VIP seating. That was the equivalent of six stories up, but the figure flipped in midair and made a featherlight landing. It wasn't due to magic, but simply great physical technique. Having absorbed the full shock of the landing by just bending its legs, the figure flashed a proud grin and made peace signs with both hands. "Victory!"

It was a child of perhaps ten who had jumped down. The most apt descriptor for that smile was "radiant like the sun." She had that kind of androgynous cuteness only children have.

Her golden hair reflected light in a way that made it look almost like she had a halo. Her eyes, bright like a puppy's, were two different colors—forest green and ocean blue. As a dark elf, a relative of the elf race, her ears were long and pointed, her skin tan.

She wore fitted, dark red dragon scale light armor, top and bottom, over a layer of basic leather protective gear. On top of that, she sported a white vest with golden threading, featuring the crest of Ainz Ooal Gown on the chest, and white pants to match. A big golden acorn hung from her neck. Her hands were protected by gloves with magic metal plates on the backs of the palms. Whips were bundled at her waist and right shoulder, and across her back, she carried a bow with peculiar decorations on the grip, handle, and limbs.

"Oh, it's Aura." Momonga murmured her name in recognition. Aura Bella Fiora was one of the guardians of the sixth level, a beast tamer-ranger who could employ fantastical and magical creatures.

She came running toward him with short steps that somehow carried her crazily fast, like an animal running flat out. She closed the distance in an instant and put the brakes on. Her sporty shoes inlaid on top with scarletite sent up a cloud of dust as they scraped along the ground. If she had calculated it out so that not a speck would reach Momonga, she'd done a brilliant job.

"Phew." She wiped her forehead even though she wasn't sweating and smiled like a puppy who wanted to play. Then she greeted Momonga in that ever so slightly too-loud voice that only children have: "Welcome to the floor I guard, Lord Momonga!" Compared to Sebas and Albedo she was less deferential and more familiar, but that was actually more comfortable for Momonga. He didn't have much experience with all of this, so being overly revered only made it harder to know how to act.

He wasn't getting any hostility from Aura's ear-to-ear grin, and Sense Enemy didn't pick up anything, either. His emergency plan had been to attack with full power and promptly retreat, but it seemed like that would be unnecessary. "Thanks. I thought I'd come bother you for a bit."

"What are you talking about? You are the master of the Great Tomb of Nazarick—its absolute ruler! No one would ever feel bothered to receive a visit from you, Lord Momonga!"

"Oh, hm... By the way, I see that you're here, Aura, but...?"

As if taking a cue, Aura turned on her heel, glared up at the VIP seats, and shouted, "Hurry up, c'mon! Lord Momonga is here! You're being rude!"

Up in the darkness of the VIP seats, Momonga saw something bouncing up and down in a fidgety way. "Oh, Mare's over there, huh?"

"Yes, Lord Momonga, he is. He's such a wimp... Get down here!"

A weak little voice replied. In fact, it was a wonder they could even hear it, considering their distance from the VIP seats, but it was made possible by the magical necklace Aura had equipped.

"I-I... Sis, there's n-no way..."

Aura sighed, exasperated. "Oh, uh, Lord Momonga, he's just a bit of a coward. He's not being rude on purpose."

"Of course. I know that, Aura. I've never for a moment doubted your loyalty to me." Momonga nodded and gave a kind answer to put her at ease.

Adults need to know their inner feelings as well as what their outward-facing stance would be. Sometimes it was necessary to tell a little lie.

Aura seemed relieved, but a moment later she turned in anger to the figure up in the VIP seats. "Our elite lord has graced us with his presence, and one of the floor guardians can't even come out to meet him?! That's the worst and you know it! If you don't have the courage to move your own butt, we're gonna try it with my foot next!"

"Nnn... I'll... I'll take the stairs..."

"You mean you're going to keep Lord Momonga waiting even longer?! Get over here already!"

"Ahh, f-fiiiine... H-here goes!" It was a pretty pathetic little shout for someone trying to psych himself up, but he did hop down.

Another dark elf. The difference between him and Aura was like night and day, but although he stumbled upon landing, it didn't seem like he'd taken any damage from the fall. He must have neutralized it with pure physical ability.

Then, he came running at a speed that matched the sound of his light footfalls. He was giving his all, naturally, but was still hopelessly slow compared to Aura.

She must have been thinking the same thing, because her brow began to twitch. "Hurry up!"

"I-I-I am!"

The child who finally arrived looked just like Aura. Same hair color and length, same eye colors, same facial features—they couldn't be anything but twins, but if Aura was the sun, then Mare was the moon. He trembled as if expecting to be chewed out at any moment. Momonga was a bit surprised by both of them.

The Mare he knew wasn't like this at all. Of course, NPCs generally just stood there rigidly with their fixed expressions; it didn't matter how long of a bio they were given, it was never reflected in their personalities. Yet here they were before him, two dark elves, with rapid-fire emotions.

"So this is how Teapot meant for them to be..." BubblingTeapot was the guild member who had set up Aura and Mare. He wished he could show them to her now.

"S-sorry to keep you waiting, Lord Momonga." Mare looked up at him nervously. The scales of his upper body dragon armor were more indigo than blue. He also wore a short mantle of dark green that almost exactly matched the leaves of the forest. Most of his clothes were white like Aura's, but he was wearing a skirt so short it left a little skin showing—only "a little" because of his white stockings. His acorn necklace looked just like Aura's, but silver. He wasn't as heavily armed as his sister; in his hands, which wore slender white gloves with a silky sheen, he clutched a gnarled staff of black wood, and that was it. Mare Bello Fiore. He was the other guardian of the sixth level.

Momonga smiled kindly—not that his empty eye sockets showed it—and took a good look at the two of them. Aura proudly puffed out her chest while Mare trembled under his gaze. Satisfied that they were indeed the crystallization of his guildmate's intentions, he nodded several times and then spoke. "More than anything I'm just glad to see you're both doing well."

"Yeah, we're great! Just lately it's been so boring. It'd be nice if some raiders would come for a change!"

"I-I don't want any raiders to come… Th-they're scary…"

Mare's words wiped the excitement off Aura's face, and she sighed. "Sorry, Lord Momonga. Please excuse us. Mare, come with me a minute."

Momonga gave a slight nod, and Aura moved away a bit, dragging Mare by his pointy ears. "O-oww! A-Aura, that hurrrts!"

Then, she started hissing at him. Even at a distance, Momonga could tell she was giving him a scolding.

"Raiders? I'm actually with Mare on that one…" *I'd at least like them to wait until I get my feet on the ground,* he thought as he watched the twins.

The next thing he knew, Mare was sitting erect with his legs tucked under him and Aura stood before him lecturing. The situation was reminiscent of the power struggle between the two of his former guildmates who were sisters, and he smiled wryly.

"Geez, but I don't think Peroroncino made Mare. Maybe Teapot had the idea that one should obey one's elder sister? …Actually, now that I think of it, both Aura and Mare have died once before… I wonder what happened with that…"

In the raid where 1,500 men attacked, the huge army got as far as the eighth level. In other words, Aura and Mare died attempting to hold the sixth level, *but did they remember it?*

What does death mean for the two of them?

In *Yggdrasil,* characters who died lost five levels and dropped one of their equipped items. That meant that characters level 5 or under were destroyed. Player characters were spared destruction by divine grace and stopped at level 1. Of course, that was speaking strictly of the rules of the game.

In actuality, spells such as Resurrection and Raise Dead could ease the level penalty, and cash store items let players get off with just losing some experience points. In the case of an NPC, it was even simpler. The guild could revive a character with no penalty by paying a fee according to its level.

Dying to lose levels ended up being a favorite way for people to rebuild their characters. Certainly in a game where an enormous amount of experience was required, losing even one level would be an extreme punishment, but in *Yggdrasil* it was pretty easy to rack up levels until the upper 90s. The developers set it up so that losing levels wasn't such a terrifying thing. Their intent was not for people to be so scared of losing levels that they didn't want to explore, but for them to venture bravely into new territory.

Under those rules, were these two who had died in the 1,500-man raid now different people? Or were they the reincarnations of those exact characters?

He did want to know, but he also felt like there wasn't any reason to wake sleeping dogs. That huge raid might have been a traumatizing experience for them. He also wondered if it was really necessary to prod so much just to satisfy his own curiosity when Aura wasn't showing any hostility. After all, these were lovable NPCs that his guildmate made. He could talk to Aura about it after all the other pending matters had been taken care of.

Plus, it was possible that the entire concept of death had changed entirely. In the real world, dying was the end naturally. But what if that were different here? Momonga thought he'd like to experiment with it in the near future, but he couldn't determine how high a priority it should be until he had more information. It was probably best to just put it on the back burner for now. At this point, he didn't know how different this world was from *Yggdrasil*, so all he had was a great many questions.

While he was pondering all of this, Aura had continued berating Mare. Momonga couldn't help but feel bad for him. He never said the kid deserved this much scolding. When the two sisters in his guild had fought, he had kept his mouth shut and just watched, but now he was different.

"How about we leave it at that?"

"Lord Momonga! But Mare's not fulfilling his duties as a gua—"

"I have no issue with his behavior. Aura, I understand very well how you feel, including your thinking that as a floor guardian Mare shouldn't be so timid, especially around me. But should the Great Tomb of Nazarick be raided, I believe that both you and Mare will fight fearlessly in the face of death to protect it. If he'll do what needs to be done when the time comes, you don't need to scold him so much." Momonga, who had walked closer to them, grabbed Mare's arm and stood him up. "And Mare, you should thank your big sister for being so kind. Even if I were upset, after seeing her chew you out like that, there'd be nothing I could do but forgive you."

Mare's eyes widened and he looked at his sister in surprise. Aura chimed in hastily, "Huh? N-no, that's not why I did it! I didn't think anything like that about you!"

"It doesn't matter, Aura. No matter what your intent was, your kindness came through. I just want you to know that I have no misgivings about Mare being a floor guardian."

"Huh? Oh, uh, okay! Thank you, Lord Momonga!"

"Th-thank you!"

He accepted their bows, but couldn't help but get the willies from the way their eyes lit up when they looked at him. He'd pretty much never been looked at with such admiration, so he cleared his throat to hide both his hesitation and embarrassment.

"Ahem, more importantly: Aura, I wanted to ask you about what you were mentioning before. You said you're bored when no one is raiding us?"

"Ah, well, no, I mean..." From her backpedaling, Momonga could see he'd phrased his question badly.

"No, I'm not accusing you of anything. Please tell me honestly."

"Well, yes, it is a little boring. There isn't anyone strong enough to train with around here," Aura answered, looking up at him, poking the tips of her index fingers together.

As a guardian, Aura's level was, of course, 100. There were not so many level 100s in the dungeon—including Aura and Mare, nine NPCs. Plus one other.

"What about sparring with Mare?"

Mare had scrunched up as though he were trying to hide, and now a shudder went through his whole body. His eyes glistened as he shook his head no. He was terrified. Aura reacted with a sigh again.

As she exhaled, a sickeningly sweet fragrance filled the air. It was different from Albedo's, a syrupy aroma that seemed to cling somehow. Recalling her powers, Momonga took a step back.

"Oh! I'm sorry, Lord Momonga!" Realizing what had happened, Aura flapped her arms around to clear the air.

One of Aura's passive skills as a beast tamer was the ability to use both buffs and debuffs at the same time. The effects drifted into the air on her breath and could have a radius of dozens of feet to a hundred or more—using an additional skill could make the range unbelievably huge.

In *Yggdrasil,* buff and debuff icons would pop up so players understood clearly when they were in effect, but in their current situation, they problematically did not.

"Umm, it's okay now. I turned it off!"

"Oh..."

"But Lord Momonga, you're undead, so psychic stuff shouldn't have any effect on you."

That's the way it had been in *Yggdrasil.* Psychic abilities had neither good nor bad effects on the undead.

"...Was I in range just now?"

"Urk." Aura scrunched up her shoulders in fear of the coming rebuke. Even Mare shrank a bit.

"...I'm not angry, Aura," Momonga said as kindly as he could. "Relax. Did you think you could affect me with a skill you weren't even using seriously? I'm just asking if I was in range or not."

"Got it! Uh, you were in range." From Aura's voice, filled with relief, Momonga realized how terrible and awe-inspiring he was to her.

A prickling pressure assailed him under his clothes in the area where his stomach would have been if he'd had one. *What if I end up weaker because of this?* The thought of it made him want to run away at full speed.

"And what was the effect?"

"Uh, I think the one from just now was...yes, fear."

"Hmm..."

He didn't feel fear. In *Yggdrasil*, friendly fire had been disabled, so players couldn't harm members of their guild or other teammates. Here, however, there was a high possibility that that had changed; he knew it would be good to confirm one way or the other right away.

"I thought it used to be the case that your powers couldn't have any negative effects on people in the same guil— Group."

"Huh?" Aura's blank expression was matched by Mare. Momonga gathered that it hadn't been the case.

"Must have been my imagination?"

"Yes, but I can control the range of the effects at will, so maybe that's how you misunderstood?"

So friendly fire was on. The reason Mare hadn't been affected was probably because he was equipped with an item that could neutralize psychic effects. Meanwhile, Momonga's god items didn't have any psychic resistance data in them. So why hadn't he felt fear?

He had two guesses: basic resistance based on his ability points or psychic effects immunity due to a special undead ability. He decided to dig a little deeper, since he wasn't sure which one was correct.

"Can you try out some other effects for me?"

Aura cocked her head and made an odd questioning noise. She seemed like a puppy again, so Momonga reached out to pet her in spite of himself.

Her smooth, silky hair was delightful to touch. When she didn't seem to mind, he wished he could just stay there petting her forever—except Mare's glazed stare freaked him out, so he stopped. *I wonder what he's feeling...*

After thinking for a moment, Momonga released his other hand's grip on the staff and stretched it out to pet Mare. Absentmindedly thinking how the texture of Mare's hair seemed somehow better than Aura's, he petted the both of them until he was quite satisfied. Then, he finally remembered what he'd gone there to do.

"Now, then, I have a favor to ask. I'm testing out a lot of things at the moment and...I want your cooperation, Aura."

At first the two of them looked like they didn't really know what to do, but by the time he took his hands away, they seemed self-consciously happy and willing.

"Okay, understood! Leave it to me, Lord Momonga!" Aura gleefully replied.

She was enthusiastic to get going, but Momonga held her back. "Before that—" He grabbed the floating staff.

Okay, just like before. As he had done when he used the ring's power, he focused his mind on the staff. Of its countless powers, the one Momonga chose was contained within one of its jewels—inside a god artifact, the Moon Orb.

Summon Moon Wolf!

As the summoning magic activated, three beasts oozed into existence out of nowhere. Nothing about this surprised Momonga, since that was how the animation had looked in *Yggdrasil.*

The moon wolves were similar in appearance to Eurasian wolves, except they gave off a silvery light. Momonga could sense a strange connection between these monsters and himself that clearly indicated who was in charge.

"Moon wolves?" Aura asked, her voice implying confusion at why he would summon such a weak monster.

Moon wolves were extremely fast, so they were often deployed as key units in sneak attacks, but they were only level 20—too weak for Momonga and Aura. But for their purposes right now, these were fine. Weaker was actually better.

"Yes. Include me in the range of your breath, too."

"What? Are you sure?"

Aura didn't seem okay with it, so he insisted, "It's fine."

Things weren't operating completely like they had been in the game anymore, so he couldn't ignore the possibility that Aura's powers weren't working correctly. In order to rule it out, he needed to be hit with her power at the same time as a third party, hence the moon wolves.

Aura huffed and puffed for a little while, but Momonga didn't feel a thing. Partway through, he turned his back to her and relaxed his mind, but there was still no effect. The moon wolves did seem affected, though, so her power must have been working. Therefore, it seemed Momonga was immune to psychic effects. In other words...

In *Yggdrasil,* when subhumans and grotesques reached certain race levels, they gained specific racial abilities. Momonga, who had reached the elite race of overlord, had the following monster powers: Create Upper-Tier Undead (four per day); Create Middle-Tier Undead (twelve per day); Create Lower-Tier Undead (twenty per day); Negative Touch; Aura of Despair V (instadeath); Negative Guard; Dark Soul; Raven-Black Halo; Immortal Blessing; Impure Providence; Black Wisdom; Evil Language Proficiency; Ability Point Damage IV; Stabbing Weapon Resistance V; Cutting Weapon Resistance V; Greater Repel Resistance III; Greater Physical Damage Immunity III; Greater Magical Damage Immunity III; Chill, Acid, Electric Attack Immunity; Magical Vision Boost: See Through.

Add to that the abilities from his class level: Boost Instadeath Magic, Master of Dark Rites, Immortal Aura, Make Undead, Control Undead, Fortify Undead, etc.

He also had the basic undead special abilities: Critical Hit Immunity; Psychic Effect Immunity; No Hunger/Thirst; Poison, Sickness, Sleep, Paralysis, Instadeath Immunity; Resistance to Ghost Magic; Physical Penalty Resistance; Breathe Anywhere; Ability Point Damage Immunity; Energy Drain Immunity; the ability to recover from Negative Energy; Night Vision, etc.

Of course, he also had weaknesses: Justice, Light, Holy Attack Vulnerability IV; Battering Weapon Vulnerability IV; Holy, Justice Area Ability Point Penalty II; Double Fire Damage, etc.

It seemed extremely likely that he still possessed both the basic undead abilities and the special abilities he had gained from leveling up.

"I see. That's good enough for now… I thank you, Aura. Any issues on your end?"

"No, everything's fine."

"Okay. Return!" The three moon wolves disappeared as if time were rewinding.

"Lord Momonga, was that why you came to our floor today?" Aura asked, but Mare nodded that he was curious, too.

"Hm? Oh right, no—I thought I'd do some training today."

"Training? You?!" Aura's and Mare's eyes practically popped out of their heads. What was this most elite caster, the ruler of the Great Tomb of Nazarick who dominated all manner of lesser beings, talking about? But Momonga had expected this.

"Yes."

The tap of the staff on the ground accompanying his simple reply was enough for them to understand. Momonga was inwardly pleased that their reaction matched what he'd anticipated.

"I-i-is that, uh, the legendary you-know-what? The most elite weapon only you can touch?"

What does she mean by "legendary you-know-what"? Momonga wondered, but it didn't seem to be anything bad given the sparkle in Mare's eyes.

"That's right. This is the Guild Weapon we all created together, the Staff of Ainz Ooal Gown." He lifted it into the air and it sparkled beautifully in the light. It was such a gorgeous display it was almost as if the staff was showing off—except it was still exuding that ominous black shimmer, so it was hard to see it as anything but evil.

Momonga didn't have a body type that could burst with pride, so to speak, but the passion was clear in his voice. "The jewels held in each of the seven snakes' mouths are all god artifacts. Since the items are part of a series, collecting them all yields great power. Gathering them took serious effort and an immense amount of time. In fact, there were many times we thought to quit. How many mobs did we hunt for the drops…? Furthermore, the power contained within even just the staff itself surpasses god tier and is on par with a World Item. Most impressive of all is its automatic intercept— Ahem…"

…I'm totally rambling…

It was only natural to want to brag—he'd crafted it with his guildmates, but since he'd never been able to take it anywhere, he'd never had the chance to show off. That was no excuse to gush right now, though. He suppressed the urge to keep boasting.

It's pretty embarrassing actually…

"Well, yeah, that's about it…"

"W-wow!"

"That's amazing, Lord Momonga!"

The sparkles in the kids' eyes made him want to break into a huge grin. Trying to keep a straight face—not that his expressions came through so well via his skull anyway—he continued speaking. "Anyhow, I'd like to do some experiments. Can you get things ready for me?"

"Yes, sir! Understood! I'll begin preparations right away. And then…is it okay if we watch?"

"Sure, I don't mind. I'm the only one who can hold it, so you should at least have a look."

"Yess!" shouted Aura, bouncing around so cute and joyful. Mare couldn't hide how happy he was, either—his long ears were twitching.

Oh, man. Hey, dignified expression of mine, no slipping, Momonga told himself, mobilizing all his willpower.

"Oh, and Aura, I've called all the floor guardians here. They should arrive in less than an hour."

"Huh? Th-then, we have to get ready to welcome the—"

"No, don't worry about that. You can just wait for them here."

"If you say so… Hm? All the floor guardians? So Shalltear will be here, too?"

"All the floor guardians."

"Ah…" Her ears suddenly drooped.

Mare seemed more or less okay. The backstory had Aura not getting along with Shalltear very well, but his case must have been different.

"How are they going to react…?" Momonga whispered under his breath.

2

A party of about fifty riders galloped across a grassy plain. All of them were equally brawny, but one stood out from all the rest.

There was no word more fitting for him than *robust*. It was plain even through his breastplate that his whole body was covered in bulging muscles. He was in his thirties. Deep creases formed when he knit his tan brow. His black hair was neatly trimmed and his black eyes gleamed with the sharpness of a dagger.

The rider next to him spoke. "Captain, we've almost reached the first village on our patrol."

"Yes, it seems that way, Vice-Captain."

This was Gazef Stronoff, pride of the Re-Estize Kingdom and captain of its guard. The village had not yet appeared down his line of sight.

Suppressing his impatience, Gazef maintained a steady speed. Though they weren't driving their horses to exhaustion, it had been quite a march from the royal capital to here. A hint of fatigue had taken up root in his core. Certainly the same could be said for the horses. It wouldn't do to burden them any further.

"But I really hope it's nothing…" The vice-captain spoke again. His voice betrayed his anxiety, and Gazef felt the same.

The mission the king had given them was to "find the imperial knights spotted near the kingdom's border and subdue them."

Under normal circumstances, it would have been faster to send soldiers from the nearby city of E-Rantel, but the empire's knights were strong and well outfitted. The gap between them and the kingdom's recruits was clear. The only soldiers in the kingdom that had a chance against the knights were the ones directly under Gazef. But it was foolish to leave everything up to them like this. Even just mobilizing some troops to guard the villages until Gazef and his men arrived would probably have been enough to stave off the enemy. There were plenty of other options as well. Just currently, they weren't being—no, they couldn't be—taken.

Gazef knew why and it irritated him to no end. He did his best to relax his grip on the reins, but he couldn't extinguish the blaze of his inner emotions.

"Captain, it's ridiculous for us to get to the village and then begin the search. And since you brought all of us, couldn't we divide up the labor? Or better yet, we could hire some adventurers from E-Rantel and ask them to find the knights. Why are we doing it like this?"

"...Don't say that, Vice-Captain. Nothing good will come of everyone finding out there are imperial knights throwing their weight around inside the kingdom's borders."

"Captain, there's no one to hear us now. I want you to tell me the truth." A faint smile played across the vice-captain's face, but it was the exact opposite of a kindly grin. "Are the nobles interfering?" The vice-captain practically spat the words, and Gazef didn't reply. Because the answer was yes. "So the damned nobles plan to use the victims as pawns in their power struggle? And since this area is directly under the king's jurisdiction, I suppose they'll use any suffering as an excuse to make snide remarks."

"Not all the nobles think that way."

"I'm sure there are some who, like you say, think of the people. Like the Golden Princess. But how many? ...If the king could just take absolute power like the emperor next door, he could ignore the damned nobles and focus on the people."

"If we force things, sides will be taken and the country will split. Causing an internal conflict with an expansionist empire next door would be even worse for the people."

"I know, but..."

"Let's drop it for now..." Leaving it at that, Gazef pursed his lips and turned his penetrating gaze forward.

Black smoke rose from beyond a small hill up ahead—and not just one or two trails. There wasn't a man present who didn't know what that meant. Gazef clicked his tongue and kicked his spurs into his horse's flanks.

The scene that flooded their vision when they crested the hill was what they had expected. The village had been burned to ashes. The scattered house wreckage still standing was like grave markers.

Gazef gave orders in a steely voice. "Company, begin maneuvers. On the double!"

•

The village was burned to the ground. Only the collapsed remains of houses still bore any resemblance to their former shape. Walking through the wreckage, everything smelled like charred ashes mixed with the stench of blood.

Gazef's face was steady, no trace of emotion, but that itself showed most clearly what he must have been feeling. The same went for the vice-captain, walking beside him.

Of the more than one hundred villagers, only six had survived. The rest had been massacred—women and children alike, even infants.

"Vice-Captain, escort the survivors to E-Rantel."

"Please don't do this! That would be the most..."

"You're right—it's a foolish plan. But we can't just leave them here like this."

E-Rantel was directly under the king's jurisdiction and protecting these villages was his job. If they abandoned the survivors, it would be a terrible blow to the king. And it was easy to see that the nobles trying to corner him would make noise about it, too.

And more importantly...

"Please rethink this. We should retreat to E-Rantel for the time being and get ourselves in order."

"That's impossible."

"Captain! I'm sure you realize, but this must be a trap. The timing of the attack on the village lines up too well with our arrival in E-Rantel. They waited for us before committing this atrocity. I'd even venture to say that the fact that they didn't kill every last person means it can't be anything but a trap." The survivors hadn't managed to escape the knights by running and hiding. The attackers just didn't kill them. Their aim was probably to force the military to divide their strength to protect them. "Captain, you can't mean that you're going to chase them down knowing full well it's a trap!"

"...That was my intention."

"Are you serious? Captain. It's true that you're strong. I'm sure you could fight one hundred knights and come out victorious. But the empire has a caster. If that old man is with them, it's risky, even for you. You're not fully outfitted right now, so losing to the Four wouldn't be out of the question, either. So I'm begging you, please withdraw. No matter how many more villages fell, losing you would be a bigger loss for the kingdom!" In response to Gazef's silence, the vice-captain continued with pain in his voice. "If you can't withdraw, then let's *all* leave the survivors and go after them."

"That...is probably the wisest choice, but it would mean abandoning lives that could be saved. Do you really think they could make it if we left them here on their own?"

The vice-captain had no response. He knew the chances were slim. If they didn't provide an escort and take them somewhere safe, they'd be gone within a few days. Still the vice-captain said—he *had* to say—"Captain. The most valuable life here is yours. We can't be worried what happens to the villagers."

Gazef knew it was killing the vice-captain to say such things, and he was angry at himself for forcing the issue, but he still couldn't accept it. "I was born a commoner. You were, too, right?"

"Yes. I aspired to the Select because I looked up to you."

"You lived in a village, right?"

"Yes, that's why—"

"Death is like a next-door neighbor when you live in a village. It's not so rare for a monster to attack and kill people, right?"

"Right..."

"Mere soldiers can't always handle a monster. If you don't have the money to hire a specialist in monster extermination—an adventurer—all you can do is lie low until it leaves."

"Right..."

"So, didn't you ever hope? Hope that a noble would appear in your hour of need? That someone with power would come and save you?"

"It'd be a lie if I said I didn't, but no one ever came. At least, the nobles of the domain we belonged to never gave us any financial help."

"So let's show them we're different. We're going to save the villagers."

The vice-captain's voice caught as he remembered his past.

"Vice-Captain. Let's show 'em that there are people out there who will risk their lives despite the danger, that there are strong who will protect the weak!"

The men's eyes met and exchanged a multitude of emotions.

Finally, the vice-captain spoke, sounding tired but aiming to convey his passion. "...Then I'll take my men and go. I may be replaceable, but you're not."

"Don't be absurd! There's a better chance we make it back alive if I go, too. We don't go to our deaths; we go to save the people."

The vice-captain's mouth worked for a moment, then closed. "I'll choose who will escort the villagers to E-Rantel right away."

•

As the sky reddened, human shapes began to appear one after another on the grassy plain. There were forty-five of them. The way they appeared out of nowhere was not due to camouflage, but magic.

One glance was enough to tell they were not mercenaries, travelers, or adventurers. They all looked the same, clad in armored clothing woven out of special metallic thread to prioritize mobility and defense. Due to magical fortification, however, these clothes had even greater defense and, in fact, were more effective than a full suit of armor. Their leather bags weren't very full and didn't seem like the kind of thing someone on a journey would carry—that is, as long as they weren't also magic. The specially made belts around their waists held multiple potions and the mantles draped across their backs radiated magical auras.

Gathering enough magical items for all those people would have been no easy feat, either of coin or in terms of time and effort. Being so well equipped was proof that they had nation-level support behind them. Despite that, there was nothing on any of their gear displaying their rank or affiliation. In other words, they were an unlawful group with reason to hide.

They looked toward the abandoned village. Gazing upon the ruins enveloped in the stench of burning and blood produced not a flicker of emotion in their eyes. They looked on coolly, as if it were a matter of course.

"We let him get away, huh?" A low voice spoke with a hint of disappointment.

"...There was nothing we could do. Have our decoy continue attacking villages. We must lead the beast to its cage." The man's sharp gaze followed Gazef and the others as they headed away.

"Tell me where the decoy should strike next."

3

Momonga prepared to cast a spell, stretching his fingers out slowly toward a straw figure set up in a corner of the arena.

The magic he specialized in was more about secondary effects, like instadeath, than simply dealing damage. For that reason, it didn't work so well on nonliving targets. A situation like this called for straightforward damage-dealing magic, but he had chosen his class's ghost tree and beefed up his repertoire with those type of spells. As a result, in terms of damage dealt, he was a few tiers behind magic users who specialized in combat spells.

Momonga peeked at the children—their eyes sparkled with curiosity. The anxiety of whether he could live up to their expectations or not weighed him down.

Next he stole a glance in a different direction, where there were two huge monsters. They stood ten feet tall with inverted triangle figures. Muscles rippled over frames that were a combination of human and dragon. Covering the muscles were scales harder than steel. The monsters had dragon-like faces and tails thick as tree trunks. Despite the lack of wings, they looked very much like dragons standing upright. In their arms, thicker than a man's torso, they each held some kind of weapon (a sword? a shield?) that was half as long as they were tall. They were dragonkin, employed by Aura via her beast-tamer skills to keep the arena clean. They were only level 55 and had no special abilities to speak of, but the punches they could dish with their strong arms paired with their seemingly inexhaustible health meant they could hold their own against higher-level monsters.

Breathing a little quickly, Momonga turned back to the straw figure. *Honestly, having everyone watching with such high expectations is putting me on the spot.* The point of this exercise was to check if he could even use a spell or not.

The reason he'd allowed Aura and Mare to watch was so he could show them his power before the others arrived and teach them how foolish it would be to oppose him. Of course, it was impossible for him to imagine these children betraying him, and there was certainly no sign that they might do such a thing, but Momonga wasn't confident they would remain loyal to him if it turned out he had lost the ability to cast spells.

Aura interacted with him as if they were old acquaintances, but from Momonga's perspective they might as well have met for the first time. Of course, her background was all based on ideas from the guild and both of the children were guild member–created treasures, but it wasn't as if all their behavioral patterns, their responses to any situation, were set in stone. There was definitely what Momonga supposed could be called a "loophole" in their settings.

If they were intelligent living things that thought and behaved autonomously, they would eventually come across a situation that their bios did not prepare them for. And how would things turn out if there was nothing in there about devoting themselves to their master even if he was weak?

Actually, there were probably more cases where loyalty was not specified at all, in which case obeying orders or not all came down to individual judgment. If disobeying was as far as it went, that was fine, but what if someone wanted to rebel against the guild master if they thought he wasn't cutting it?

Being more skeptical than necessary was a problem, but it was also stupid to blindly trust them. *I'll just have to feel it out as I go.* That was what made the most sense to Momonga under the circumstances.

His other aim in having the twins there was to get advice in the event he couldn't cast a spell. They thought he was there to test the staff. He already knew magic items worked, so he could wield as much deception as necessary.

My plan is perfect.

He patted himself on the back and wondered if he had always been so sharp and composed, but there was no one who could answer that question for him.

Momonga cleared the doubts from his mind and considered the magic he'd been able to use in *Yggdrasil*. The total number of magic spells in *Yggdrasil,* from tiers one to ten, plus super tier, was well over six thousand. These were split into various trees, but of the total, Momonga could use 718. Normally a level-100 player could use about three hundred, so that was an insane amount.

Not only that, but he'd memorized them all so he could choose the most appropriate spell for every situation—including this one. First, since friendly fire was on, he had to know what the area of effect would look like, so he would have to select a spell not based on how many enemies, but based on the area. *And if this is my target, then...*

In *Yggdrasil,* all he'd had to do to cast a spell was tap an icon, but he couldn't do that anymore, so he had to find another way. He thought he might already have it partially mastered. He focused on the powers deep inside him, just as he had when he'd turned off Negative Touch. *Just imagine there are icons floating in the air...* He laughed to himself. *I got it.*

He had a perfect grasp of what the area of effect would be and how much time it would take before he could cast again. The confidence in his ability came with a serious high—the fulfillment and satisfaction of knowing that his magic was truly his own power. He'd never felt like this in *Yggdrasil*.

As if transmuting the delight that had bubbled up inside him—his swiftly calming mind intensified the high—he gathered it at his fingertips and spoke the word of power: "Fireball!"

A ball of flames grew from the tip of his finger, shot off at the straw figure he was pointing at, and hit just where he'd aimed. The ball burst on impact, instantly scattering the flames it had contained. The expanded flames raged through the area, even scorching the ground, in a flash.

The whole thing had only taken a second. Nothing was left of the straw figure but burned-up remains.

"Heh-heh-heh-heh..." Momonga let slip a laugh only he knew the meaning of and the twins looked on, puzzled.

"Aura, ready another straw figure."

"Oh—yes, sir! Right away! Hurry and set it up!" One of the dragonkin stood a new figure next to the charred one.

Momonga walked leisurely over, turned toward the straw figure, and cast a spell: "Napalm!"

It went slightly astray but suddenly formed a column of flames that then engulfed the area and swirled up into the sky. After a beat, Momonga cast another spell at the figure that had been reduced to debris. "Fireball!"

The figure was obliterated on impact.

The spells' cooldowns were the same as in *Yggdrasil*. Actually, since for an area-of-effect spell he didn't have to first select the spell and then aim by moving the cursor showing the area, he might have been able to cast even faster.

"Perfect." His satisfaction took the form of this remark, voiced of its own accord.

"Lord Momonga, should I prepare some more straw figures?" Aura did seem puzzled. She knew from before that Momonga possessed incredible power, so she probably didn't understand what was such a big deal about stunts like this. But that was exactly the impression he'd wanted to make on the twins, so their confused expressions were proof of his success.

"No, that won't be necessary. I want to test something else now." Once he'd declined Aura's request, he set about his next objective.

"Message." First, he would try to contact a GM. The way the Message spell worked in *Yggdrasil* was that if the player being contacted were in the game at the time, the caller would hear a cell phone–like ring, but if they weren't, it would just disconnect. Now it was maybe a cousin of that spell. Momonga felt like he was putting out a feeler to search for something. The sensation was difficult to describe, and he was experiencing it for the first time in his life. It continued for a little while and then, with nothing to connect to, the spell timed out.

Well, that's discouraging.

He repeated the same spell, this time not aimed at a GM. He was calling the old members of Ainz Ooal Gown. He attempted it with 1 percent hope, feeling 99 percent like nothing would come of it, and as expected, there was no response. After calling all forty members and confirming no response from anyone, he slowly shook his head. He'd known it was hopeless, but getting slapped in the face with reality was quite a downer. He cast the spell once more, at Sebas.

It connected!

So it was clear that Message was indeed—alas—working. There was still the possibility that it would only connect to characters in this world, but...

"Lord Momonga." The deeply deferential voice echoed in his head. Momonga wondered if Sebas was bowing on the other end like a businessman in the real world would have been.

Sebas must have been unsure how to interpret the silence caused by Momonga's extraneous musing because he spoke again, sounding perplexed. "Is...something wrong?"

"Oh, uh, sorry. It seems I spaced out for a moment. By the way, what's it like out there?"

"We're on a grassy plain, and I haven't been able to confirm the existence of any intelligent life."

"A grassy plain... No bogs?"

The Great Tomb of Nazarick used to be located deep in a swamp inhabited by frog-like people known as tsveiks. The whole area was covered by mist, and there were poisonous bogs here and there.

"No, just a grassy plain."

Momonga laughed in spite of himself. *Who knows what the heck is going on now?*

"So Nazarick as a whole has been teleported to some unknown location…? Sebas, is there anything up in the sky? Any signs or signals?"

"No, nothing like that. Just the same night sky as the sixth level."

"What?! A night sky, huh? There's nothing else in the area that catches your eye?"

"No, not in particular. Aside from the Great Tomb of Nazarick, I don't even see any man-made structures."

"I see, I see…"

What could he say? The only thing left for him to do was rip his hair out (although somewhere in his mind he had been prepared for this possibility).

Sebas's silence indicated he was awaiting direction. Momonga glanced at the band on his left wrist. There were about twenty minutes until the other guardians would arrive, in which case there was only one order that made sense to give.

"Be back in twenty minutes. Once you've returned to the Tomb, come to the Amphitheatrum. I'm assembling all the guardians, so I'll have you report what you've seen."

"Understood."

"Okay, get as much information as you can before then."

After getting Sebas's confirmation, he ended the spell. Just as he was thinking he'd take a break, having finished everything he needed to do for the moment, he remembered the two children and their expectant gazes.

He needed to show them the power of the Staff of Ainz Ooal Gown, since he'd said he would. He took the staff into his hand but couldn't decide what magic to unleash. It was as if all its countless powers were begging to be used. *I should probably go for something pretty showy.* So he chose the Fire Orb and from among its powers cast Summon Primal Fire Elemental.

Obeying Momonga's will, power stirred within a jewel in one of the snakes' mouths. Sensing that the flow of power was adequate, he pointed the staff. A huge sphere of light grew at the end and an incredible storm of flames whipped up around it. The vortex rapidly expanded to a diameter of thirteen feet and a height of about twenty feet.

The crimson purgatory kicked up a hot wind, and out of the corner of his eye, Momonga saw the dragonkin move in front of Aura and Mare to protect them. His robe flapped in the waves of heat. It could've easily burned him, given the temperature, but Momonga had compensated for the weakness to fire he shared with all undead with perfect resistance, so he was unaffected.

After increasing its size by consuming all the air in its vicinity, the swaying tornado of flames emitted a glow like fusing iron and took on a humanoid shape.

The primal fire elemental was one of the highest-level elementals, falling in the upper 80s range. Momonga felt the same connection with it that he had with the moon wolves.

"Whoa." A gasp escaped Aura's lips as she marveled at the monster. It was impossible to call forth such an elite elemental with regular summoning magic, and the look on her face was like a kid who'd gotten the toy she'd always wanted.

"Want to try fighting it?"

"Huh?"

"Wh-what?"

She was lost for a moment, but then the natural smile of a child played across her face. Actually, for a child it was a bit—well, *rather*—twisted; Mare's expression was more childlike.

"You'll let us fight it?"

"Sure, I don't mind. It's no big deal if it gets defeated." Momonga shrugged. The staff's power allowed him to summon one a day. In other words, it didn't matter if this one got taken down, because he could summon another one the next day.

"Uh, I just remembered something I have to do..."

"Mare!" She grabbed him with an iron grip when he tried to make a run for it. Apparently she wasn't going to let him escape. She snagged him with her smile. To Momonga, it was the smile of an adorable little girl, but he wondered if it looked different to someone with the same face; Mare was scared stiff.

Aura dragged him in front of the primal fire elemental. His eyes darted around seeking succor, finally finding Momonga. In reply to his radiant ear-to-ear grin, Momonga joined his palms to mimic a prayer. The light on Mare's face went out.

"Well, don't overdo it, you two. It'd be silly to get hurt."

"We won't!" Aura responded cheerfully. Mare's voice was there, too, but gloomy, like he was being escorted to his doom. Momonga figured they wouldn't get hurt as long as Mare was there, so he used his connection to the primal fire elemental to order it to attack.

The twins engaged the roaring flames of the attacking elemental with Aura forward and Mare in back. Aura double wielded her whips to lash the hovering monster into submission, and Mare's magic steadily racked up damage.

"Yeah, I figured this would be no problem for them..."

The battle may have been one-sided, but he continued to watch while he went over in his head the other things he had to investigate. He'd already confirmed that magic and some items worked, but there were still other items he wanted to check—most importantly, scrolls, staves, and wands. Objects like these contained magic. Scrolls were single use while staves and wands came with a certain amount of casts.

Momonga possessed quite a few of these. He was the type that felt using up consumables was a waste. He refused to use the highest-grade recovery potions, even on the final boss. He'd gone beyond cautious to plain stingy, so his inventory had just piled up. In *Yggdrasil*, they'd been stored in his item box, but where were they now?

Recalling how he used to open his item box, he stretched his fleshless hand into the air. He felt it slip into something; it was almost like breaking the surface tension of water. He was sure for an onlooker it must have looked like part of his arm had disappeared into the air. Then, as if he were opening a window, he made a broad sliding motion to the side. A window *did* open, right in the air, and inside were several staves lined up all neat and tidy. This was definitely *Yggdrasil*'s item box.

He moved his hand to scroll through what he supposed one could call his "inventory screen." Scrolls, wands, weapons, armor, decorations, jewels, potions, and other consumables—he had a vast number of magical tools.

Momonga's face broke into a relieved smile. *With all this, I should be able to protect myself even if everyone in the Tomb turns against me*

Still absentmindedly keeping his eye on Aura and Mare's fierce battle, Momonga summarized all the information he'd collected so far.

Are the NPCs I've met programs?

No. They were beings with consciousness just like humans. It was impossible to capture such subtle emotions with code. He needed to assume that they were no longer programs but had somehow become equivalent to humans.

And what is this world?

That was unclear. Considering *Yggdrasil*'s magic existed, it would be valid to suppose he was inside the game, but taking into account the previous answer, that couldn't possibly be the case. That said, it was either the game world or some other world, one of the two. Not that either made any sense.

How should I conduct myself?

He'd confirmed that he could use his powers as he could in *Yggdrasil*. So, if all the NPCs and monsters in the Great Tomb of Nazarick were also based on *Yggdrasil* data, he would have no enemies. The problem would be if there were something not from *Yggdrasil*, but all he could do was cross that bridge when he came to it. For now, he had to just act with the dignity of a ruler—assuming he could muster such a thing.

What's the plan?

Work to gather information. He didn't know what this world was, and at the moment, he was like an ignorant tourist. He needed to keep his wits about him and cautiously gather as much information as he could.

Say this is some other world—should I try to get back to mine?

Good question. If he'd had any friends, he'd probably try to go back. If his parents were still alive, he'd risk his life to find a way back. If he'd had a family to take care of or a lover...

But he had none of those things.

He went to the office, worked, came home, and slept. Up until now, he'd log onto *Yggdrasil* and keep things ready in case any of his guildmates wanted to come back, but he didn't even have that anymore. Was there any point in going back to such a world?

But, if he *could* get back, then he knew he should put in the effort. One could never have too many options. The world outside the Tomb could very well be hell.

"Okay, what do I do?" Momonga's lonely words to himself evaporated into the air.

4

The primal fire elemental's gigantic body disappeared as if melting into the air and the heat that had been thrown around the area rapidly dissipated. Momonga also felt the bond of dominance he'd been vaguely aware of break.

The primal fire elemental had extraordinary destructive power and stamina, but for Aura, who demonstrated impressive evasive action and had complete immunity to the fire damage that had been hitting everything in the area, it might as well have been target practice.

Of course, if she had gotten hit, she would have lost a significant portion of her health, but Mare, as a druid, would never let that happen. He used an appropriate mix of buffs and debuffs to support her.

Their style of fighting was a magnificent division of roles between forward and rear positions. Momonga was struck both by that and by how raw the action had felt—it had been a real fight, not something from a game.

"Magnificent… You were both…wonderful!"

The children smiled at his heartfelt words of admiration. "Thank you, Lord Momonga! It's been a while since we've gotten such a workout!"

The two of them casually wiped the sweat from their faces, but the moment they did, it beaded up again and began to drip down their tan skin.

Momonga silently opened his item box and took something out for the first time in this world: the Bottomless Pitcher of Water.

Yggdrasil had systems for eating and thirst, etc., but since Momonga was undead, none of them applied to him, so he had never used the item himself. He'd been using it for his mounts.

The pitcher was made out of a transparent material that seemed like glass and was filled to the brim with fresh water. Perhaps due to how cold the water was, countless droplets had condensed on the outside of the container. Next, he took out two clean glasses, filled them, and offered them to the twins. "Aura, Mare, please drink this."

"What? We couldn't possibly, Lord Momonga."

"Y-yeah, we don't need to trouble you for that. I can make water with my magic."

Aura waved her hands in polite refusal, and Mare shook his head quickly back and forth. Seeing them like that made Momonga wince.

"Oh, c'mon, it's water. Just a small token of my thanks for all your hard work."

"Ahhh..."

"Ohhh..."

Aura and Mare, blushing, nervously reached out their hands to take the glasses.

"Th-thank you, Lord Momonga!"

"I can't believe *you're* pouring drinks for *us*!"

Does it really make you that happy?

This time Aura didn't refuse, but took the glass in both hands and gulped it down. The movements of her throat were clearly visible, and water that overflowed from the corners of her lips ran down her lustrous neck and disappeared into her chest. Mare, meanwhile, held the cup in one hand and took measured sips. The difference in their personalities was made abruptly apparent just from the way they drank.

Watching them, Momonga brought a hand to his own throat. It felt like there was a membrane stretched directly over his cervical spine.

He hadn't felt thirsty since entering this body. Or tired. He understood that it was only natural for an undead to not feel any of those things, but the idea of not being human anymore seemed like it had to be a joke.

He felt around his body some more. Skin, flesh, blood vessels, nerves, organs. He was missing all manner of things; he had a body made solely of bone. He'd known that, but now he groped around so it would sink in.

His sense of touch was slightly dull compared to when he was human, almost like there was a thin cloth between him and anything he went to touch. Meanwhile, his other senses performed outstandingly. His hearing and vision were extremely sharp.

Since his body was built entirely of bones, it seemed like it could break at any moment, but he also had the sense that each bone was more solid than steel.

Although this body was completely different from his old one, there was a strange satisfaction and sense of fulfillment knowing it was his. Perhaps that was why he wasn't frightened by his transformation.

"Want another glass?" He held up the Bottomless Pitcher and offered once the children had finished their water.

"Umm, nope! That was enough for me!"

"I see. Mare, how about you?"

"Oh! U-um, I-I'm okay. M-my throat's not dry anymore."

Momonga nodded, took the glasses back, and put them away into the air.

"I thought you were more scary, Lord Momonga," Aura said softly.

"Oh, really? I can be scarier if you like..."

"No, I like you better like this! Way better!"

"Then I'll stay like this." Aura's animated response had thrown him off a bit.

"Y-you're not this nice only to us, are you?"

Momonga didn't know how to respond to her quiet murmurs, so he just patted her on the head several times.

"Eh-heh-heh-heh..." She was like a puppy presented with its favorite food. Mare looked on jealously. Suddenly they heard a voice.

"Oh? Am I the first?" It sounded younger than one might expect from the tone. At the same time, a shadow spread across the ground, rose up out of it, and took on the shape of a door. Then, someone walked slowly through.

Her whole body was wrapped in a soft-looking raven-black ball gown with a full, wide skirt. She covered up on top with a bolero cardigan featuring frills and ribbons. Add to all that her fingerless lace gloves and almost all her skin was hidden from view. Only her shapely face—*unparalleled* was the right word to describe it—was visible, its almost waxy white skin exposed. Her long silver hair was gathered to one side and up so not a strand of it fell in her face. Her crimson eyes had a weirdly jubilant look in them.

She was fourteen or possibly younger. There was still some child in her, and her beauty was borne of that mix of cuteness and adult attractiveness. One thing that was out of balance, however, was how big her chest was for her age.

"Teleportation is restricted in Nazarick for a reason! Don't just go using a gate! You entered the arena the normal way, so couldn't you have just kept walking, Shalltear?" An exasperated voice sounded right next to Momonga. The icy tone had nothing of the puppyishness of just a moment ago. On the contrary, it was full to overflowing with hostility.

Next to Aura, Mare began trembling again. It was probably wise of him to be inching away from his sister. Even Momonga was a bit alarmed by the sudden change in her.

The girl, Shalltear, who had arrived using the highest level of teleportation magic, cast not so much as a glance at Aura, but stood squirming a bit before Momonga. She smelled pleasantly like perfume.

"You reek," Aura muttered softly, adding that maybe her undead body rotting was to blame.

Perhaps because she had caught Momonga instinctively lifting his arm to check if he smelled, a dark blue vein stood up on Shalltear's forehead.

"Oh, come now, you can't say that—Lord Momonga is undead, too..."

"Huh?! What are you talking about? Lord Momonga's not regular undead. Pretty sure he's like 'super undead' or 'godly undead' or something."

Hearing Shalltear and Mare express their satisfaction with such an explanation ("Oh...," "Right..."), Momonga felt somewhat insignificant. *I don't know what it's like here, but at least in* Yggdrasil *I was just plain undead...* More to the point, "super undead" and "godly undead" didn't exist.

"S-still, what you said was kinda bad."

"Y-you think so? Okay, then, take two. Ahem… 'Maybe it's 'cause of your rotting dead flesh.'"

"I… Yes, I suppose that will do." Accepting Aura's second take, Shalltear slipped her arms around Momonga's neck to embrace him.

"Ahh, my master, the sole being I cannot conquer." Her wet tongue showed itself between her parted red lips. It moved over them as if it were its own separate animal. From her open mouth came sweet-smelling breath.

All of this would have been extremely becoming of a bewitchingly beautiful adult, but at her age, something was off. The awkward mismatch was even a bit endearing. In the first place, she wasn't tall enough, so instead of embracing him, it just seemed like she was trying to hang from his neck.

Despite all that, Momonga was unaccustomed to attention from women and was plenty bewitched. He nearly took a step backward but made up his mind to stand still.

Was her personality always like this? He couldn't get the question out of his mind. But since the one who wrote her backstory was Peroroncino, it was entirely possible that this was just how she was. That guy loved porn games more than anything and had even adopted "Porn games are my life!" as his personal catchphrase. And that good-for-nothing had written the bio of Shalltear Bloodfallen. She was the guardian of levels one through three and a true vampire, as well as a little girl who'd been given a pile of X-rated video game character traits.

"I think that's enough…"

Shalltear responded to the low, hard voice and sneered at Aura. "Oh, hello, squirt. I didn't see you there."

Momonga didn't feel like bothering to point out that they'd just been talking a moment ago.

Ignoring Aura and her twitching, irritated expression, Shalltear addressed Mare. "It must be hard for you to have such an odd elder sister. You should get some distance from her as soon as possible. If you don't, you might end up the same way!"

Mare's face went sickly pale—he knew she was using him to pick a fight with his sister.

But Aura smiled. "Shut up, Miss Fake Boobs."

She'd dropped a bomb.

"How'd you know?!"

"Ooh, she broke character," Momonga said to himself. There was no sign of her forced elegant cool.

"One glance is enough to tell! Look how bizarrely poofy they are. How many layers of padding did you use?"

"Wahhh! Wahhh!" Shalltear flailed her hands as if to erase the words out of the air. Now she looked her age.

Meanwhile, Aura had an evil grin on her face. "If you use that much padding...I bet they must shift around when you run, huh?!"

"Yeek!" Shalltear emitted a strange scream now that she was caught.

"Bull's-eye! Neh-heh-heh! Your boobs slip, so that's why you used a gate—so you could get here in a hurry without having to run!"

"Shut it, pip-squeak! You don't have *any*! I at least have a litt— I mean, I'm pretty big!" Shalltear frantically fired back, but Aura only grinned even more evilly. Shalltear took a step back as if she'd been shoved. The fact that she was trying to inconspicuously shield her chest was kind of sad.

"I'm still only seventy-six! I've got plenty of time ahead of me! It must be tough being undead with no future. You don't grow!"

"Ugh," Shalltear groaned and retreated farther. She had no comeback for that, and it showed plainly on her face. Aura noted this and stretched her slit-like grin even farther.

"You should be satisfied with what you got—pft!"

"Now that you said it you can't take it back!"

Shalltear's gloved hands began to exude a shimmering black haze. Aura had her whips ready to intercept. Before the two of them stood a flustered Mare. Momonga felt like he was watching a scene from the past and couldn't decide whether to stop them or not.

Peroroncino, who had created Shalltear, and BubblingTeapot, who had created Aura and Mare, were brother and sister. They used to have good-natured squabbles sometimes, like this. Momonga almost felt he could see the shadows of his former guildmates fighting behind the two NPCs.

"WHAT A RACKET." Momonga was basking in reminiscences of his old guildmates when the hard, twisted voice of something not human speaking human words stopped Aura and Shalltear's quarrel short.

Standing in the direction from which the voice came (who knew how long he'd been there) was a grotesque throwing a chill into the air. He looked like an eight-foot-tall bipedal insect. If there were such a thing as a combination of an utterly demonic mantis and an ant, it'd probably look like this. From his sturdy tail that was double his height and the rest of his body sprouted countless icicle-like spikes. His horizontally closing lower jaws were surely powerful enough to sever a human arm with no trouble.

Two of his arms carried a silver halberd and the other two held a horrifying yet excellently made mace giving off a sinister black aura and a broadsword so warped it seemed impossible for it to ever be sheathed.

He was wrapped in a chill that sparkled like diamond dust and his light blue exoskeleton was like armor. His back and shoulders bulged like icebergs.

This was the guardian of the fifth level, "Sovereign of the Frozen River," Cocytus. He struck the ground with the blade of his halberd and the earth around it slowly froze.

"YOU AMUSE YOURSELVES TOO MUCH BEFORE A SUPREME BEING."

"She's being disrespectful to—"

"I'm just telling the truth—"

"Arrrrgh..."

Mare panicked as Shalltear and Aura glared at each other again, eyes fearsomely flashing. Momonga was over it all by now and warned them both in a voice he made deep on purpose, "Shalltear, Aura, that's enough playing around for now."

Both of them jumped and then hung their heads in unison. "I'm sorry!"

He nodded to generously accept their apology and then turned to the newly arrived figure. "Thanks for coming, Cocytus."

"I COME IMMEDIATELY WHEN YOU CALL, SUPREME ONE."

White breath escaped from between Cocytus's mandibles and in response came a cracking noise as if the moisture in the air were freezing solid.

It was a cold on par with the heat of the primal fire elemental. Just being near him was enough to cause all sorts of low-temperature status effects and physical damage, but Momonga didn't feel a thing. Though really, there was no one in the room who didn't have some way to resist fire, chill, and acid attacks.

"Have you been bored with no raiders these days?"

"THERE CERTAINLY HASN'T BEEN MUCH GOING ON..." His mandibles clicked. It sounded like the threatening clicks of an angry hornet, but Momonga chose to think he must be laughing.

"BUT THAT SAID, I HAVE THINGS TO DO, SO I CAN'T SAY I'VE BEEN BORED."

"Oh! 'Things to do'? Do you mind telling me what?"

"TRAINING SO THAT I MAY BE OF USE TO YOU AT ANY TIME."

Cocytus, not that it was apparent from the way he looked, was a warrior, both personality-wise and by design. Of those in the Great Tomb of Nazarick who used weapons, he had the highest attack power.

"To be of use to me? Thanks."

"HEARING THAT SINGLE WORD MAKES IT ALL WORTH IT. OH, IT SEEMS DEMIURGE AND ALBEDO HAVE ARRIVED."

Following Cocytus's line of sight, Momonga saw two shadows near the entrance of the arena. Albedo was in front. A man followed behind her as if in attendance. When they'd gotten closer, Albedo smiled and bowed deeply to Momonga. The man also gave an elegant bow before speaking. "Sorry to keep you all waiting."

He was about six feet tall with skin the shade of a suntan. He had Asian features and his jet-black hair was slicked back. The eyes behind his round glasses were not so much slivers as closed. He wore a three-piece suit with a necktie and had the air of a shrewd businessman or lawyer.

Even though he presented himself as a gentleman, he couldn't hide his evil nature. Behind him stretched a silver-plated tail with six spines on the tip. This man, scattering dark flickering flames, was "Creator of the Inferno"—Demiurge. He was the demon who commanded NPC defense operations and the guardian of the seventh level.

"This is everyone, then."

"Lord Momonga, it seems we're still missing two." It was a voice that wormed its way into hearts and drew one in with its richness. All Demiurge's words came with a passive skill called Incantation of Influence. It was a power that caused the weakhearted who heard him to instantly become his puppets. That said, no one in the room was affected. It only worked on targets of level 40 and below, so all those present merely heard it as a particularly luscious voice and nothing more.

"Their presence isn't necessary. They've both been assigned to prioritize other tasks. We don't need to interrupt them for this."

"If that's all right, then..."

"IT SEEMS MY COMRADE IS NOT HERE, EITHER..."

Aura and Shalltear stopped short. Even Albedo's smile froze.

"He's...only a guard for one part of one of my floors..."

"Y-yeah..."

Shalltear forced a smile and Aura chimed in while Albedo nodded.

"Ahh, the Prince of Fear? Well, we should probably notify the domain guardians as well. Please pass the information along to Crimson, Grant, and the others. I'll leave it up to each floor guardian."

There were two types of guardians in the Great Tomb of Nazarick. One was the type that all those before Momonga now were, floor guardians who were each in charge of one or more levels. The other was domain guardians who guarded part of a level. Put simply, domain guardians worked under the floor guardians to protect one section of a level. Since there were so many of them, they were somewhat underappreciated, and in Nazarick the word *guardian* generally indicated a floor guardian.

Once everyone had indicated their understanding of Momonga's order, Albedo spoke. "Now, then, let us perform the ritual of allegiance."

The guardians all nodded, and before Momonga could get a word in, they'd arranged themselves with Albedo in front and the other guardians lined up behind her. Their expressions were all stiffly ceremonious. Any hint of a jokey atmosphere had vanished.

Shalltear, at the end of the line, took a step forward. "Guardian of the

First, Second, and Third Levels, Shalltear Bloodfallen. I bow before you, O Supreme One." She dropped to one knee and put a hand over her chest, bowing her head low. After Shalltear, Cocytus stepped forward.

"GUARDIAN OF THE FIFTH LEVEL, COCYTUS. I BOW BEFORE YOU, O SUPREME ONE."

He took the same humble posture as Shalltear and bowed to Momonga. Next, the two dark elves stepped forward.

"Guardian of the Sixth Level, Aura Bella Fiora. I bow before you, O Supreme One."

"G-Guardian of the same, Mare Bello Fiore. I b-bow before you, O Supreme One."

As expected, they also got down on one knee and bowed their heads low. Shalltear, Cocytus, Aura, Mare. They were built differently, so there should have been some discrepancy in the size of their steps, but their kneeling positions formed a straight line.

Then Demiurge took a graceful step forward. "Guardian of the Seventh Level, Demiurge. I bow before you, O Supreme One." Though his tone was cool, he made an extremely heartfelt bow without breaking his elegant demeanor. Finally, Albedo stepped forward.

"Captain of the floor guardians, Albedo. I bow before you, O Supreme One." Smiling faintly at Momonga, she kneeled in the manner of the other guardians. But for Albedo, that wasn't the end. With her head bowed, she made her voice carry and gave her last report. "Excepting Guardian of the Fourth Level, Gargantua, and Guardian of the Eighth Level, Victim, the floor guardians have gathered to prostrate ourselves before you… Your orders, O Supreme One! We offer our complete devotion to you."

Being faced with their six bowed heads was practically enough to make his gulp audible despite a lack of anything to gulp with. The air was tense. Or maybe it was only Momonga who felt on edge.

I don't know what to do… Normal people probably never experience something like this even once in their lives.

In the confusion, he accidentally activated some of his skills and emitted an aura throughout the area. A halo appeared behind him. Without even the composure to cancel them, he frantically fought to remember everything he'd seen in movies or on TV to get an idea of how to conduct himself.

"Raise your heads." All of their heads rose together in so crisp a motion that he practically expected to hear a *whoosh*. It was so simultaneous that he wondered if they'd been practicing.

"Well, then... For starters, I appreciate you all gathering here."

"Please save your appreciation. We offer you not only our devotion, but our very selves. It is most natural that we should heed your call."

None of the other guardians tried to cut in. As captain, Albedo was truly their unified voice.

Seeing all their earnest expressions turned his way, Momonga felt a lump in the throat he didn't even have. The pressure to behave like a ruler was weighing him down.

But that wasn't all. His orders would determine their future. He started to feel indecisive. The worry that the Great Tomb of Nazarick might collapse due to a decision he made flitted across his mind.

"Lord Momonga, you seem irresolute. That is only natural. You must wonder whether it is even worth accepting our help." Her smile had vanished and a determined look tensed her features. "However, if you honor us with your orders, we the floor guardians will suffer any trials to carry them out with all our bodies and souls. We vow to serve in such a way as will bring no shame upon our Creators, the Forty-One Supreme Beings of Ainz Ooal Gown."

"We vow it!" The other floor guardians echoed Albedo in chorus. Their voices were filled with an unstoppable power—their loyalty was like a priceless diamond sneering at Momonga for worrying they might betray him.

It was as if the darkness before his eyes had vanished in the morning light, and a shiver went through him. He realized how wonderful the NPCs his guildmates had made really were. The radiance of Ainz Ooal Gown's glory days was here now. He was so happy to have the fruit of his guildmates' labor with him that his dignified expression broke. Of course, there were no major changes to his bony face, but the beautiful red spark in his eyes burned more brightly.

With no trace of his former anxiety, Momonga spoke smoothly, like the guild master he was. "Wonderful, guardians. It is my firm belief as of this moment that you can understand my aims and are capable of accomplishing them without error." He surveyed their faces once more. "Now, then, there may be some points that are unclear, but I want you to listen carefully. It appears the Great Tomb of Nazarick has unexpectedly become involved in some sort of situation, and it's unclear how it happened."

The floor guardians' serious expressions didn't flinch.

"The cause is unclear, but we know for sure that the Tomb has been teleported out of the swamps and into a grassy plain. Is there anyone who saw any signs this might happen?"

Albedo gazed over her shoulder at the faces of each floor guardian. After reading their expressions, she said, "No, my apologies, but no one had any idea this would happen."

"Then I'd next like to hear from each floor guardian. Did anything strange happen on your levels recently?"

Now they spoke up individually for the first time.

"Nothing strange happened in the seventh level."

"Nor in the sixth."

"L-like my sister said."

"THE SAME GOES FOR FIVE."

"Nothing strange happened in the first, second, or third levels."

"Lord Momonga, I would like to investigate the fourth and eighth levels immediately."

"Very well, I'll leave that up to you, Albedo, but take care in the eighth level. If something happened there, it's possible you may not be able to deal with it."

After Albedo deeply bowed in acknowledgment, Shalltear spoke.

"Then I'll investigate the surface."

"Oh, I already sent Sebas out to explore the surface."

Albedo had been there when he'd given the order, so she wasn't surprised, but the others couldn't hold their shock back from appearing on their faces.

The Great Tomb of Nazarick had four NPCs with superior melee combat skills. Cocytus had the highest attack power when armed. Clad in heavy armor, Albedo had no equal when it came to guarding. Sebas was the best in a pure fight, and when he showed his true form, his total combat ability probably outstripped the previous two. Then, there was one who outstripped all three of them.

The guardians' shock must have been at the fact that Momonga would send Sebas, who boasted no weaknesses and all manner of strengths in a head-on fight, out to do a task so simple as reconnaissance. They took this as a sign of how wary he was about the unusual situation they were in and the reality of the crisis began to sink in for them, too.

"Well, it's about time to wrap up, but—" Momonga caught sight of Sebas jogging toward him. When he arrived, he slowly lowered himself to one knee like the others.

"Lord Momonga, I apologize for my lateness."

"No matter. More importantly, what's it like out there?"

Sebas looked up and cast a momentary glance at the guardians.

"This is an emergency. It's only natural that we should inform the floor guardians."

"Yes, my lord. For a half-mile radius, it's all grassy plain. I could not confirm any man-made structures. I saw a number of small animals as one might expect to be living in such a place, but there were no humanoids or large life-forms."

"Are the small animals monsters?"

"No, the creatures did not appear to have any combat ability to speak of."

"Aha… And this grass, is it the sharp, stiff type that stabs you as you walk through it?"

"No, just plain meadow grass. There is nothing special about it."

"You didn't see any floating castles or anything?"

"No, none. There was no sign of any man-made light in the sky or on the ground."

"I see. A starry sky, then… Nice work, Sebas." Momonga expressed his appreciation but felt a bit discouraged about how little information he'd been able to get.

Still, now he more or less knew that they were not in the world of *Yggdrasil,* although there remained the question of how he could use his in-game equipment and cast spells like usual.

It wasn't clear why they'd been teleported or where they'd ended up, but it seemed like they should raise Nazarick's alert level. They might be in someone else's territory. Suddenly taking up residence in someone else's territory without permission would surely invite anger. They'd be lucky if "anger" was as far as it went.

"Guardians. First, raise the alert level by one on each floor. There are too many unknowns right now, so don't let your guard down. Take any raiders alive. Capturing them without injury would be ideal. It goes without saying, but we don't want to complicate things while we're in this uncertain situation."

Everyone bowed together in understanding.

"Next, I'd like to hear about how things operate here. Albedo, how do you share security information among floors?"

In *Yggdrasil,* they'd just been NPCs operating according to their programs. There shouldn't have been any movement of information or mobs among floors.

"The security of each level is left up to the individual guardians, but we do have a system for sharing information, which Demiurge oversees."

Momonga was slightly surprised but then nodded his head in satisfaction.

"Splendid. Defense Operations Coordinator Demiurge and Floor Guardian Captain Albedo, I trust you to work toward a more perfect system."

"Yes, my lord. To clarify, we can except levels eight, nine, and ten from the system?"

"Victim has eight covered, so that one is fine. Actually, I'm making eight off-limits. I take back the order I gave you earlier, Albedo. As a general rule, only those with my express permission will be allowed to enter the eighth level. Undo the seal that prohibits direct travel between the seventh and ninth levels, and let's have the security system cover the ninth and tenth levels as well."

"I-is that all right with you?" Albedo's astonishment was plain on her face.

Behind her, Demiurge's eyes opened wide, and he said what they were actually thinking. "You will permit lowly minions to enter the domain of the Supreme Ones? Is the situation so serious as that?"

Minions were the monsters that members of Ainz Ooal Gown did not create, the mobs that spawned automatically. Come to think of it, with very few exceptions, there were no minions in the ninth or tenth levels. Momonga wasn't sure what to say.

Albedo seemed to think those areas were some kind of holy ground, but the truth couldn't have been further from that. The reason there were no mobs assigned to the ninth level was simply that by the time a group of raiders broke through the eighth level where all the strongest monsters were, they figured they didn't have much chance of winning, so they decided they would just lurk in the Throne Room like proper villains.

"I have no problem with it. This is an emergency, so let's up our guard."

"Understood. I'll choose the very best, most noble minions for the job."

Momonga nodded and turned to look at the twins.

"Is it possible to hide the Great Tomb of Nazarick somehow? I'm not sure if illusions alone will cut it and thinking about the energy required to maintain something like that gives me a headache."

Aura and Mare put their heads together. After a moment, it was Mare who spoke. "I-it would be difficult to use magic if we need to hide all the parts that are aboveground… But maybe if we covered the walls with dirt and grew plants out of it…?"

"You intend to soil the walls of glorious Nazarick?" Albedo addressed Mare over her back. Her tone was sweet and gentle, but the emotions contained were confrontational.

Mare's shoulders jerked. None of the other guardians spoke, but they all seemed to be in agreement with Albedo.

To Momonga, however, her comments were unnecessary heckling. They weren't in a position to be concerned with such things. "Albedo, don't interrupt. I'm talking with Mare." Even he was surprised at how deep his voice was.

"Ah, my apologies, Lord Momonga!" She bowed low, her face frozen in fear. Sebas and the guardians' expressions instantly stiffened as well. Although the reprimand was directed at Albedo, they must have taken it personally.

From the sudden shift in mood, Momonga realized he'd said too much and regretted it, but he continued his discussion with Mare. "Is it possible to cover the walls with dirt and hide us?"

"Y-yes. That is, if you'll forgive me doing such a thing..."

"But if we were spotted from a distance, wouldn't a huge mound of dirt seem out of place...? Sebas, are there any hills in the area?"

"No, unfortunately it seems to be flat; however, I can't say for sure that I didn't overlook something due to its being nighttime."

"I see... But if we want to conceal our walls, Mare's plan is a brilliant one. What if we mounded up dirt in the area to create dummy hills?"

"In that case, we would stand out a little less."

"Okay. Mare and Aura, work together on that. Go ahead and take anything you need from the levels. We'll conceal the tall parts you can't cover later with illusions that work on anyone not from Nazarick."

"Y-yes, sir. Understood."

That was all Momonga could come up with for the moment. He felt like he was probably missing a lot of things, but they could always discuss them later. It had only been a few hours since the crisis began.

"Okay, that's it for today. Everyone take a break and then begin your tasks. It's hard to tell when we'll be able to take it easy for a bit, so don't work too hard." The guardians bowed their heads in understanding. "Finally, there is something I would like to ask each of you. First, Shalltear: What kind of person do you see me as?"

"A concentration of beauty. You are truly the most beautiful person in this world. Jewels don't hold a candle to your fair body," Shalltear replied promptly. It was obvious from the unhesitating speed at which she responded that what she said was what she really thought.

"Cocytus?"

"YOU ARE STRONGER THAN ALL THE GUARDIANS AND TRULY FIT TO BE ABSOLUTE RULER OF THE GREAT TOMB OF NAZARICK."

"Aura?"

"You're merciful and exceedingly considerate."

"Mare?"

"I think you're s-super nice."

"Demiurge?"

"You are wise in judgment and always make use of your energy to get things done. And I think the word *inscrutable* describes you well."

"Sebas?"

"You were the leader of the Supreme Beings. And you are the merciful one who did not forsake us, but stayed."

"Last but not least, Albedo."

"You are he who holds the highest position among the Supreme Beings and our exalted master, as well as the man I love."

"I see. I think I have a sufficient understanding of everyone's thoughts now. I'm entrusting a part of the work my friends used to do to you. Strive to be ever loyal!" Momonga teleported away as the guardians humbly bowed before him again.

The scenery changed at once from the arena to Lemegeton and its golems. Once he'd looked around to make sure no one was there, he heaved a sigh. "I'm exhausted..." He wasn't experiencing any physical fatigue, but he could feel the mental weariness weighing down his shoulders.

"Why do they all think so highly of me?" *They must have me mistaken for someone else.* As he was listening to them talk he'd wanted to laugh and point out their error. "Ah-ha-ha-ha," he chuckled dryly and then shook his head—the looks on their faces and the mood in the room had told him they weren't joking.

In other words, they'd been completely serious.

If he didn't live up to their appraisal, they might be disappointed. The more he thought about it, the weaker he felt. And there was one other problem. Remembering it made him wince so hard it seemed like it would show on his skull. "What should I do about Albedo? I can't face Tabula like this..."

Intermission

The pressure all but forcing their foreheads into the dirt vanished.

They were all aware their creator and master, worthy of their worship, had departed, yet no one stood up. Some time passed before someone let out a sigh of relief. The tense mood relaxed.

The first one to stand was Albedo. The places where her knees had pressed her white dress into the ground had gotten slightly dirty, but she didn't seem to care one bit. She fluttered her wings to shake the dust off her feathers. As if given momentum by Albedo's example, the others stood. Then scattered thoughts began to be voiced.

"T-that was really scary, huh, sis?"

"Seriously. I thought I was going to be crushed."

"I'd expect nothing less from Lord Momonga, but to think that his power would affect even us guardians..."

"I KNEW THAT AS ONE OF THE SUPREME BEINGS HE WAS STRONGER THAN US, BUT I DIDN'T REALIZE BY HOW MUCH."

They all shared their impressions of Momonga. The pressure that had shoved them all toward the ground was the aura Momonga had been emitting.

Aura of Despair. It caused the fear status effect along with ability penalties. Normally it shouldn't have worked on NPCs the same level as him, but the Staff of Ainz Ooal Gown had boosted its effects.

"Lord Momonga has shown us his caliber as a ruler."

"Right? He had that authority all along, but he didn't exercise it until we gave our titles. The moment we presented ourselves as guardians, he unleashed some of his great power."

"YOU MEAN HE SHOWED US HIS RULER SIDE IN RESPONSE TO OUR OATH OF LOYALTY?"

"That must be it."

"Yeah, he wasn't giving off an aura at all when he was with us. He was super nice. He even gave us something to drink when we were thirsty!"

The other guardians bristled. They were envious to the point where it showed. Albedo's reaction was especially big. Her hands shook, and it seemed like her fingernails were about to rip through her gloves.

Mare's shoulders jerked and he spoke up in a loudish voice. "S-so that was Lord Momonga being all serious as the ruler of the Great Tomb of Nazarick, huh? Amazing!"

The mood changed instantaneously.

"You're exactly right. He responded to our feelings by behaving in the manner of an absolute ruler—I'd expect nothing less of our Creator, the pinnacle of the Forty-One Supreme Beings and our merciful master who remained with us to the end."

Everyone seemed enchanted, listening to Albedo's words, but only Mare's expression contained relief.

The Forty-One Supreme Beings were their Creators. Naturally, everyone was enveloped in incomparable happiness at having witnessed the true nature of one who deserved absolute devotion.

The greatest joy of not just the guardians, but anyone created by the Forty-One Supreme Beings, was to be of use. After that came being paid attention. This was only logical, of course. For someone created to be useful to the Forty-One Supreme Beings, what greater joy could there possibly be?

Sebas spoke to disperse the lax atmosphere. "Well, I'm going to head back. I don't know where Lord Momonga went, but I should probably being serving at his side."

Albedo looked awkward for a moment, but recovered. "Got it, Sebas. Attend him respectfully, and if anything comes up, let me know immediately. If he calls for me, I'll go running at once, no matter what I have to cast aside."

Demiurge, listening to this, had a faint look on his face that showed what a piece of work he felt she was.

"Oh, but if he calls me to his bedchamber, tell him I'll need a little time. I should bathe first. Of course, if he says to come as I am, I don't mind at all. I'm keeping myself as clean as possible and paying meticulous attention to what I wear so he can summon me at any time. In other words, though it's only natural, Lord Momonga's wishes take priority—"

"I understand, Albedo. If I waste too much time here, I won't have as much to serve Lord Momonga. That would be terribly rude to him, so apologies, but I take my leave. Excuse me, everyone." After saying his parting words to all the dumbfounded guardians, he jogged off.

Demiurge spoke as if to dismiss Albedo's look that said she hadn't finished. "Well, it sure is quiet. What's wrong, Shalltear?" Everyone turned to look at her. She was still kneeling.

"WHAT IS IT, SHALLTEAR?"

She lifted her head only after being addressed a second time. Her unfocused eyes glistened.

"IS SOMETHING WRONG?"

"Th-that awesome presence was so thrilling that my underwear are in quite a state."

Silence.

No one knew what to say, so they just looked at one another. Shalltear had the most twisted fetishes of all the guardians, and all they could do was facepalm when they remembered her necrophilia. Mare was the only one who didn't get it and stood there looking perplexed. But there was one present who wouldn't let that be the end of it—Albedo.

Something like jealousy caused her mouth to open. "You bitch!"

The insult caused Shalltear's lips to curl into an alluring smile.

"Huh? Lord Momonga is one of the Forty-One Supreme Beings, as well as extremely beautiful. It's a reward to be hit with such a wave of power. You're crazy if you didn't get wet! Maybe you weren't made pure at all—maybe you're just frigid! Hm? You big-mouthed gorilla!"

"You lamprey!"

They glared at each other. The other guardians didn't think it would devolve into a death match, but they still looked on with anxiety.

"I was created the way I am by the Supreme Beings, and I have no complaints. Do you?"

"You know, I'm pretty sure the same goes for me!"

Shalltear slowly stood up, closing the distance between them slightly. Their eyes remained locked. They moved closer and closer together until finally they were bumping up against each other.

"You must think you've won because you're convinced you get to be close to Lord Momonga just because you're captain of the floor guardians, but isn't that a bit far-fetched?"

"Ha! Well, I do intend to achieve absolute victory while you're busy guarding the most remote areas of the Tomb."

"Pray tell what you mean by 'absolute victory,' Captain."

"A bitch like you ought to understand! *Yes*, I mean *that*."

During the exchange their gazes didn't budge. They continued staring expressionlessly deep into each other's eyes.

With a ruffling noise, Albedo's wings stretched out imposingly. In response, a black haze began to come off Shalltear.

"Uh, Aura, I'll leave the girls up to the girls. If something happens, I'll jump in to stop them, so just let me know."

"Wha—? Demiurge! You're gonna shove this off on me?"

Demiurge backed away from the standoff, waving his hands in surrender. Cocytus and Mare followed. They didn't want to get involved.

"GOOD GRIEF. IS THIS REALLY WORTH FIGHTING OVER?"

"Personally, I'm quite curious what the outcome will be."

"WHAT DO YOU MEAN, DEMIURGE?"

"Could be in terms of beefing up our war potential or the future of the Great Tomb of Nazarick."

"What does that mean, Demiurge?"

"Mm..." Demiurge wondered how to answer Mare's question. For a moment the sadistic desire to spoil that innocent mind by filling it with adult knowledge reared its head, but he dismissed it without hesitation.

Just like a demon should be, Demiurge was cruel and cold-blooded, but that was to outsiders of Nazarick. He saw others created by the Forty-One Supreme Beings as precious comrades in his loyalty.

"A great ruler should have a successor, right? Lord Momonga stayed with us until the end, but he could still lose interest in us and go where the others went. It'd be nice if he'd leave us someone for us to give our loyalty to if he leaves..."

"Uh, so you mean you wonder who will be the heir's mo—"

"THAT SEEMS A BIT DISRESPECTFUL. IT IS OUR

DUTY AS GUARDIANS AND CREATIONS TO AVOID THAT FATE BY REMAINING LOYAL TO LORD MOMONGA AND WORKING HARD SO HE STAYS," Cocytus interrupted.

Demiurge turned to face him. "Of course, I understand that, Cocytus, but wouldn't you like to be loyal to Lord Momonga's son as well?"

"AH. THAT DOES SOUND PRETTY GOOD..." Cocytus imagined giving Momonga's child piggyback rides. But he didn't stop there. He imagined giving him fencing lessons, drawing a sword to protect him from the oncoming enemy, and taking orders from him once he'd grown up. "OH, HOW WONDERFUL... I CAN SEE IT NOW, JUST WONDERFUL... HE CAN CALL ME UNCLE."

Demiurge averted his eyes from Cocytus and his uncle fantasies, wincing a bit. "I'm also very interested to see to what extent children could be of use in a plan to strengthen the Great Tomb of Narazick. I wonder. Mare, want to try making some babies?"

"Huh? What?!"

"That said, I suppose there's no one for you to do it with... If there are any humans, dark elves, elves, or closely related species out there, I'll capture one for you, so how about it?"

"Huh? What?!" Mare thought for a moment and then nodded. "If it would be useful to Lord Momonga, then...sure. But how do you make a baby?"

"Right, I'll tell you when the time comes. But hm, if we go off performing breeding experiments on our own, Lord Momonga might scold us. Nazarick's upkeep costs must be pretty precariously balanced."

"Y-yeah. Once I heard that a single Supreme Being was spawning minions here on a very strict budget. If we make the population jump weirdly, we're sure to get scolded. I-I would hate for Lord Momonga…to scold me…"

"Well, same here. No interest in getting scolded by a Supreme Being… If we could build a ranch somewhere outside of Nazarick, that might work, though…" Leaving off there for that idea, Demiurge tossed a question at Mare about something that no one had mentioned yet. "By the way, Mare, why are you dressed like a girl?"

He tugged at the edges of his skirt as if to hide his legs even a little more. "Th-this is what BubblingTeapot chose. She said I was a boy, so I don't think there's any mistake about my gender…"

"Hm, she must have put some thought into it. Then, that must be the proper attire for you, but…I wonder if all little boys should be dressed the same way?"

"I-I'm not sure about that."

Although they had mostly disappeared, once one of the Forty-One Supreme Beings' sacred names came into things, all one could do was accept the judgment. That meant that the way Mare was dressed was the most correct way within the Great Tomb of Nazarick. If anyone was going to tell him to stop dressing that way, it would have to be another Supreme Being.

"I guess we need to consult Lord Momonga. It may very well be the case that all boys should dress that way... Cocytus, are you quite ready to come back to us?"

At the sound of his colleague's voice, Cocytus emitted a sigh of contentment from the bottom of his heart and then shook his head several times. "WHAT A LOVELY NOTION. IT CERTAINLY IS SOMETHING TO HOPE FOR."

"Oh yeah? Good for you... Albedo, Shalltear, are you still fighting?"

The pair still staring each other down looked up when he called to them. But the one who answered Demiurge's question was standing off to the side looking exhausted—Aura.

"The fight...is over. Now they're just—"

"The issue is simply who will be his first wife."

"We concluded that it would be bizarre for the absolute ruler of the Great Tomb of Nazarick to have only one queen. But now we have to decide who his primary will—"

"That's very interesting, but tell me more later. More importantly, Albedo, could you give us some orders maybe? We've got a lot of things that need to get moving."

"Yes. Yes, you're right. I need to give orders. Shalltear, let's discuss this further at a future date. I'm sure it will take more time than we have now, anyway."

"I have no objections, Albedo. There's nothing that will take us so long to discuss as this."

"Okay. Very well, I'll come up with our plan going forward." Albedo had put on her captain of the floor guardians face, and all the guardians responded by bowing their heads in respect.

They bowed, but they didn't kneel. She was worthy of respect as their captain, but she was not absolute. There wasn't that much of a gap in status between those created by the Forty-One Supreme Beings. That said, it was the Forty-One Supreme Beings who had bestowed upon her the rank of captain, so she was given the respect appropriate for her position—and no more. Their behavior was a manifestation of that belief. And it didn't bother Albedo, because she knew it was a most correct way to think.

"First..."

Chapter 3 The Battle of Carne Village

Chapter 3 | The Battle of Carne Village

1

There was so much stuff randomly lying around the dressing room adjacent to Momonga's private quarters that there was barely anywhere to walk—from things like robes that he could equip to full suits of armor he had bought but then threw in there after discovering he had no use for them. And it wasn't just protective gear. There were weapons from staves to great swords, too—really just all kinds of things.

In *Yggdrasil*, players could create infinite unique items by inlaying existing items with data-containing crystals that defeated monsters dropped. Players who preferred a certain style often stocked up on those type of items.

Which explained this room.

Momonga casually chose a great sword out of the pile of countless weapons. It wasn't sheathed, so its silver blade gleamed in the light. The letter-like markings etched into the blade's cheek also caught the light and were clearly visible. He moved his arm up and down, testing the large sword's heft. It was extremely light—like a feather. Of course, it wasn't because the sword was made out of light material. Momonga was just that strong.

As a magic user, he had high magic ability points and low physical ability points. Even so, by the time he hit level 100 he'd amassed quite a few physical ability points as well—so much so that it was a cinch for him to bludgeon lower-level monsters to death with a staff.

The moment Momonga attempted to slowly change to a fighting stance, the sound of metal hitting something hard rang throughout the room. The sword that should have been in his hands had fallen to the floor.

The maid standing by immediately picked up the great sword and offered it to him, but he didn't take it. He just stared at his empty hands.

This.

This was confusing.

The existence of NPCs who behaved as if they were alive made him think this world wasn't the game, but these odd physical limitations made it feel like it had to be.

In *Yggdrasil,* since Momonga had never learned a warrior class, it would have been normal for him to not be able to equip a great sword. But if this were a real world, common sense said he should be able to "equip" anything.

Momonga shook his head and gave up thinking about it. He didn't have enough information, so no answer would come, no matter how hard he racked his brains now.

"Clean this up," he ordered the maid and then turned to face the large mirror that practically took up a whole wall. In it was a skeleton wearing clothes.

If the body you were used to changed into some weird other thing, you'd think you'd be frightened. But Momonga wasn't frightened at all. It didn't even feel unnatural. He felt like there must be some reason for that beyond the fact that he had logged so many hours in *Yggdrasil* with this body.

He also felt that in addition to his looks, his mind had changed quite a bit, as well. First, there was that thing where whenever his emotions fluctuated in a big way, it was like something suppressed them to level him out. And his desire had weakened. He didn't feel like he wanted to eat or sleep. He didn't *not* feel sexual desire, but it didn't build even when Albedo pressed her softness up against him.

Assailed by the feeling he'd lost something very important, his eyes unconsciously moved near his waist. "I lost it before I even got to use it, huh...?" The emotion went out of his extremely quiet utterance partway through.

He had the awfully levelheaded thought that perhaps especially the mental changes could be the result of an undead's perfect resistance to psychic attacks.

Right now, I'm an undead body and mind with the vestiges of a human clinging to them. That's why when my mood changes past a certain point, it gets suppressed. He wondered if there was any danger of going completely flat if he continued being undead.

Of course, even if I have *changed, it doesn't mean much. No matter what this world is like, or what kind of being I am, I still have my will.*

Besides, there were beings like Shalltear. It might be too soon to blame everything on being undead.

"Create Greater Item." The moment he cast the spell, full plate armor covered him from head to toe. It was rather expensive looking—the fluted type, gleaming raven black, with purple and gold accents.

He tested some movements. His whole body felt heavy, but it wasn't so bad that he couldn't move. He would have thought there would be gaps between his body and the armor, considering he was all bones, but it fit perfectly.

So, just like in Yggdrasil, *I can equip an item if I create it using magic?* Impressed, he looked through the slit in his close helmet at the mirror and saw a splendid warrior standing there—it was impossible to take him for a caster. He nodded emphatically and swallowed despite the lack of spit. He felt like a child who was about to say something he knew would make his parents mad.

"I'm going out for a bit."

"The guard is ready for you," the maid replied promptly, but…

This. He hated this.

The first day the honor guards trooped after him, it was a little overwhelming. The second day, perhaps because he'd gotten used to them, he'd wished he'd had someone to brag to. And the third day…

He suppressed a sigh.

It was too much—walking around with an entourage, receiving deferential bows from everyone he met. If he could just let them follow him without thinking too hard, he might have been able to endure it, but that wasn't possible. He had to act the part of ruler of the Great Tomb of Nazarick and never show even a hint of weakness. For a regular guy like Momonga, it was mentally exhausting. Even if any large emotional fluctuations reversed to level out, it still felt like his brain was being simmered on low heat.

And then there were the beautiful (*you could probably say "super beautiful"*) women who waited on him constantly, practically never leaving his side. He would have thought that as a man that would make him happy, but he ended up feeling more like his personal space was being invaded.

This mental fatigue must be another vestige of my humanity.

In any case, it was no good for the ruler of the Great Tomb of Nazarick to be so mentally burdened in this crisis. There was the danger he might commit an error in some critical situation.

I need to recharge. Having reached that conclusion, Momonga opened his eyes wide. Of course, his face didn't move at all—the flames in his eyes just burned brighter. "No, that's not what I meant. I'm going to go make some rounds on my own."

"P-please wait, my lord. If something should happen to you while you are out alone, we would not be able to die as your shields."

Faced with someone who had resolved to give up her life if she could protect her master, he felt heartless for trying to go on a solo walk just to relax.

Still, it had been a little over three days since they'd found themselves in this strange situation, about seventy-three hours. After presenting himself with the dignity of the master of the Great Tomb of Nazarick for that long, his entire being was begging for a rest. So, although he felt bad, he racked his brains for an excuse.

"There is...something I must do in utmost secrecy. I will not allow any escorts."

A brief silence.

After what felt like an awfully long time to Momonga, the maid answered, "Understood. Be careful, Lord Momonga."

Her buying his excuse felt like a stab in the chest, but he dismissed it. *There's nothing wrong with taking a little break. I'll go see what it's like outside. Yes. It's crucial for me to see where we've been teleported to with my own eyes.*

The more he thought about it, the more excuses he came up with, probably because he was aware that what he was doing was wrong. Shaking off the nagging guilt (which manifested almost like someone was holding him back by his hair, not that he had a scalp), he used his guild ring.

* * *

He'd teleported to a large room. There were long, narrow stone platforms for laying out corpses (not that there were any now) on either side. The floor was made out of some kind of polished white stone. Behind him was a staircase that descended until it reached a large double door: the entrance to the Great Tomb of Nazarick's first level. The torches in the sconces built into the walls were unlit; the only light was the pale glow of the moon coming in through the main entrance. This was the part of the Tomb closest to the surface, the Central Mausoleum.

Even though just walking across the spacious room would take him outside, Momonga couldn't move his feet—he'd encountered something that unexpected.

Across the room he saw a crowd of grotesques. There were three types of monsters—four each for a total of twelve.

One of these types had hideous demonic faces with fangs. Their bodies were covered in scales and their strong arms were equipped with sharp claws. They had long snakelike tails and blazing wings of flame. They fit the image of a demon very well.

The second type of monster had female bodies sporting black leather bondage gear and crow heads.

The final type was a demon that wore armor open wide in front to display their magnificent abs. If it weren't for their bat wings and the horns sprouting from either temple, they wouldn't even look like monsters. Although their faces were those of beautiful men, their eyes glimmered with a desire that could never be fulfilled.

Their names were Evil Lord Wrath, Evil Lord Envy, and Evil Lord Greed.

All of their eyes turned at once to focus on Momonga, but none of the monsters made a move. It was a gaze worthy of the word—their eyes exerted an almost physical pressure.

All these monsters were a level somewhere between 80 and 90 and had been positioned as guards around Demiurge's residence, the Red-Hot Shrine where the gate to the eighth level was. Normally, undead mobs under Shalltear's control would be stationed this close to the surface, so why were Demiurge's bodyguards here?

With the appearance of a demon—who had probably been there behind them from the beginning, but difficult to make out in the shadows—that mystery was solved.

"Demiurge..."

When his name was spoken, a puzzled look appeared on his face. It could have been either that he wondered why his lord and master was in such a place or that he was surprised by the appearance of an unfamiliar monster.

Momonga bet on the smaller chance and continued walking. Even if his true identity hadn't been revealed by him standing there, it was too suspicious to remain. He decided to walk along the wall and try to slip past the demons without paying them any attention.

He knew painfully well that their gaze was following him. He wanted to look at his feet, but he willed his weak spirit into submission and walked proudly, chest out.

When the distance between them had closed, the demons, as if by previous arrangement, all got down on one knee and bowed their heads. Bowing at the front of the line, naturally, was Demiurge. His movements were so smooth and refined he reminded Momonga of a nobleman out of a story.

"Lord Momonga, what in the world are you doing here without your guards? And what are you wearing?"

They'd seen through him instantly.

He figured there was no helping the fact that he got caught by the one said to be most intelligent in all of the Great Tomb of Nazarick, but he realized it might have been obvious, anyway, because he had teleported. Only someone with a guild ring could teleport freely within the Tomb, so it was a dead giveaway.

"Ahh, well...I have my reasons. And as for why I'm dressed like this, I'm sure you already know."

There were various shades of emotion crossing Demiurge's graceful features. Several breaths later, he answered, "My apologies, Lord Momonga, but I am unable to fathom the depths of your profound—"

"Call me Dark Warrior."

"Lord Dark Warrior...?" Demiurge looked like he wanted to say more, but Momonga endeavored to ignore it. He knew it was an embarrassingly generic name, but it fit right in with the other monster names.

There wasn't any deep reason for the name change. Now the only ones present were Demiurge's underlings, but they were all right near the entrance. There would probably be lots of minions coming through and he didn't want them all calling him "Momonga, Momonga."

A light of understanding had gone on in Demiurge's expression. What had he decided Momonga was feeling? "I see... So that's why!"

Huh? You see what? Momonga stopped himself from asking.

He was just an ordinary guy. He couldn't imagine what line of reason Demiurge had used or what kind of conclusion he had reached with his overflowing wisdom. He just stood there under his close helmet in a nonexistent cold sweat hoping his true intentions wouldn't be found out.

"Lord Mo— Dark Warrior, I have grasped one part of your profound intentions. It is certainly a show of consideration befitting our ruler, however, it would not do for me to overlook you being out without an escort. I deeply understand what a bother this must be, but I beg that you will pity me with your mercy."

"I suppose I have no choice. I will allow one guard to accompany me."

An elegant smile spread across Demiurge's face.

"I appreciate you granting my selfish request, Lord Dark Warrior."

"You don't need the 'Lord' with 'Dark Warrior'..."

"Surely you can't be serious! Such a thing would be unforgivable. Of course, if it were for an infiltration mission or I was on a special mission and had orders from you to that effect, I would obey them, but do you think there is anyone in all of Nazarick who could refer to you, Lord Momonga—I mean, Lord Dark Warrior—without 'Lord'?"

Momonga was overwhelmed by Demiurge's ardent speech and nodded several times. That said, inside, he had the feeling that this repeated emphasis on "Dark Warrior" was meant to poke fun at the absurdity of it, and he began to regret choosing the name so hastily.

"How rude of me. I am taking up your precious time, Lord Mo— Dark Warrior... Then, you all stand by here and explain where I've gone."

"Understood, Master Demiurge."

"Well, it seems like your minions have agreed. Shall we, Demiurge?"

Demiurge bowed as a token of his subordination, and Momonga slipped past him to head out. Demiurge straightened up a moment later and accompanied him.

"Why was Lord Mo— Ahem, Dark Warrior dressed like that?"

"I don't know, but there must be some reason."

The evil lords who had remained quietly voiced their questions.

They hadn't known it was him just because he'd teleported—there was another way. Momonga could not perceive them, but all the minions in the Great Tomb of Nazarick—or rather, all the minions that belonged to Ainz Ooal Gown—gave off a wavering signal. They used this signal mainly to determine if someone was an ally or not. And the Forty-One Supreme Beings—currently just Momonga—"felt" to the minions like absolute rulers. It was such a bright signal that it could be sensed even at a distance. That was why even though he was covered in armor, there was no mistaking him. They would have known it was him instantly, even if he'd strolled in instead of teleported. And it was easy to distinguish that signal from any others.

The double door leading to Nazarick's first level opened, and someone walked up the stairs. The signal that seemed to emanate to them was that of a floor guardian.

Reaching the top of the stairs, captain of the floor guardians, the beautiful Albedo, came into view. Registering the arrival of the person their direct master had been waiting for, the evil lords got down on one knee. Albedo took their obedience in stride. She looked around the room without even stopping to notice them.

She turned to the evil lords only after not managing to find whom she was looking for. Then she walked in front of them and asked no one in particular, "I don't seem to see Demiurge around. Do you know where he is?"

"Well… Actually, someone by the name of Lord Dark Warrior came here alone a little while ago, so Master Demiurge left to accompany him."

"Lord...Dark Warrior? I don't know any minions by that name. And Demiurge—a guardian—accompanied him? Isn't that a bit absurd?"

The evil lords glanced at one another, unsure what to do. Seeing this, Albedo smiled gently. "Might a bunch of minions be daring to hide something from me?"

Though there was kindness in her words, the evil lords sensed the iciness of a final warning and concluded this was not something they should hide.

"Master Demiurge judged that this Lord Dark Warrior was the one whom we serve."

"Lord Momonga was here?!" Her voice was a bit frantic.

An evil lord replied calmly, "Well, his name was Lord Dark Warrior, but..."

"What about his guard? Did they know he was coming here? If Demiurge agreed to meet me here, he must have known Lord Momonga was coming! Ah, but more importantly, I need clothes! Draw me a bath!" She fingered her dress.

Since she had been working in various places without rest, her clothes were dirty and the ends of her hair were tangled. Even her wings were a bit of a mess. But for such a peerless beauty as Albedo, that amount of grit was hardly a minus at all; in the same way that one subtracted from a hundred million meant practically nothing, her beauty was hardly detracted from. But from Albedo's point of view, she was not fit to present herself to the one she loved above all others.

"The nearest bath is in...Shalltear's room? She'll be suspicious, but I have no other choice. You guys bring me some clothes from my room! On the double!"

Albedo was about to race off, but one of the evil lords called out to her. It was an envy. "Mistress Albedo, if you'll excuse me, would it not perhaps be better to go as you are?"

"...What are you talking about?" She stopped, and the reason she bristled was that she felt she was being asked to show herself to him filthy.

"Ah, I meant that the fact that such a beautiful woman as yourself has been working so hard for him might make a good impression and be advantageous for you in the end."

"Not only that," another evil lord continued, "if you take a whole bath and make all the preparations to go before Lord Momonga—Dark Warrior—that would take quite some time. If you missed him…it would be such a waste."

Albedo moaned. It annoyed her, but they were right. "That makes sense… It seems it's been so long since I've seen Lord Momonga that I'm not thinking quite straight. It's been…eighteen hours. Don't you think eighteen hours is just too long?"

"I do. It's too long."

"I need to get the groundwork of our operations laid so I can guard him personally! Now, then, grumbles aside, first I must see Lord Momonga. Where did he go?"

"He went outside just a moment ago."

"I see." Her reply was curt, but she was smiling in anticipation of seeing Momonga and her wings fluttered adorably. Her footsteps were quick as she bustled by the evil lords.

Then she stopped and addressed them once more. "I just want to ask one more thing: Do you really think Lord Momonga will take it as a plus if I show up all dirty?"

•

The scenery that stretched out before Momonga after he left the mausoleum was breathtaking.

The part of the Great Tomb of Nazarick that was aboveground took up more than two thousand square feet. It was protected by a thick wall twenty feet high, which had two entrances: the main and rear gates.

The graveyard's undergrowth was trimmed short, creating a refreshing atmosphere. On the other hand, however, a large tree cast gloomy shadows here and there with its drooping branches. Countless white gravestones formed disorderly rows.

The neatly trimmed undergrowth and disorderly gravestones combined to create severe discord. Statues of angels and goddesses made with notable artistic merit were scattered about, warping the chaotic design to brow-furrowing levels.

There were fairly large mausoleums in each of the cardinal directions and then a huge one in the center of the graveyard. The Central Mausoleum was surrounded by armed warrior statues about twenty feet tall.

This Central Mausoleum was the entrance to the Great Tomb of Nazarick and the place from which Momonga had just come. Standing at the top of the broad white staircase, he silently looked out at the world.

Helheim, the world the Great Tomb of Nazarick was from, was eternally dark and cold. Perpetual night made for dismal scenery, and the heavens were covered by thick, dark clouds. But here was different.

Here there was a stunning night sky.

Gazing up at the stars, he sighed in amazement and shook his head several times as if he couldn't believe it.

"Wow, even for a fantasy world, this is… This beautiful sky is proof that the air isn't polluted here. Probably no need for heart-lung machines in this world…"

He'd never in his life seen such a clear night sky.

Momonga was about to cast a spell, but he realized his armor was in the way. Certain magic users had a skill that let them cast spells in armor, but he hadn't learned it, so his heavy armor would impede his magic. Just because he'd created the armor with magic didn't mean it came with amazing bonuses. There were only five spells he could use under these conditions, and unfortunately the spell he wanted to use was not among them.

Momonga put his hand into space and took out an item. It was a necklace with a bird wing charm. He put it around his neck and focused his consciousness there.

Then the one spell it contained was unleashed. "Fly!"

Freed from the yoke of gravity, Momonga glided lightly into the air. He went to ascend all at once, increasing his speed as he flew. Demiurge rushed to follow, but Momonga didn't pay him any mind. He just kept flying straight up.

How far up am I?

Momonga's body slowed to a halt. He practically tore his helmet off, and when he looked at the world below, he said nothing—no, he was unable to say anything.

The night sky banished the earth's darkness with its pale light. Each time the wind made the grass sway, it was like the world was sparkling. The stars and a great celestial body reminiscent of the moon shone in the heavens.

Momonga sighed as he spoke. "It's just stun— No, a clichéd word like *stunning* doesn't even begin to capture it. I wonder what Blue Planet would say if he could see this..." *If he could see this world that doesn't seem to have any air, water, or soil pollution...*

Momonga remembered his old friend, the one who had smiled self-consciously when he got called a romanticist at an off-line gathering of guild-mates, who was so kind—a man who loved the night sky. No, what he loved was nature, with its vistas that were mostly lost now due to pollution. He'd started playing *Yggdrasil* to experience scenery it was impossible to see any-more in the real world. And the thing he'd worked hardest on was the sixth level. The night sky there, in particular, was a realization of his ideal world.

He'd always get so excited when he was talking about nature—really, a bit too excited.

How nuts would he have gone seeing this world? How passionately would he have gushed to me, that low voice of his getting higher and higher? Craving a dose of Blue Planet's wisdom for the first time in a while, Momonga looked to his side.

Of course, no one was there. There was no way anyone would be there.

Dimly feeling something akin to loneliness, Momonga heard the sound of flapping wings—Demiurge had transformed.

Black wings made of some kind of moist-looking membrane had sprouted from his back, and his face had turned from a human one into something vaguely frog-like. This was his half-demon form.

Some grotesques had multiple forms. In Nazarick, for example, Sebas and Albedo had other forms, too. Those types of grotesques took some trou-ble to make, but they were consistently popular because people enjoyed having multiple forms like a final boss. Many of them were set up so they took penal-ties in human or half form but received bonuses in their full grotesque form.

Looking away from Demiurge, who now had an appearance quite befitting a demon, Momonga turned once again to the twinkling stars, sighed in wonder, and uttered some words as if speaking to his friend who wasn't there. "Being able to see just by the light of the moon and the stars—this definitely can't be the real world, huh, Blue Planet? Everything sparkles like a box of jewels."

"Perhaps it *is* a box of jewels. This world must be beautiful because it contains jewels you are meant to adorn yourself with, Lord Momo— Dark Warrior," Demiurge answered with what seemed like flattery.

The sudden interruption made it feel like his memories of his friend were being trampled upon, and he grew irritated for a moment. But looking at such a beautiful world made all his anger fade away. Actually, looking down at the world like this made it seem so puny; he felt like maybe acting like the ruler of some league of evil wouldn't be such a bad idea.

"It truly is beautiful. Perhaps this untouched box of jewels exists to be mine for the taking." Momonga held his hand up near his face and made a fist. Almost all the stars in the heavens fit inside. Of course, they were only hidden from view by his hand. He shrugged at what a childish thing he'd done and murmured to Demiurge, "No, I shouldn't monopolize it. The Great Tomb of Nazarick, my friends in Ainz Ooal Gown—they should be adorned as well."

"That's a very attractive idea, my lord. If you so wish it, and if I might get your permission, I would mobilize Nazarick's entire army and take this whole box of jewels for you. Nothing would make me happier than to do that and offer it up to you, whom I respect most highly."

Momonga chuckled softly at the melodrama. *Demiurge must also be a bit drunk on this ambiance…*

"But that sentiment is nothing but foolish when we don't even know what kind of beings inhabit this world. It's possible that we're nothings here. But…hmm… Taking over the world does sound kind of fun."

"Taking over the world"—I sound like the villain from a kids' TV show.

It wouldn't be such an easy thing to do, either. There'd be the issue of how to rule the world after it was taken over, how to maintain public order and stop rebellions before they started—so many problems crop up when various countries get brought under unified rule. *If you think about all that even a little bit, it makes it seem like there are no benefits to world conquest.*

Even Momonga knew all that. He'd said it out of a childish desire: The world was pretty, so he wanted to have it. Also, it seemed like something the infamous guild master of Ainz Ooal Gown would do. And the last reason… was that his tongue slipped.

No, there was one more.

"Ulbert, Luci★Fer, Variable Talisman, and Belliver…?" He'd just recalled the former guild members who had joked that they should conquer at least one of *Yggdrasil*'s worlds.

He felt safe in the knowledge that Demiurge was the smartest guy in Nazarick and would therefore probably get that he was about as serious as a kid making a joke.

If Momonga had seen the look that played across the froggy face behind him, he wouldn't have let the conversation end there.

Instead of looking at Demiurge like he should have been, he gazed at the boundary line of the heavens that embraced both the earth and the stars, the horizon.

"An unknown world… But am I really the only one here? Couldn't some of the other guild members be here, too?"

It wasn't possible to make alts in *Yggdrasil*, but he could imagine a scenario where someone who had once quit made a new character and came back for the last day. HeroHero was logged out, but there was even still the possibility that he was here. Momonga being in this world was strange enough. If he considered the fact that the entire situation was an unknown, he couldn't completely deny the possibility that guildmates who quit the game had been sucked in, too. Message hadn't worked, but there were any number of potential explanations for that, like that the geography was different or the effect of the spell had changed.

"In that case, I should spread the name of Ainz Ooal Gown throughout the world…" If someone from his guild were here, they would hear of it, and once they did, they would surely come to find him. He was confident that their bonds of friendship were at least that strong.

Tossed on the ocean of his thoughts, Momonga looked at Nazarick—a huge spectacle was just beginning. A span of dirt more than one hundred yards wide began to undulate like the sea. The little swells rising one after the other out of the plain slowly moved in one direction; swallowing each other up, they gradually began to form one mass, and eventually it grew to the size of a hill and swept toward Nazarick. The attacking dirt broke on the solid walls and scattered. It was just like the spray of a tsunami.

"Earth Surge... Not only did he use a skill to expand its area of effect, he's using a class skill as well?" Momonga whispered, impressed. There was only one person in Nazarick who could use magic like that. "I'd expect nothing less of Mare. Seems like leaving the camouflage work up to him was the right choice."

"Indeed. Besides Mare's efforts, we are utilizing undead, golems, and other minions who do not experience fatigue to do some of the work, but unfortunately they are making little progress. When they move some earth, the land is left bald—we'll need to grow some plants in order to conceal it, which only makes more work for Mare..."

"The walls of our castle are so vast—it makes sense it would take some time to cover them. The problem will be if we are discovered partway through. What precautions have we taken?"

"An early warning network is already in place. We can now detect any sentient being that comes within about three miles instantly without their knowledge. "

"Splendid. But are there minions in that network?" Hearing Demiurge's affirmative, Momonga thought they should create another warning network without minions, just in case. "I have an idea for that warning network—please use it."

"Understood. I'll include it after consulting with Albedo. By the way, Lord Dark Warrior—"

"Ah, that's enough, Demiurge. You can just call me Momonga."

"I see. Lord Momonga, may I inquire what your plans are?"

"I'm thinking to go check up on Mare, since he's carrying out my order so perfectly. I'd like to give him a reward, but I wonder what would be appropriate..."

A smile played across Demiurge's face, a kindhearted one unbecoming to a demon. "I think your talking to him will be plenty reward enough… Ah, my apologies. Something has come up. I won't be able to—"

"You're forgiven. Go, Demiurge."

"Thank you, Lord Momonga!"

At the same time Demiurge flapped his wings, Momonga began his descent. On the way, he put his helmet back on.

The dark elf situated at Momonga's landing spot looked up as if he sensed something. Surprise broke out across his face when he laid eyes on the armored figure.

When Momonga alighted softly on the ground, Mare came scampering over, skirt fluttering. *Argh, I can almost see underneath.* Not that Momonga had any interest in seeing, but he did wonder what was going on under there.

"L-Lord Momonga, w-welcome! I m-most humbly th-thank you for coming!"

"Mmm… Mare, you don't have to be so scared and don't feel like you have to rush around. If it's hard for you, I don't even mind if you drop the formalities…when it's just the two of us, at least."

"I-I can't do that, not toward a Supreme Being. Sis ought to do better, too. W-we can't be so impolite."

He didn't really want to make children stand on ceremony, but… "Is that so? If that's what you've decided, then I have nothing further to say. Just know that I don't mean to force you, Mare."

"Y-yes, sir! B-by the way, what brings you here, Lord Momonga? D-did I do something wrong?"

"No, Mare, I came to praise you."

Mare had been looking a little twitchy because he thought he was about to be scolded, but his expression flipped to surprise.

"The work you're doing is extremely important. We may have a warning network, but it's entirely possible that regular people in this world are over level 100. If that's the case, the most important thing we can do is prevent them from discovering us."

Mare nodded.

“So I want you to know how satisfied I am with your flawless work and how much peace of mind I get by entrusting this to you.”

One of Momonga’s ironclad rules from his days as a working adult: Good bosses praise their subordinates’ work as appropriate.

The guardians had a much higher opinion of Momonga than he warranted. In order to not lose their loyalty, he had to act the part. He’d maintained their golden legacy all this time, but to disappoint and be betrayed by the guardians and other NPCs made by the guild members would brand him as unfit to be guild master. That’s why he had to try to be a great ruler.

“Do you understand, Mare?”

“Yes, Lord Momonga!” He may have been dressed like a girl, but the firm resolve on his face marked him clearly as a boy.

“Okay, then, I’d like to give you a reward for your good work.”

“B-but! It’s only natural that I should do this work!”

“It’s also natural to give a reward for a job well done.”

“N-no, it’s not! We exist to serve the Supreme Beings! It’s a matter of course that we should get things done well!”

They repeated this exchange several times, but their opinions continued to run parallel to one another. Beginning to sense futility, Momonga decided to offer a compromise.

“Then let’s say this. There’s no problem if it also rewards you for continuing your loyal work in the future, right?”

“I-if you’re sure it’s okay…”

Momonga compelled him to be calm and took out the reward. It was a ring.

“L-Lord Momonga, I think you t-took out the wrong…th-thing!”

“It’s no—”

“You’re mistaken, my lord! That’s a Ring of Ainz Ooal Gown—a treasure only Supreme Beings may possess! There’s no way I can accept such a gift!”

Momonga was taken aback by how hard Mare was trembling.

It was true that the ring was a one-in-a-hundred item made exclusively for members of Ainz Ooal Gown. Since forty-one of them had been passed out, there were fifty-nine that had no designated user—no, fifty-eight. In that sense, they were quite rare. But part of why he wanted to give it as a reward was how useful it would be.

Mare seemed like he was ready to bolt, so in order to calm him down, Momonga reached out carefully. "Relax, Mare."

"I-I-I can't! Y-you just said that a ring of the Supreme Ones was going to be my reward!"

"Mare, just think about it. Transportation by teleportation is prevented within the Great Tomb of Nazarick, but isn't that inconvenient sometimes?"

Hearing this, it seemed Mare was able to begin to calm down.

"In the event we are attacked, I want each floor guardian to act as commander on their level. If they can't teleport, if they can't escape easily, that won't work very well. That's why I want you to have the ring." The ring resting on Momonga's upheld palm gleamed in the moonlight. "Mare, having your loyalty pleases me greatly. I understand quite well that as our subject you feel you can't accept a ring that is our sign, but I think you grasp my intentions now—take it as an order."

"B-but why m-me? Could it be that you're giving them to all the guardians...?"

"I plan to, but you're the first because I think highly of your work. If I gave them to people who hadn't done anything yet, the rings' significance as a reward would be diminished. Or are you saying I should lower their value?"

"N-n-not at all, my lord!"

"Then take it, Mare. Take it and continue serving Nazarick and myself."

Trembling, Mare slowly bowed and accepted the ring.

Seeing him like this, Momonga felt a bit guilty. His other aim in giving away the ring was to make it so it wouldn't be immediately apparent who it was anytime someone teleported.

When Mare slipped the ring on, it changed size to fit his slender finger. He looked at it on his hand a few times and sighed in amazement. Then, he turned directly toward Momonga and bowed deeply. "L-Lord Momonga! Th-thank you so much for giving me such a valuable reward! I'll do my best to be word—worthy of such a treasure!"

"I'm counting on you, Mare."

"Yes, my lord!" Mare finished with a boy's valiance on his face.

Why did BubblingTeapot dress him like this? To be the opposite of Aura? Or was there actually a reason?

As Momonga wondered about this, it ended up being Mare who asked *him* about *his* getup.

"U-umm, Lord Momonga... Wh-why are you dressed like that?"

"O-oh, uh...because..."

Because I wanted to run away. There was no way he could say that.

Mare looked up at him full of expectation, eyes sparkling. *How do I get out of this?* If he messed up here, his performance to date as a great boss would all have been for nothing. There was probably no world where a subordinate would accept a superior who wanted to run away.

If only I were more *confused, then I would be leveled out automatically,* thought Momonga, who now had a new predicament to escape from—when a helping hand came from behind.

"It's simple, Mare."

Upon turning around, Momonga was captivated. Standing in the moonlight was a woman who could have been called beauty incarnate. Illuminated head to toe by the pale light streaming down from the heavens as she was, if she had said she were a goddess, he would have been convinced. She shifted her black wings.

It was Albedo.

Right behind her was Demiurge, but she was so beautiful, it took a moment to notice him.

"The reason Lord Momonga is wearing armor and the reason he was hiding his name until a little while ago was that he didn't want to disturb our work. If Lord Momonga were to show up, everyone would naturally stop what they were doing and demonstrate their submission to him. But that is not what Lord Momonga wishes. So he created the persona of Dark Warrior, to say that it was unnecessary to stop our work to pay him respect."

Momonga nodded vigorously to her.

"Right, Lord Momonga?"

"How very like you to perceive my every intention, Albedo."

"As captain of the floor guardians, it's only natural. No, I'm confidant that even if I weren't captain, I would still know your heart, Lord Momonga."

The less-than-thrilled look on Demiurge's face after she bobbed her head with a smile made him wonder a bit, but Momonga couldn't really say anything, since Albedo had gotten him out of a jam.

"I-I see…," said Mare, seeming impressed.

Momonga looked over at them and saw something that made him do a double take. For one moment, Albedo had opened her eyes so wide it looked like they would fall right out of her head and rolled them, like a chameleon or something might do, to look at Mare's finger.

Her face returned to normal before Momonga could even think anything of it. She was back to her beautiful self, like her previous expression had been a hallucination.

"…Did you need something?"

"Ah no, nothing. Okay, well then, Mare, sorry to bother you. Take a break and then keep working on the camouflage."

"I will! Then, if you'll excuse me, Lord Momonga."

Momonga nodded gently, and Mare scampered off, stroking his ring.

"And what in the world brings you here, Albedo?"

"I heard from Demiurge that you were here and thought I would come pay my respects. I apologize for appearing before you in such a filthy state."

She said she was "filthy," but it didn't really seem that way to Momonga. Certainly there was some dust on her clothing, but it didn't mar her beauty.

"You needn't apologize for that, Albedo. Your radiance could not be dimmed by a little dust. I do feel bad for running around such a flawless beauty like you, but this is an emergency. Sorry, but I'm going to need you to keep bustling about Nazarick a bit longer."

"For you, Lord Momonga, I would run any distance."

"I'm grateful for your loyalty… Oh, Albedo. I should give you one of these, too."

"One of…what? I wonder…" As Momonga took out a ring, she lowered her eyes a bit and tried to keep her features neutral. Of course, it was a Ring of Ainz Ooal Gown.

"You need one of these, too, since you're the captain of the floor guardians."

"...Thank you, my lord."

After Mare's reaction, the lukewarm reception was a bit of a letdown, but he soon realized he'd misread her. Albedo's lips were twitching as if she were desperately trying to hold her expression together. The jerking of her wings was probably also the result of her trying not to flap them. The hand she'd taken the ring with (at some point her fist had opened) was shaking. With all those signs, he'd have to be stupid to not understand how she really felt.

"Strive to be loyal. Demiurge...I'll have one for you another time."

"Understood, Lord Momonga. I shall endeavor to be worthy of such a great ring."

"Ah. Well, I finished what I came to do. I guess I'll head back to the ninth level before I get scolded."

Albedo and Demiurge saw him off with a bow as he teleported away with his ring.

He had the feeling that right as the view before his eyes was changing, he heard a woman's voice shout, "Sweet!" but he figured he had misheard, since Albedo would never use such an inelegant expression.

2

They were nearing the village's edge.

Behind them, Enri heard the clanking of metal—and at a regular pace, too.

Praying in her mind, she glanced back. As she'd thought—as she'd worried the *worst-case scenario* might be—a knight was chasing them.

But we're so close! She wanted to hurl the words in frustration, but she held them back. She didn't have any energy to waste.

She took ragged breaths one after the other. Her heart was beating so fast she thought it would explode; her legs shook and it felt like she might run out of strength and collapse to the ground at any moment.

If she had been alone, she probably would have despaired and lost the energy to run. Her little sister, whose hand she held, gave her strength. Yes, the wish to save Nemu's life was the only thing keeping Enri going now.

She threw another glance over her shoulder as they ran. The distance between them had not changed much. Despite the armor, the knight wasn't slowing down. The difference between a trained knight and a village girl was painfully clear.

She was sweating and her entire body was assailed by a coldness. At this rate, she wouldn't be able to escape with Nemu.

"Let go of her hand...," she heard a voice say.

"You might be able to make it on your own.

"Do you want to die here?

"It might be safer to split up."

"Shut up, shut up, shut up!" She ground her teeth and gasped a rebuke at herself.

I'm the worst big sister.

Nemu looks like she's about to cry, so how come she doesn't?

It was because she believed in Enri. She believed her big sister would save her.

Clasping the hand that gave her the energy to run and the courage to fight, Enri thought, *Who could abandon a sister like this?!*

"Agh!" If Enri was severely fatigued, Nemu was completely exhausted. She cried out as she tripped and nearly fell.

The reason she didn't fall was that the two of them were connected by their tightly held hands. But having to pull her threw Enri off-balance as well.

"Hurry!"

"I-I am!"

But when they tried to run again, Nemu's leg cramped up and wouldn't move right. When Enri panicked and went to pick her up, she realized in horror that the knight was right next to them.

The sword the knight held was slick with blood. And that wasn't all. His armor and helmet had both been splattered.

Enri stared the knight down, shielding Nemu.

"There's no point in resisting." There was no tenderness in his words. They were said with more of a sneer. His slimy tone seemed to imply that he could kill them either way.

Enri's chest burned with rage. *What is he talking about?!*

The knight slowly raised his sword. Faster than he could cut her down, Enri smashed her fist into his iron helmet as hard as she could. "You think I'm that easy?!"

"Gwah!"

She'd put all her anger, and all of her will to protect her sister, into her fist. She wasn't scared of hitting metal. It'd been a punch that contained her whole body and soul. She heard the crunch of bone, and the pain shot through her entire body a moment later. The knight staggered from the impact.

"Let's go!"

"Yeah!"

Bearing the pain, they were just starting to run when Enri felt something red-hot on her back. "Ngh!"

"You little—!!"

The humiliation of having underestimated a village girl must have made the knight angry. What had saved her, in fact, was that he'd lost his composure and swung so carelessly. But now she'd run out of luck. She was injured and the knight was mad. The next blow would surely be fatal.

Enri glared bitterly at the sword raised over her head. She could look at it with the sternest expression in the world, but its ominous sparkle told her two things. One: In a few seconds, she would almost certainly die. Two: As a mere village girl, there was nothing she could do to escape.

There was a bit of her own blood on the tip of his sword. It reminded her of the awful pain spreading out from the wound with each beat of her heart and the hot sensation she'd felt when she'd been cut. She'd never been in this much pain before, and it scared her so much she felt sick.

If I throw up, maybe the burning in my chest will go away, too…

But Enri was trying to find a way to survive. She didn't have time to vomit.

Although she was nearly discouraged, there was one reason she couldn't give in to despair: the warmth in her heart for her sister.

I have to at least save Nemu.

That thought didn't allow giving up as a choice, but the knight in full plate armor blocking their path sneered at her determination.

The sword came down.

Whether achieved by some trick of extreme concentration or her brain being activated by the life-threatening situation, it felt like time had slowed down; Enri flailed for a way to survive—for a way to save Nemu.

But there was nothing. If she had an idea, it was only to use herself as a shield—a last resort where she would take the sword with her flesh and make sure he couldn't get it out. She'd grab onto him somewhere, or maybe even onto the blade itself as it cut into her—in any case, she'd grab as hard as she could and never let go. Not until the last of her life flickered out.

If that was the only option she had, then she just had to accept it.

The smile of a martyr appeared on her face. *This is about all I can do for my little sister now.*

It was unclear whether Nemu would be able to escape the hell their village had become on her own. It was entirely possible that there was a lookout making sure no one ran into the forest. But if she could make it through this, she at least had a chance. For that slim chance, Enri would bet her life—no, everything.

Even so, fear of the imminent pain made Enri shut her eyes. She braced herself in the raven-black darkness for the agony that would come…

3

Seated in a chair, Momonga gazed at the mirror directly in front of him. The image reflected in the mirror, about three feet in diameter, was not Momonga's. Instead, it reflected a grassy plain from somewhere else, as if it were a television. The grass calmly swayed in the breeze as if to prove that it wasn't a still image.

Showing the flow of time, the sun that had just started to rise gradually banished the darkness over the plain. The pastoral scene coming into view was a far cry from the hopeless landscape of the Great Tomb of Nazarick's onetime world, Helheim.

Momonga lifted a hand and slowly moved it to the right. The view reflected in the mirror slid to the right as well.

It was a Mirror of Remote Viewing. Since it would display a specified location, it was an item that PK (player killers) or PKK (PK killers) would find handy, but because players could conceal themselves easily enough with anti-intelligence magic and it was vulnerable to counterattacks from reactive barriers, it was also an item of questionable utility.

But as an item that could display what was happening outside, there were plenty of reasons for Momonga to use it in his current situation. As he watched the grassy plain go by from overhead, he thought it looked like a location from some movie.

"So if I move like this, it'll scroll the screen. And I can switch the angle like this..." Drawing circles in the air, he kept changing his view. For hours now he'd been using trial and error to search but had yet to find any sentient (and preferably human) beings. He silently focused on the monotonous task, but since all that came up was the same grassy plain, his motivation began to dwindle. He glanced out of the corner of his eye at the other person in the room.

"What is it, Lord Momonga? Whatever you require, I am at your service."

"N-no, it's nothing, Sebas." The butler was smiling but everything he said was somehow prickly. He respected Momonga absolutely, but it seemed he was a bit miffed about him going out without an escort—it'd been like this ever since Momonga had returned from the surface and Sebas had caught him to give him "advice."

"I just can't get used to this..." Momonga let his inner thoughts slip out.

Whenever he was with Sebas, he couldn't help but think of former guild member Touch Me. Not that there was anything strange about that, considering Touch Me had created Sebas. *But why did they have to be so similar that they're both equally scary when they're mad?* Grumbling inwardly, he turned his attention back to the mirror.

Once he figured out how to control this thing (it was taking a while), he was planning to teach Demiurge to use it. This was the idea he'd had for the warning network.

Even though it would be easier to leave this up to his subordinates, he was doing it himself with the questionable aim of getting them to think, *That's our ruler, all right,* when they saw him working. That's why he couldn't just get fed up partway and abandon the project. *I gotta figure out how to get the viewpoint up higher. If only there were a user manual...*, he thought as he continued working.

How long had he been doing this?

Probably not that long, but if he didn't get results, he would feel like he'd been wasting his time. With a glazed look on his face, he moved his hand absentmindedly and the view changed dramatically. "Whoa!" He shouted a mix of surprise and triumph. It was like the cheer of a programmer in his eighth hour of overtime who made a random edit that somehow got his code to work. There was applause in response—from Sebas obviously.

"Congratulations, Lord Momonga. I can only say that I would have expected nothing less."

He'd only been using trial and error, so it didn't seem like the type of work that deserved so much praise—it made him a little suspicious—but the look on Sebas's face was genuine admiration, so he decided to accept the sentiment. "Thanks, Sebas, but I'm sorry to make you hang around here with me for so long."

"What are you saying, Lord Momonga? As a butler, the reason I was created was to stand by and obey your orders. There is nothing whatsoever to feel sorry about. However, it is true that some time has passed. Would you like to take a break?"

"No, that won't be necessary. I'm undead, so I don't get negative status effects like fatigue. If you need a break, though, you can take one; I don't mind."

"I thank you for your kindness, my lord, but what butler can rest while his master is still at work? I also experience no physical fatigue, thanks to an item. I will accompany you until you are finished."

Momonga had realized something about his conversations with the NPCs. They talked using some video game expressions as if they were totally normal: skills, classes, items, levels, damage, negative status effects… There was something sort of funny about saying all those words with a straight face. Putting that minor issue aside, he was glad he could give orders using game lingo.

He told Sebas he understood and threw himself back into operating the mirror. Then, after repeating similar movements over and over, he finally figured out how to adjust the height of his viewpoint. Grinning, he earnestly set about searching for people.

After a while, something that looked like a village appeared. It was about six miles south of the Great Tomb of Nazarick. The village was surrounded by wheat fields, and there was a forest nearby. *Pastoral* was definitely the word for the scenery. At a glance, it didn't look as if the civilization were terribly advanced.

As he zoomed in, something seemed off. "Are they having a festival?" Though it was early morning, there were people going in and out of houses, running. Everyone seemed to be in a hurry.

"No, that's not it…," Sebas, who had moved beside him, answered in a steely voice as he watched the scene with a piercing gaze.

Sebas's hard tone gave Momonga a bad feeling, and he furrowed his brow as he zoomed in farther.

Knightlike figures in full plate armor were brandishing swords at simply dressed people who seemed to be the villagers.

It was a massacre.

The villagers fell one by one each time a knight raised a sword. They must not have had any means of resistance. All they could do was flee in desperation while the knights just chased them down and killed them. Horses the knights must have ridden in on were standing in the fields eating the wheat.

"Tch!" Momonga clicked his tongue and went to change the view. This village held no value for him. If he thought he could have gotten some information, there might have been a point to saving it, but like this, no.

I should ignore them. As he made this coldhearted judgment, Momonga suddenly felt confused. There was a slaughter in progress and all that came to mind was what Nazarick stood to gain. The emotions he would have taken for granted—pity, anger, uneasiness—were completely missing. He felt like he was watching animals on TV, or insects in the dirt, playing out survival of the fittest.

As an undead, am I already counting humans as a different species?

Nah, couldn't be.

He hurried to justify his thoughts with an excuse.

I'm not some hero.

I may be level 100, but as I said to Mare, normal people here might be that. I can't just go charging into a situation when I'm in a world where anything could be possible. The knights may be killing the villagers in a very one-sided way, but there could be a reason for it: disease, crime, a lesson. There are any number of possible reasons. If I step in as a third party to drive the knights away, I might make an enemy of the country they serve.

Momonga put a hand to his head—to his skull. It was absolutely not the case that the scene failed to faze him because he had ceased to be human and transformed completely into an undead, immune to psychic effects.

His hand slipped and a different part of the village showed up on the screen. Two knights were breaking up a struggle between a villager and another knight. They forcibly dragged the villager away and made him stand up, with one knight restraining his hands. Then, as Momonga watched, the other stabbed him with his sword. The blade went clear through the flesh and came out the other side. *That's probably fatal.* But the sword didn't stop there. The knight stabbed once, twice, three times, over and over, as if taking out his anger. Finally he kicked the body away, and it fell, splurting blood, to the ground.

Momonga and the villager's eyes met. Or perhaps he just thought they did.

Nah, this has to be a coincidence.

Unless there was anti-intelligence magic involved, there was no way the villager could know he was being observed.

His mouth worked frantically, spilling a bloody froth. His eyes were already glazing over, and it was impossible to tell where he was looking. Still he clung to life and was able to get some words out. "Please, my daughters…"

"What will you do?" Sebas asked, as if he'd been waiting for the right time.

There's only one answer. "Ignore them. We've nothing to gain by saving them," Momonga answered calmly.

"Understood."

Momonga casually glanced over at Sebas; behind him appeared a vision of his former guildmate.

"Right, Touch?"

But then Momonga remembered something Touch Me had once said.

"When someone's in trouble, it's only natural to help them."

Back when Momonga had started playing *Yggdrasil,* there were people going around hunting grotesques like him. The quote was a memory from those times. He'd kept getting PK'd and was almost to the point of quitting the game when Touch Me had reached out to help him. If it weren't for that, Momonga wouldn't be here.

He slowly exhaled and broke into a resigned smile. With that quote in his mind, he couldn't very well not go and help them.

"I'll repay the debt I owe you. I have to test out my combat abilities in this world at some point, anyway..." Talking to someone who wasn't there, he zoomed out to look at the entire village. He combed over it, searching for villagers who were still alive.

"Sebas, put Nazarick on the highest alert level. I'm going ahead. Albedo is standing by in the next room; tell her to fully arm herself and follow—but no Ginnugagap. Also, prep reinforcements. If something happens and I become unable to retreat, send in a party with good stealth abilities or invisibility."

"Understood. But if you need an escort, then I would—"

"If you escort me, then who will relay orders? If there are knights rampaging through that village, there's the possibility another group could appear near Nazarick while I'm gone. If that happens, I need you here."

The scene in the mirror changed and he saw a young girl send a knight staggering with a punch. Then she took a younger girl—was it her little sister?—by the hand and tried to escape. Momonga immediately opened his item box and took out the Staff of Ainz Ooal Gown.

Meanwhile, the girl's back had been cut. There was no time to lose. The spell glided out of his mouth. "Gate."

Momonga traveled by way of the most reliable teleportation spell in *Yggdrasil*. It could cover any distance and had a failure rate of 0 percent.

His view changed. Momonga felt a tiny bit of relief that there had not been any magic blocking his teleportation. If there had been, he wouldn't have been able to save the village, *and* it might have ended with someone getting the jump on Nazarick.

The scene before him was the one he'd been watching a moment before—the two scared girls. The older one, probably the elder sister, had shoulder-length hair in a braid. Fear had drained the blood from her healthily tanned face. Her eyes brimmed with tears. The younger one had buried her face in the older girl's back; her whole body was trembling.

Momonga looked coolly at the knight standing before them. He must have been thrown off by Momonga teleporting in; he'd forgotten he'd been swinging his sword and was just staring at him.

Momonga had lived a nonviolent life. And he felt this world was real, not a game. Despite that, confronting an opponent with a sword didn't scare him one bit. His calm made a coolheaded decision for him.

He opened his empty hand, stretched it out, and promptly cast a spell.

"Grasp Heart."

Magic tiers went from one to ten, and this was a ninth-tier spell—one that caused instant death by crushing the enemy's heart. It was one of Momonga's specialties, since he was strong in ghost magic, which often came with effects like instadeath.

The reason he'd chosen this as his opening move was that even if his opponent resisted it, there was stun as a secondary effect. In that case, he planned on taking the two girls and jumping through the still-open gate. *When the strength of your enemy is unknown, you need to have an evacuation strategy and plan B ready.*

But in this case the prep was unnecessary.

Simultaneously with the sensation of something warm being squashed in Momonga's fist, the knight silently crumpled to the ground.

Momonga looked down coldly at the lifeless body.

He'd had a hunch it would be this way, but sure enough, he felt nothing upon killing a human... His mind was like the surface of a placid lake—no guilt, fear, or confusion. *Why?*

"Hmm, so it seems I've quit being human in mind as well as in body..."

Momonga walked forward. As he passed the girls, who must have been frightened following the death of the knight, the elder sister made a hesitant noise.

One look was enough to tell he had come to save them, and yet they were panicked as if he had done something insane. *What do they expect?*

He wanted to know the answer, but he didn't have time for a Q and A. He confirmed in passing that the elder sister's shabby clothes were torn and her back was bleeding; he hid the two of them behind him and shot a penetrating glare at a new knight who had appeared next to a nearby house.

The knight registered Momonga as well and took a step back, as if he were scared.

"So you're fine chasing little girls around, but I'm too much to handle?" Momonga sneered in response to the knight's terror and set about selecting his next spell. For his first move, he had chosen a pretty advanced one. Grasp Heart was from the magic tree he specialized in, so he got the ghost magic boost, and a boosted rate of instadeath success, as well. But there was no way to tell how powerful the knights really were like that.

I should use something else on the next one, not instadeath, as a chance to test not only how strong beings in this world are, but also how strong I am myself.

"Well, since you're here, I'm going to have you help me with my experiment."

In comparison to how strong Momonga's ghost magic was, his basic attack magic was fairly weak. Plus, metal armor was weak against electric magic, so in *Yggdrasil* most players added electric resistance to their armor. This all meant that using electric magic would be a good way to see how much damage the knights could take.

He wasn't going for the kill, so he didn't need to use a skill to boost it. "Dragon Lightning!"

White lightning appeared writhing like a living thing from his hand to his shoulder. A beat later it leaped off the end of his finger pointed at the knight like an electric discharge from a cloud. It was impossible to dodge or guard against.

The energy took the form of a dragon and lit the knight up glaringly white for just a split second. Ironically, it was beautiful.

The flash dimmed and the knight fell to the ground like a marionette whose strings had been cut. The strange odor of his charred flesh beneath his armor could be smelled faintly.

Momonga had been prepping for his follow-up attack and was astounded to see how fragile the knights were. "How weak… They die this easily?"

To Momonga, Dragon Lightning—a fifth-tier spell—was way too low level. When he, as a level 100, went out grinding, he'd been using mainly spells in eighth tier and up. He barely used five at all.

Seeing that his opponents were so fragile sent all his worry out the window. There was, of course, the possibility that those two had been particularly weak. Still, it was hard to feel nervous at this point. Nonetheless, he kept his option to teleport away open.

It was possible that they specialized in attacking. In *Yggdrasil,* an attack that chopped a player's head off would just be counted as a critical hit and deal a lot of damage, but in the real world, it would be instantly fatal.

Since he could no longer be nervous, Momonga decided to be cautious. It would be stupid to die from carelessness.

First, I need to test more of my powers. He used a skill, Create Middle-Tier Undead: Death Knight. This was one of his special abilities. He could create all sorts of undead mobs, but this one was his favorite tank. Its total level was low at 35, and its attack level was even lower, comparable to a level-25 mob. On the other hand, it had good defense but still only about what a level-40 mob would have. In other words, in terms of levels, this monster was useless to Momonga.

However, the death knight had two handy special abilities. One was that it would pull all enemy attacks. The second was that it could withstand any attack once, with one HP (hit point) remaining. Momonga had been able to make good use of it as a shield for those reasons.

And that was why he was creating one now.

When the Create Undead skill was used in *Yggdrasil,* the monster would instantly shimmer out of thin air near the player, but it seemed to work differently in this world.

A black fog oozed out of the air and covered the knight whose heart had been crushed. It puffed up but then began to melt into the corpse. Then, he abruptly stood up with jerky, inhuman movements. Momonga heard the two girls shriek, but he didn't have time to care about that—he was just as surprised as they were.

A black liquid glugged noisily out of the slit in the knight's helmet. It must have been coming out of his mouth. The viscous fluid darkness flowed to cover his entire body without missing a spot—it was like seeing someone get preyed on by a slime. Once the darkness had enveloped him completely, his shape began to warp and change.

After several seconds, the darkness drained away and what was standing there could definitely be called the vengeful spirit of a dead knight.

He'd grown to a height of around seven and a half feet and his body had gotten insanely thick. It made more sense to call him a beast than a person. In his left hand, he held a huge tower shield that covered three-quarters of his body, and in his right, a flamberge. Normally this blade of more than four feet would be wielded with both hands, but this giant could easily hold it in one. A horrifying aura of reddish black twisted around the waved blade, undulating like the beating of a heart. His huge body was covered in full plate armor made of black metal with a pattern of crimson arteries going through it here and there. It was quite the embodiment of violence, with sharp spikes jutting out in various places. His helmet had horns like a demon and an open face that left his rotting features visible. In his vacant orbits, his hatred for living things and anticipation of slaughter burned red. He stood in his ratty raven-black mantle awaiting orders, his posture appropriately imposing.

Momonga could feel the mental connection to the summoned monster, just like he had with the primal fire elemental and the moon wolves. He used it to give an order. "Kill the knights"—he pointed at the knight he'd killed with Dragon Lightning—"who are attacking this village."

"Yarrrrrgh!" the knight howled. It was a scream that would make anyone's skin crawl. The air vibrated with his bloodlust. He ran off, swift as the wind, and made a beeline like a hunting dog on the scent of its prey. It seemed his perception ability, Hate, was working.

Watching his death knight get smaller and smaller in the distance, Momonga was made vividly aware of a difference between this world and *Yggdrasil*—the difference of freedom. A death knight was supposed to stand by near its summoner (Momonga) and intercept enemies. It wasn't supposed to take orders and act on its own. That difference could prove fatal in a world containing so many unknowns.

Momonga clawed at his face in frustration. "He's gone! What's the point of a shield who leaves the one he's supposed to protect? Sure, I'm the one who gave the order, but…," he mumbled.

He could make more death knights, but since he didn't know the strength of his enemies or what the situation was, he felt he should save up casts of spells that were limited. But Momonga was a rear guard magic user and had no one to go out front and tank for him. He felt naked.

I guess I should make one more. I'll see if I can do it without using a dead body this time, he was thinking, when someone came through the still-open gate just as it was beginning to expire and fade away.

The figure was covered head to toe in demonic black armor. Not a single patch of skin showed among the thorny raven-black plates. It was equipped with a raven-black kite shield, and in its hands, wearing gauntlets with spikes like claws, it casually held a bardiche giving off a faint, sickly green glow. Draped over its shoulders was a mantle the color of fresh blood, and its surcoat was also bloodred.

"My apologies. Getting ready took some time." From beneath the horned close helmet came the charming voice of Albedo.

She had learned all the classes that had good defensive abilities or seemed appropriate for an evil knight to know—like dark knight. For that reason, she had the best defense out of all the level-100 warrior-type NPCs (Sebas, Cocytus, herself) in Nazarick. In other words, she was the best tank they had.

"Oh, that's fine. Actually, your timing's perfect."

"Thank you. Then, how will you dispose of these lower life-forms that are still alive? Would you rather I dirty my hands in your place?"

"...What did you hear from Sebas?"

Albedo said nothing.

"He didn't tell you? We're saving this village. Our enemies at the moment are the ones in the armor like that guy lying over there."

Albedo indicated her understanding and Momonga looked elsewhere.

"Let's see..."

The two girls shrank and tried to hide themselves under Momonga's unreserved gaze. *Maybe having seen the death knight is what is making them shake so hard. Or was it the howl? Or what Albedo had said?*

Maybe all of it.

Momonga thought he would first try to show them he wasn't an enemy. Healing the elder sister's wounds seemed like a fine way to do that, so he reached toward her, but the girls didn't see it the way he did.

A wet patch appeared between the elder sister's legs. And then the younger sister's.

"..."

The smell of ammonia drifted into the vicinity. Waves of fatigue Momonga wasn't even supposed to experience surged over him. He didn't know what to do. It seemed like asking Albedo for help would be a bad idea, so he decided to continue as he had been.

"...It looks like you're injured." As an adult, Momonga had been trained to look past all manner of things.

Pretending not to notice they'd wet themselves, he opened his item box and took out a bag. An infinity haversack, unlike its name, was limited to around a thousand pounds. The items inside could be given menu shortcuts, so it was *Yggdrasil* basics for players to use a bag like this for things they wanted to use often.

In one of his many infinity haversacks, Momonga finally found a red potion. It was a minor red potion, which healed 50 HP in *Yggdrasil*. Every player ended up using them early on in the game. But to Momonga, this item was useless—this type of potion used justice energy to heal, but for an undead like Momonga, justice had the opposite effect and worked as a poison. However, it wasn't as if all his guildmates were undead. That was why he hadn't thrown them away.

"Drink this." He casually thrust it toward her.

The older girl grimaced in horror. "I-I'll drink it! Just please don't make my si—"

"Sis!" The younger girl tried to stop her, looking like she was about to cry. Momonga racked his brains.

Why the tender family drama when all I did was save them and then offer a potion out of the kindness of my heart? Seriously...what the heck!

They don't trust me at all. I was going to ignore them, but instead I saved their lives—it wouldn't be weird at all if the three of us were tearfully hugging right now. Or rather, that's what it would look like in a movie or a manga. But this is the complete opposite!

What's the problem? Do you have to be good-looking to get that kind of ending?

As various questions came up in Momonga's fleshless, skinless head, he heard a gentle voice. "He tried to give you lower life-forms a potion out of kindness, and you refused?! You deserve to die ten thousand deaths..." Albedo instinctively raised her bardiche. It was clear she was determined to promptly chop off both of their heads.

Considering how he was being treated after risking danger to save them, Momonga understood how she felt, but he couldn't allow her to go through with it or the whole point of coming would be lost.

"W-wait. Don't be too hasty. There's an order to everything. Lower your weapon."

"...Understood. I obey your word," she replied in a velvet tone and returned her bardiche to its former position.

Still, the thick air of violence coming off Albedo was more than enough to scare the two girls so much their teeth were chattering—even Momonga could feel it in the pit of the stomach he didn't have.

Anyway, we can't get out of here soon enough. There's no telling how bad things will get if we stay.

Momonga offered the potion again. "This isn't dangerous; it's medicine that will heal you. Hurry and drink it." His tone contained a bit of kindness even as he tried to compel her, implying she'd die if she didn't.

She reacted by opening her eyes wide, grabbing the potion, and downing it in one go. Then came surprise.

"No way..." She touched her back. She twisted around and whacked herself a few times as if she couldn't believe it.

"The pain is gone, right?"

"Y-yes." She nodded, looking utterly astounded.

So a minor healing potion will do for a wound like that.

That was fine, but Momonga had another question. There was no avoiding it. Everything depended on her answer.

"Do you two know what magic is?"

"Y-yes. There's an apo-pothecary who sometimes comes to our village, my friend. He can use magic."

"I see. That makes things much easier to explain. I'm a caster." He cast some spells. "Anti-Life Cocoon. Wall of Protection from Arrows."

A glowing dome appeared in a ten-foot radius around the girls. There weren't any other visible effects, but changes could be felt in the air. Normally he would perfect the setup with an anti-magic spell, but he didn't know what kind of magic this world had, so he just left it. They'd just have to consider themselves unlucky if another caster showed up.

"I used a spell that puts up a barrier that won't let any living things through, as well as a spell that weakens projectile attacks. If you stay there, you should be pretty safe. And just in case, I'll give you these, too." After giving a simple explanation of the magic he had cast, he took out two shabby-looking horns and tossed them over. Apparently the Wall of Protection from Arrows didn't register them as something to be stopped, so they fell near the girls. "These are items called Goblin General's Horns. If you blow them, an army of goblins (little monsters) will appear and obey your orders. You should use them to protect yourselves."

In *Yggdrasil*, apart from some consumables, most items could be customized by inlaying them with data crystals. However, there were also "artifacts," which were dropped as fixed data and couldn't be augmented. These horns were a lower-tier example of one of those.

Momonga had used one once: It had summoned about twelve fairly strong goblins, two goblin archers, a goblin mage, a goblin cleric, two goblin riders with wolves, and a goblin leader.

For an army, it was pretty small, not to mention weak. To Momonga, these items were junk; he was surprised he hadn't gotten rid of them. This had to be the best use for them.

And yet, there was one good thing about the Goblin General's Horns. The goblins it summoned didn't disappear after a set time, but stuck around until they died. They would be able to buy the girls some time.

Having given his brief explanation, Momonga set off, referring to the image of the entire village still in his mind, and Albedo accompanied him. However, before they had gotten more than a few steps, a voice called out to them.

"U-umm, th-thank you for saving us!"

"Thank you!"

Hearing their voices put their appreciation into words, Momonga stopped. He turned to look at the two teary-eyed girls and replied curtly, "Don't worry about it."

"A-and I know it's shameless of me, but...we don't have anyone to rely on but you. Please, please save our mom and dad!"

"Got it. If they're alive, I'll save them," he promised casually, and the older sister's eyes widened. She seemed stunned, as if she shouldn't believe he'd just said that. Then, she returned to herself and bowed.

"Th-thank you! Thank you! Thank you so much! And may I ask..."—she swallowed hard—"...your name?"

When he went to give his name, "Momonga" wouldn't come out. *"Momonga" was the name of the guild master of Ainz Ooal Gown. What am I now? What is the name of the last player remaining in the Great Tomb of Nazarick...?*

Oh, I see.

"You would do well to remember my name. I am Ainz Ooal Gown."

4

"Yarrrrrrrrgh!"

The howl set the air vibrating. It was the signal that one slaughter would give way to another. The hunters would be the prey.

Londes Di Grampp cursed his god for the umpteenth time. In the past ten seconds, he'd probably cursed him enough for a lifetime. *If God really exists, he should get down here right now and smite this evil being.* Why was Londes, a pious believer, being forsaken?

There is no God.

He had always made fun of the unbelievers who spouted such nonsense, asking them where the magic the priests used came from, then, but he was beginning to be convinced that he'd been the foolish one all along.

The monster before him—if he had to give it a name, he'd call it a "death knight"—advanced a step, looking pleased.

Londes backed up two steps instinctively to put more space between them. His armor was rattling as he trembled. The tip of his sword wavered in the air. It wasn't just him—all the swords of the eighteen men surrounding the death knight were shaking.

Though their bodies were ruled by fear, no one fled. But it wasn't out of bravery. The chattering of their teeth proved that if they could, they'd forget everything and run away just as fast as they could.

They simply knew it was impossible.

Londes shifted his line of sight slightly, seeking salvation. They were in the center of the village. The sixty villagers they'd rounded up were watching them, terrified, from around the square. The children were hidden behind the slightly raised wooden platform used for events. Several people carried clubs, but they weren't ready to fight—not dropping their weapons was the best they could manage.

* * *

When Londes and the other knights attacked the village, they had come from all four directions and driven the villagers into the center of town. Then, after searching the empty houses, taking care not to overlook level hideouts, they had planned to douse them in alchemical oil and burn them down.

There were four knights still on their horses stationed in the area. They were on watch with their bows at the ready so they could kill anyone who tried to flee the village. This was a plan they'd used many times with no weaknesses.

The killing was taking a bit longer than expected, but it had been progressing smoothly. They had gathered the remaining living villagers in one area. After some moderate culling, they would release a handful.

At least, that's how it was supposed to have gone.

Londes remembered the moment things took a turn. Elion had tried to slash at some straggling villagers from behind as they were running to the square and gotten sent flying into the air.

It was so absurd no one could understand it. His armor may have been made lighter with magic, but it was still heavy, and he was a grown, built man. Who could make any sense of the sight of him arcing lightly through the air like a ball?

He flew more than twenty feet before crashing to the ground. The crash made a hideous noise, and then he didn't so much as twitch.

Even harder to believe was the sight where Elion had been moments before. The horrifying undead death knight slowly lowered the huge shield it had used to bash him out of the way.

That had been the beginning of their despair.

"Yeaaagh!"

A high-pitched shriek sounded, as if all hell had broken loose. One of his comrades in the circle, no longer able to bear the fear, turned tail and ran. In an extreme situation like this, with such a delicate balance, one weak link could break the entire group. But no one followed him, and they had a very good reason not to.

A black blur whipped through Londes's peripheral vision. For having such a giant build, far surpassing the height of an average human, the death knight was certainly quick on his feet.

His comrade was permitted to run a total of three steps. As he went to take his fourth, a silver flash cut his body in two like it was nothing. The left and right halves collapsed to either side and his pink entrails slopped out, sending a sour stench into the air.

"Krrrrrr," the death knight growled as he stood there bathed in blood, with his flamberge at the low end of its slash.

It was a purr of delight. That much could be read from his face, even if it was hard to look at because it was rotting off. The death knight was enjoying this. As the one with unquestionable authority, as a killer, he was enjoying the feeble resistance the humans put up—their fear, their despair.

Though they all held swords, no one moved to attack. At first, they had, despite their fear, but even if they were lucky enough to slip past his defense, they couldn't put so much as a nick in his armor. And in response, the death knight didn't even bother with his sword; he just knocked them flying with his shield, hitting them hard, but not so hard they'd die. His aim in holding back was "play." It was clear he relished the pathetic humans' frantic struggle.

He only swung his sword like he meant it when someone tried to run away. The first who had tried to run was Lilick, a good-natured enough fellow, if an obnoxious drunk. In a flash, all four of his limbs had been severed, and as the finishing touch, his head was lopped off. Seeing one of their own die was enough for the others to learn they couldn't run.

Attacking was futile and they'd be killed if they ran. In that case, there was only one thing to do: Die as this monster's plaything.

Everyone was wearing close helmets, so it was impossible to tell, but they all must have realized their fate. Some were sniffling, grown men crying like children. They'd been the strong who had robbed the weak of their lives, and they'd gotten used to it; they weren't prepared to face the reverse.

"God help us..."

Some murmured between their sobs.

"Oh God..."

If Londes wasn't careful, he felt like he'd soon be on his knees either praying or blaspheming.

"You bastards! Get that monster under control!"

A voice that grated on the ears like an out-of-tune hymn rang out among the supplicating knights. It had come from a knight right next to the death knight. Trying to tiptoe away from his comrade who'd been cut in half, he just looked ridiculous.

Londes frowned at the ungainly figure. Since the close helmet hid the face and the voice was strained due to fear, it was hard to tell who it was. *Yeah, but there's only one guy who takes that tone.*

Commander Belius... Londes grimaced. He'd been chasing village girls out of vulgar desire, then cried for help after getting into a fight with their father. When someone got them apart, he'd taken his rage out on the father by stabbing him over and over. That's the kind of guy he was. Back home he was a man of some means and only joined the company because he thought it would look good. They'd probably been doomed from the moment he was selected as commander.

"I'm too important to die here! Buy me some time! Be my shields!"

Of course, no one moved. Sure, he was commander, but nobody cared for him very much, so there was no way they would risk their lives for him. The only one who reacted to the shout was the death knight, who slowly turned in Belius's direction.

"Yeek!"

I'm impressed he could even get words out, much less get his voice to carry, standing that close to the death knight. Londes was oddly impressed.

Belius's terrified voice thundered on. "Money, I'll pay you! Two hundred gold pieces—no, five hundred!"

He was offering quite a sum. But he might as well have been telling them he'd pay them if they survived jumping off a 1,500-foot cliff. No one moved a muscle, but there was one response—well, half of someone moved.

"Oghabowww..." The right side of the knight who had been split in two grabbed Belius's right ankle. He spluttered blood as he spoke in words that wouldn't form. "Ugyahhhh..." Belius screeched. All the knights and villagers who were within view of the situation froze solid.

A squire zombie. In *Yggdrasil*, when a death knight killed something, an undead with the same level as the defeated opponent would spawn. The game had a system such that anything that died by the sword of a death knight would be loyal to it for all eternity.

Belius's screech cut off abruptly and he collapsed onto his back, as if something inside him had snapped. He must have passed out. The death knight approached the now-defenseless commander and stabbed him with the flamberge. Belius's body spasmed. "Agh— Aghghhhhgh!" Jerked awake by the pain, he screamed in a way that made everyone wish they could plug their ears. "Shabe— Shave me! Preazh! I' joo amyfing!" He'd frantically grabbed hold of the flamberge sticking out of him, but the death knight ignored that and began sawing up and down. A chunk of his flesh, plate armor and all, was cut off, sending a heavy splatter of blood flying. "Gyak, gyak. I'll—arhghghhg—I' pay you. Urgghhg—shabe meee." His body spasmed violently several times and then went limp. The death knight, satisfied, moved away from the meaty wreckage.

"No, no, no..."

"Oh God!"

Several of the other knights, driven nearly insane, began to scream. The moment they ran they'd be killed, but to stay put was a fate worse than death. They knew both those things and so were helplessly paralyzed.

"Pull yourselves together!" Londes roared, cutting their shrieking short. It was so silent it felt like time had stopped. "We are retreating! Signal the horses and mounted archers! Everyone else buy us time until the whistle is blown! We're not going to die like that! Now, go!"

Everyone sprang into action at once. They moved in such perfect coordination it was like the paralysis of the previous moment had been a lie. They acted with the force of a waterfall. By following their orders like machines, they ceased thinking and could perform miraculous feats. They would probably never achieve such exquisite order ever again.

The knights confirmed with one another what each of them would do. There was one knight with one of the whistles they used to communicate—they had to protect him. He backed away a few steps, cast away his sword, and went into his haversack for the whistle.

"Yarrrrrgh!" As if in response, the death knight charged. He was heading straight for the key knight. *Is he aiming to destroy our means of escape and plunge us further into despair?* Everyone was chilled to the bone.

The raven-black flood surged closer. It was clear to everyone that whoever stood in its path would be killed, but they formed a breakwater anyway. They replaced their fear with an even more terrible fear, fueling themselves to act.

The shield was brandished and a knight went flying.

The sword flashed and a knight's upper and lower body were severed.

"Dazen! Maurette! Take your swords and cut off the heads of those who've been killed—quickly or they'll come back as monsters!"

The men who were named hastily ran toward the dead knights. The shield was brandished again, and one was bashed and sent flying; the other attempted to block the flamberge coming down on him and was cut, sword and all, in half.

In the space of a few breaths, four of Londes's comrades had lost their lives. Shuddering, he watched—like a true martyr—as the storm of raven black bore down on him.

"Yahhhhh!" Though he had no chance of winning, he couldn't go down without a fight. He screamed a battle cry and swung his sword as hard as he could at the oncoming death knight.

Perhaps the extreme situation had pulled out all the stops in Londes's body. Even he was astonished by what a powerful attack he'd unleashed. It was the best swing of his life.

The death knight countered with his flamberge.

One swing sent Londes's vision spinning. Below, he saw his headless body crumple to the ground. His sword sliced the air, making not so much as a scratch.

At the same time, a horn resounded through the area.

•

At the sound of the horn, Momonga—Ainz—looked up. Around him were scattered the corpses of the knights who had been on watch. Enveloped in the thick stench of blood, Ainz had been performing experiment after experiment, but wasn't prioritizing the right things...

He cast away the knight's sword he held. The beautifully polished blade was dirtied when it fell to the earth. "And I used to always be so jealous of people with abilities like *Reduce* Physical Damage..."

"Lord Ainz Ooal Gown."

"Ainz is fine, Albedo."

His simple reply seemed to confuse her. "Oh, tee-hee! I-is it really all right to be so rude as to abbreviate the name of our Supreme Ruler?!"

Ainz didn't think it was such a big deal. It did make him happy, however, to hear that she held the name of Ainz Ooal Gown so sacred. His tone naturally softened. "I don't mind, Albedo. Until my old friends show up, this name is my name. So I allow it."

"Understood, b-but I will still attach the title. A-ahem...my master, Lord A-i-nz, tee-hee-hee! B-by the way..." She squirmed a bit, perhaps out of shyness. But since she was covered head to toe in full plate armor, none of her beauty shone through. The sight was so strange it was a bit awkward. "C-could it be that, tee-hee-hee, you're letting me specially call you by this shortened—?"

"No. Being called such a long name every time would be annoying. I'm going to have everyone call me the same thing."

"Oh. Of course. I assumed..." Her mood suddenly darkened.

Next, Ainz asked her a question with a bit of anxiety, "Albedo... Do you find anything wrong with me calling myself by this name?"

"I think it fits you extremely well. I think it's appropriate for the man I love—ahem—for the one who kept the Supreme Beings together."

"...Originally, it was a name that stood for all forty-one of us, including your creator Tabula Smaragdina. So how does it strike you that I leave all your masters out of this and take the name as my own?"

"I realize this may invite your displeasure, but...I will be so bold as to humbly offer one thought. If it causes you to furrow your brow in the slightest, please order me to kill myself... If one of those who abandoned us were to leave you, Lord Momonga, who stayed with us all this time, out of it and take the name, I may have felt it was wrong. But if it is you, my lord, and all the others' whereabouts are unknown, what else could I feel but happiness?" Albedo bowed her head in a swift motion and Ainz said nothing.

Nothing after the word *abandoned* had registered. All his former guildmates had left for a reason. After all, *Yggdrasil* was a game, not something one could sacrifice reality for. That went for Momonga, too. But did he harbor some suppressed rage toward his guildmates? For "abandoning" him?

"Hrm, maybe, maybe not. Human emotions move in mysterious, complicated ways. There's no answer... Albedo, lift your head. I've understood your thoughts. Yes, this is my name. Until some of my friends come to raise objections, it will refer to me only."

"Understood, sublime lord and master. Nothing makes me happier than that the man I love should call himself by that sacred name."

"Love," huh...?

Despite his dark thoughts, Ainz chose to avoid the issue for the moment. "Ah... I thank you."

"Oh, but Lord Ainz. Are you sure it's all right for me to be wasting your time like this? Of course, I am satisfied simply standing at your side, but... well, hm. Yes, a stroll might be nice."

That wouldn't do. He had come to save the village.

He already knew the girls' parents were dead. Remembering their corpses, he clawed at his face. When he'd seen their dead bodies, it was as if he'd seen two bugs lying dead in the road. He'd felt no pity, no sadness, no anger—nothing.

"Well, let's put aside the idea of a stroll, but it's true that we're not in any particular hurry. It seems the death knight is doing his job."

"I'd expect nothing less of an undead you created, Lord Ainz. I marvel at his magnificent efficacy."

The undead made with Ainz's powerful magic and skills were stronger than normal undead. Still, this one was only about level 35. Compared to the overlord wisemen and grim reaper thanatoses he could make using experience points, the death knight wasn't so fancy. If such a weak monster was still out there fighting, it just meant that none of the enemies in the area were terribly strong.

In other words, they weren't in any danger.

Realizing that, he wanted to pull a victory pose, but he suppressed the urge, knowing he had to act his part. He did, however, do a mini–fist pump under his robe.

"It probably just happens to be the case that the knights who attacked this village are weak. Anyhow, let's go check on the survivors."

Ainz was about to leave when he realized there were some things he needed to do first. For starters, he turned off the Staff of Ainz Ooal Gown's effects. The evil aura it had been giving off flickered and went out like a flame blown in the wind. Next, he went into his item box and took out a mask that would cover his whole face. Into it was carved a difficult-to-pin-down expression—tears or perhaps anger. It was a bit ornate. If someone had told him it looked like the masks of Barong or Rangda from Bali, he would have had to agree.

Despite how weird it looked, it didn't have any powers. It was an event item, and it wasn't possible to augment it. The only way to obtain it was to have been in-game for two hours or more during the period between seven and ten PM on Christmas Eve. Or rather, if one was there (and therefore dateless on the most romantic day of the year), it was forcibly added to the player's inventory—a type of cursed item. In that sense, it was considered a cursed item. Its name was Mask of the Jealous, or the jealousy mask.

"Are the admins on crack?"

"We've been waiting for this!"

"There are some peeps in my guild who don't have it, but we can PK for it, right?"

"Screw being human!"

That was the kind of stuff that was written in the *Yggdrasil* thread on a major forum site about the mask Ainz now donned.

Then, he took out some gauntlets. They were the typical, unsophisticated iron gauntlets one could get anywhere, with no outstanding features. They were known as járngreipr and were something the guild had made for fun. Their only effect was to boost the wearer's strength.

He equipped them, and with that, all of his skeletal exterior was covered.

Naturally, there was a reason he was taking pains to conceal himself. He finally realized the fatal error he'd been making.

Ainz was used to his bony body from *Yggdrasil,* so there was nothing horrific about it to him, but it seemed to strike fear into the hearts of the people who lived in this world. That must be true, because it wasn't only the little girls who thought he was there to take their lives—the armed knights had been frightened, too.

In any case, by changing his equipment he succeeded in downgrading his impression from evil monster to evil caster…hopefully. He wondered what to do about his staff but decided to take it. It wouldn't get in the way.

"If you were gonna pray to your god to save you, maybe you shouldn't have been massacring people?" Ainz spat a line only an unbeliever could spit in the direction of a knight who'd died with his fingers knit together in prayer. Then he cast a spell. "Fly!"

He glided lightly into the air and Albedo followed him a moment later.

Death Knight, if there are any knights left alive, leave them. We can use them. In response to Ainz's thought came compliance. He understood what the death knight was feeling and what kind of situation he was in, even at a distance; it was a vague sensation, difficult to describe.

He flew quickly in the direction the horn had sounded. The wind whipped at him—he hadn't been able to go this fast in *Yggdrasil.* His robe got twisted around his body in an irksome way, but the flight was brief.

Soon he was above the village; he looked down. One part of the ground in the square was darkened as if it had gotten wet. It was scattered with corpses. A handful of knights were left barely standing. And the death knight stood with perfect posture.

Ainz counted the surviving knights, who were breathing weakly; it seemed like moving was too much trouble for them. Four. More than he needed, but that was fine.

"That's enough, Death Knight." His voice seemed to boom a bit, out of place. It was nonchalant, like someone who'd gone to the market and was telling a merchant what they'd like to buy. That was about how this situation registered to Ainz.

Accompanied by Albedo, he touched down gently.

The knights, despondent, stood stock-still staring at Ainz. They'd been holding out for a savior, but instead the worst possible person showed up, crushing their hopes.

"How do you do, gentlemen? My name is Ainz Ooal Gown."

No one replied.

"If you surrender, I'll guarantee your lives. If you still want to fight, then..."

A sword was tossed to the ground. This was followed by the rest, and soon all four had been readily cast aside. No one said a word.

"...Well, you all seem quite exhausted, but your heads are held awfully high for being in the presence of this death knight's master."

The knights silently dropped to one knee and hung their heads—not as subjects, but as prisoners awaiting their beheading.

"I'll send you gentlemen home alive. And I want you to tell your boss—your owner—" Ainz glided over to one of the knights using Fly and, with his free hand, slipped the kneeling man's close helmet off to look into his groggy eyes. Their eyes met through Ainz's mask. "Not to cause trouble here. Tell him if you cause any more trouble here, I'll bring death to your country next." The knights nodded over and over, their entire bodies trembling. They were so desperate it was funny. "Now flee! And make sure to tell your master." He jerked his chin, and the knights practically fell over themselves as they scrabbled away.

"Acting takes so much energy...," Ainz murmured as he watched the knights' silhouettes grow smaller and smaller. If the villagers hadn't been watching, he would have wanted to rotate his shoulders. Just like inside the Great Tomb of Nazarick, acting this dignified part was a huge burden on a normal guy like Ainz. But the act wasn't over—it was time to put on a different hat.

He suppressed a sigh and walked toward the villagers. He knew Albedo was behind him because he could hear the clank of her armor. *Clean up the squire zombies,* he mentally ordered the death knight on his way. As the distance between him and the villagers closed, the mix of horror and confusion on their faces became clearly visible.

The reason they weren't upset about him letting the knights go was that a more terrifying monster had arrived, he eventually realized. Since he was strong—stronger than the knights—he hadn't thought of things from the point of view of the weak. Ainz reconsidered and pondered a bit.

If I get too close, it'll probably backfire. Ainz stopped at a reasonable distance and addressed them in a kind, familiar tone. "Okay, you're safe now. I hope you can relax."

"Wh-who…a-are you?" A man seeming to present himself as a representative of the villagers spoke without taking his eyes off the death knight.

"I saw that this village was being attacked, so I came to help."

"Wow…" Relieved murmurs went around the group, but Ainz could tell they were still uneasy.

Oh, well. I guess I'll change tactics. He took a tack he didn't particularly like. "Of course, it's not as if I did it for free. I'd like to get paid some amount times the number of lives I saved."

The villagers all looked at one another. The looks said they weren't sure they could come up with money, but Ainz could see that their skepticism was reduced somewhat. Saving people with the base aim of money made him less suspicious.

"I-in this state, I don't—"

Ainz cut him off by raising a hand. "Why don't we discuss that later. On my way here, I saved a pair of sisters. Give me a little time to bring them here." He would have to ask those two to keep their mouths shut. They'd seen him without the mask.

Ainz headed off at a leisurely pace without waiting for the villagers' reply, wondering if memory manipulation magic would work.

Chapter 4 A Duel

Chapter 4 | A Duel

1

The village headman's house was right off the square. Inside, the floor was dirt. The main room was big enough to serve as a workshop, and there was an adjacent kitchen. Some shabby chairs and a table had been set in the middle of the open area.

Ainz sat in one of the chairs and looked around the room. The light coming through the latticed door banished the darkness to the shadows, so he could see fine without Night Vision. He observed the woman working in the kitchen and noted various agricultural implements. There was no machinery to be seen. He judged that science hadn't advanced very much in this world, but realized immediately how superficial he was being. In a world with magic, how far would science even need to advance?

Ainz moved his arms, setting them lightly on the table to move them out of the sun. His gauntlets weren't that heavy, but the table was shoddily made, so it rocked and clattered. The chair made a horrible squeaking noise under his weight whenever he moved.

Impoverished was the word for these people.

Ainz leaned his staff against the table so it wouldn't be in the way. It sparkled in the light and, especially in this plain room, made it seem like they were in the land of mythology. He simultaneously recalled the villagers' speechless amazement; their eyes had practically fallen out of their heads.

He was bursting with pride that the staff he and his guildmates had made caused such genuine awe. But Ainz suppressed that buoyant feeling to the level of faint happiness and furrowed his nonexistent brow.

He couldn't force himself to enjoy the forced chill out. Granted, it would be difficult to get through this situation feeling giddy. With all of this on his mind, Ainz prepared himself to use his brain—they were about to start negotiating the price of the rescue.

Of course, Ainz's aim was information, not monetary compensation. But just saying, "Please give me information," would be terribly shady.

In a village this small, it probably didn't matter, but if more people—especially those in positions of authority—interacted with him and realized he knew nothing about the world, it could be used against him.

Am I being overly cautious? he wondered, but this was like trying to cross the street by just running into it—at some point he'd get in a fatal accident. That fatal accident would be a collision with someone stronger than him.

Ainz was stronger than anyone he'd met in this village, but that didn't mean he'd be stronger than anyone in this world. And he was an undead. He'd gotten a pretty good idea of the standing of undead here from the way the girls had reacted. Humans would revile him, and he stood a good chance of being attacked. He couldn't be too careful.

"Sorry to keep you waiting." The village headman sat in the seat opposite Ainz. His wife stood behind him.

The headman was tan with deep wrinkles. He had a brawny physique, and it was clear from one look that it'd been built by hard labor. Much of his hair had gone white—almost half of his head. His cotton clothes were dirty, but he didn't smell. Judging by the look of deep exhaustion on his face, he was probably in his late forties, but it was hard to tell—it seemed like he'd aged considerably in the past hour or so.

His wife was probably around the same age. Ainz got the feeling she'd been a trim beauty at one point, but hard work in the fields had worn most of her charm away. Spots had appeared on her face, and all that was left was a thin old lady. Her shoulder-length black hair was messy, and although her skin was tanned from the sun, she had a gloomy air about her.

"Here you go." She placed a shabby cup on the table. The reason there wasn't any for Albedo was simply because Ainz had had her go check out the village.

He refused the steaming water with a raised hand. He wasn't thirsty and he couldn't take off the mask, anyway. After seeing how much work went into it, though, he felt bad for not declining in advance.

Making hot water was hard work. First, she had to use a flint to make a spark. Then, she had to arrange thinly sliced wood chips to make a fire. From there, she moved it to the earthen oven to build the flames up. It took quite a while to heat the water.

In some sense, it was interesting for Ainz to see how water was boiled by hand without electricity—he'd never witnessed it before. In the past in his world, people used to cook with gas or something; he imagined it must have taken about the same amount of labor. *I should take this opportunity to learn about their technology, too.*

He turned back to the headman and his wife. "I'm sorry I put you to so much trouble..."

"N-not at all. No need to bow." The both of them were flustered at Ainz's politeness. They probably never imagined the one who had been ordering the death knight around up until a bit ago would bow his head to them.

For Ainz it was nothing strange. It was only natural to behave amicably with the people one was about to negotiate with.

Of course, he could always use some magic like Charm Person to get info out of them and then manipulate their memories with an elite spell as he had with the two sisters, but he wanted to save that for a last resort. In any case, it would cost a ton of magic points (MP).

Even now there was a heavy, leaden feeling at his core. Even just to overwrite a couple minutes of memory to make it so he had been wearing the mask and gauntlets from the beginning seemed to have cost quite a lot of MP. It was a serious loss.

"Well, then, shall we skip the formalities and get down to business?"

"Yes, but before that... Thank you so much!" The headman bowed his head so aggressively Ainz thought he would whack the table. A beat later his wife followed with her thanks and a bow.

"If you hadn't come, we would have all been killed! We are so grateful!"

Ainz was startled by the depth of their gratitude. *I've never been thanked so profusely in my whole life. Well, the two sisters before thanked me the same way, but… Ah, I guess I had never saved someone's life before, so it makes sense…*

The vestige of Satoru Suzuki, the man he'd once been, was a bit self-conscious in the face of their genuine thanks, but he couldn't say it felt bad.

"Please raise your heads. As I mentioned before, you don't need to worry about it. I did it expecting something in return."

"Of course, we understand. But please, still, allow us to thank you. It's thanks to you that so many of us were saved."

"Well, then, padding my fee a bit will suffice. Shall we begin the negotiations? As headman, you must be very busy."

"There's no one who deserves my time more than the one who saved our lives, but yes, let's begin."

Watching the headman slowly raise his head, Ainz got the gears in his brain moving. He had to get the information he required through conversation alone, without relying on magic.

What a pain. I was trained as a businessman, but I wonder how effective my techniques will be. He made up his mind and began to speak, feeling half like whatever would happen would happen.

"To get right to the point, how much can you offer?"

"We have nothing to hide from you to whom we are so indebted. I'd have to check to see how much silver and copper we can come up with, but for copper it would probably be about three thousand pieces."

I have no idea how much that is! Ainz shouted in his head.

He had asked in entirely the wrong way. He ought to have taken a different approach. He'd been a horrible businessman in his former life, after all, so of course his technique was horrible.

The number of coins sounded high, but he couldn't just accept without knowing their value. Accepting too low of a sum or overcharging would stand out too much and had to be avoided. *I guess I should just be glad they didn't offer four cows or something.*

Just as he was about to get depressed, his mood stabilized. Thankful for his undead body, he consoled himself by considering that he'd learned at least one thing: Silver and copper pieces were the currency circulated in villages. He wanted to know what other denominations there were, but he wasn't confident he could lead the conversation in that direction.

The bigger issue was the monetary value of a copper piece. He would run into a lot of trouble from here on out if he didn't know it. Not knowing the value of the currency would make him stick out way too much. He wanted to stay on the down low as much as possible while he was still clueless about the world, so he furiously spun his brain's gears, even just to avoid any more mistakes.

"Carrying so much small change would be a burden, so would it be possible to make it a little more compact?"

"My apologies. If I could, I'd like to pay you in gold pieces, but…we don't really use them in this village, so…"

Ainz suppressed a relieved sigh. This was just the chance he'd been looking for. Now he just had to think how to take it. He felt like his head might start steaming from the effort.

"Then how about this: I'll buy some of this village's goods at a reasonable price, and then you can pay me with the coins I give you." Ainz surreptitiously opened his item box beneath his robe and picked up two of *Yggdrasil*'s gold coins. One featured the relief of a woman's profile, and the other, a man's. The former was currency that came into use after the huge update, "'The Fall of Valkyria," and the latter, naturally, was the old kind. Monetarily they were both the same value, but he was more attached to one of them.

The old currency had been with him since he'd started playing; they had used it when they formed Ainz Ooal Gown and for most of the time the guild had existed. When the update was released, the guild was in its heyday and he'd already collected pretty much all of the gear he wanted, so he'd been just throwing the new coins into his item box.

The handful of coins that appeared in the air the first time he'd gone hunting as a skeleton mage, the mountain of coins he got when he snuck into a dungeon solo and frantically fought off all the active mobs that attacked him, the golden sparkle when he sold data crystals acquired in a successful raid with the guild…

He dismissed the nostalgia—but put away the old coin and took out the new one. "If I wanted to shop with this, about how much would it be worth?"

"Th-this is…?"

"It's a coin from a far-off—truly distant—country. Can I not use it here?"

"I think you can… One moment, please."

Feeling relieved to hear as much, he watched as the headman stood up and brought something over from the back of the room. Ainz had seen one once in a history book: a money changer's scale.

From then on it was the headman's wife's job. She first held the gold coin up to a disc-shaped object, seeming to compare sizes. Once she was satisfied with those results, she placed it on one side of the balance and put a weight on the other side. He had the feeling she said something about currency by weight.

Ainz rummaged around in his memory to guess the significance of what she was doing. *First, she must have compared it to this country's currency for size, and now she must be checking it for content.* His gold coin was lower than the weight. She added another weight to balance them out.

"It's as heavy as about two of our gold coins. E-err, do you mind if I make a slight scratch on the sur—?"

"Bah! Don't be rude! My most humble apologies. My wife has been most—"

"It doesn't bother me. You can destroy it if you like, but if the inside turns out to be solid gold, then you'll have to buy it from me…"

"N-no, I'm sorry." The headman's wife bowed and returned the coin.

"Don't worry about it. It's a matter of course when considering a deal with someone. So, what do you think about that gold piece? That relief is gorgeous, right? A work of art!"

"Yes, it's quite beautiful. What country is it from?"

"It's from a country that no longer exists."

"Oh, I see…"

"So it's worth two of yours, hm? But considering the artistic value, I would think it could be appraised a bit more highly. How about it?"

"That may be… However, we aren't merchants, so it's difficult for us to assess artistic value…"

"Ha-ha-ha. Indeed, I see. So then if I shop with this coin, we'll say it's worth two of those, all right?"

"O-of course."

"Very well. It so happens I have several of these coins, so I wonder what amount of goods you'll be able to sell. Of course, I will pay a fair price. You can charge me the same as you charge anyone in the village. Please take your time in investigating the matter."

"Lord Ainz Ooal Gown!" The suddenness of the headman's voice practically gave Ainz's nonexistent heart palpitations. His earnest expression was firmer and more striking than before.

"...Ainz is fine."

"Lord Ainz?" He seemed puzzled for a moment, but then quickly nodded a few times before continuing. "I understand just what you mean, Lord Ainz."

Ainz imagined a big question mark popping up over his head. He had a feeling there was some kind of misunderstanding, but since he had no idea what the headman was talking about, he couldn't say anything.

"I know you don't wish to be seen as cheap and that for your reputation you'd like to reach a compromise. It must cost a fortune to hire someone as strong as you, Lord Ainz. And that's why you want some material goods in addition to the three thousand copper pieces."

Ainz was completely confused by the headman's proposal and was glad he was wearing a mask. The reason he'd presented the gold coin and asked how much he could buy with it was to get a general idea of what things cost in this world. *How did things end up going in this direction?*

He didn't interrupt, so the headman continued. "However, all we can afford to offer is three thousand copper pieces. It's only natural that you would doubt us, but we have nothing to hide from you, our savior." The headman's expression was brimming with sincerity, and there was not the faintest suggestion that he might be lying. *If I get tricked here, I've got only my inability to judge character to blame.* "And of course I don't expect that someone as powerful as you would be satisfied with the paltry sum our small village can offer. If we went around the village collecting, perhaps we could scrape up something more adequate, but we've lost a lot of workers—if we pay more than the amount I mentioned, we won't be able to make it through the next season. And that goes for goods as well. Since we've lost hands, there will be fields that don't get tended. I predict extreme hardship for us in the near future if we give up produce now. I'm ashamed to ask this of you who have just saved our lives, but would you at least be willing to split everything with us?"

Oh! Is this my chance? Ainz felt as if he'd walked out of a dense forest to find a panoramic view. He pretended to be deep in thought. He could see where he wanted to go. He just prayed he would get there. After waiting a few moments, he replied, "I understand. I don't require any compensation."

"What?! Wh-why not?" The village headman and his wife's eyes widened in surprise.

Ainz raised a hand to signal he was going to continue talking. He guided the conversation, thinking what information he should give them and what he should keep to himself. It was a pain, and he wasn't 100 percent certain he could pull it off, but he had to. "I'm a caster and until quite recently had been holed up in a place called Nazarick to research magic."

"Aha, I see. So that's why you're dressed like that, huh?"

"Ah, well—er, yes," he mumbled, fingering the jealousy mask. *If casters dress so bizarrely here, I wonder what the cities look like...* Bali's Barong and Rangda walking down the street came to mind. He'd begun to hope this wasn't such a shocking world as all that when he realized something strange: The word *caster* made sense to them.

In *Yggdrasil*, the word *caster* had a broad meaning. It lumped the countless magic user classes—priests, clerics, druids, arcaners, sorcerers, wizards, bards, miko, talisman wielders, mountain hermits, etc.—all together. *What a coincidence if it were the same here.*

"I don't need compensation, but..." Ainz stopped here to judge their reaction. "A caster makes use of various things—fear, knowledge. You could call these the tools of our trade. But, as I mentioned, I've been holed up doing magic research, so I don't have much current knowledge of this area. I'd like to get some information from the two of you, and then have your understanding that no one is to know you sold it to me. Let's do that instead of monetary or material goods compensation."

"There's no such thing as a free lunch," so the saying goes. Of course he would ask for *something*. Anyone in negotiations with someone who just saved their lives and who said they didn't need anything in return would probably feel like something was fishy, so he had to make it seem to them like they'd compensated him—even if that compensation were intangible.

In other words, if he could convince them that selling him information he needed was a fair trade, they wouldn't get suspicious.

And in fact, both the headman and his wife nodded intensely. "You have our understanding. We'll never tell anyone."

Great! Ainz was glad his business know-how was worth something after all and did a mini–first pump under the table. "Oh, good. And I won't be using magic or anything to enforce your promise. I trust you."

Ainz stretched out a gauntleted hand. Initially startled, the headman seemed to realize what was going on and took it. Ainz was relieved they had handshakes in this world. If he had been given a look like, *What are you doing?* all he would have been able to do was cry.

Of course, he didn't trust them completely. If they were offered a reward, and it was good enough, they might spill the beans. By sealing the deal on their character alone, it just depended on their character. It wasn't about which was better, just Ainz chose to bet on the village headman's decency. If word got out, then it got out. He could just use the fact as a trump card in his next dealings with this village. Recalling their expressions of gratitude and the sincerity of their interactions with him, though, somehow he felt they wouldn't betray him.

"Well, then, I hope you can teach me many things."

•

"What the heck?!"

"Is something the matter?"

"Oh no, just talking to myself. Excuse me. I didn't mean to shout."

For one moment, Ainz fell out of character, but he picked up the act again right away. If he'd had a human body, he would have no doubt broken out in a cold sweat.

The village headman said only, "I see," and didn't probe any further. Maybe casters already had a reputation as weirdos in the village. That was no problem with Ainz.

"Would you like something to drink?"

"Oh no, that's okay. I'm not thirsty, but thank you for asking."

The headman's wife had left. He'd had her go outside to help with the cleanup and such. Ainz and the headman were the only ones left in the room.

The first question Ainz asked was about the countries in the area. The response had been all places he'd never heard of. He'd been prepared for anything, but surprise won out once reality was shoved in his face. At first, he'd been running his brain over many possibilities, but in general, he'd been thinking he must have been in the world of *Yggdrasil*. He could use *Yggdrasil* magic, so he figured there must be some connection. But now he was met with names of places he was completely ignorant of.

The countries in the area were the Re-Estize Kingdom, the Baharuth Empire, and the Slane Theocracy. *Yggdrasil*'s world was based on Norse myths—he'd never heard of any places like these.

His eyes were swimming, and he felt like he might collapse, but he steadied himself by putting his hands on the table. He'd just ended up in an unknown world. He'd been prepared to accept it, but he couldn't suppress his astonishment.

The shock was just too big. It was his first time being hit so hard by something since becoming undead. In order to calm down, he decided to review what he knew about the surrounding topography.

First, the Re-Estize Kingdom and the Baharuth Empire. Their territories were divided by a mountain range. From the southern edge of the mountains stretched a forest, and about where the forest ended was where the Re-Estize Kingdom's domain, containing the castle town and this village, began. The two countries had poor relations, and there was fighting on the plains near the castle town what seemed like every year during the past several.

Then to the south was the Slane Theocracy. To get a rough idea of how their territories fit together, it was easiest to think of an upside-down T tilted so it pointed up and to the right, but slightly melted so the long edge bent to go straight up. On the left was the Re-Estize Kingdom; on the right, a bit larger, was the Baharuth Empire; and below the bar was the Slane Theocracy. Supposedly there were other countries as well, but that was all the info the village headman could provide. As for the countries' relative power, the headman of a tiny village wouldn't know that, either. In other words…

"I screwed up…"

The village headman seemed to think the knights had come from the Baharuth Empire due to the crests on their armor, but in terms of which countries actually shared borders, it was possible the whole thing could have been a plot by the Slane Theocracy. It had been a mistake to let all the knights go. He should have grabbed at least one and gotten some info out of him. Now it was too late.

Assuming it had been the Slane Theocracy, then maybe he should strike some kind of deal with the empire. The kingdom was fine—he'd already earned some goodwill there for saving this village.

Ainz pondered whether he could really be the only one who'd come to this world. *That can't be. There's a huge chance other players are here. Even HeroHero might be here. What I need to think about is what will happen if I encounter other players.*

If a large number of players had come, knowing Japanese people, many of them would group together. Ainz wanted to be part of that if possible. He would make any concessions as long as they didn't have to do with Ainz Ooal Gown.

The issue would be if that group saw his guild as an enemy. That wasn't completely out of the question—Ainz Ooal Gown had role-played evil and done a lot of PK-ing, so they were widely detested. He wasn't confident that hatred had died out. He might even be antagonized out of a sense of justice or righteous indignation.

To avoid that, the first thing to do would be to make as few enemies as possible. If he killed locals—or especially if he carried out any unnecessary slaughter of humans—it could upset players who still had their humanity. Of course, if he had a reason they found convincing (for instance, saving a village like this one that was under attack), then it might be a different story.

In short, I need to have a really good reason for everything I do from now on. In other words, I didn't want to do this but…I need a procedure.

In the event this group held a grudge against Ainz Ooal Gown, Nazarick probably wouldn't be able to avoid combat. Considering their current war potential, they could annihilate thirty level-100 players in one go. And if they used a World Item, the Tomb would transform into an impregnable fortress. They'd probably be able to fight off any enemies like they had before.

But it wasn't hard to imagine how stupid trying to withstand a raid without backup would be. And each time they unleashed the World Item's power, Ainz's level would go down. If they were attacked in waves, they would eventually be worn down to the point where they couldn't use it anymore.

Ainz knew focusing on warfare was dangerous because it could lead to bias and a narrower view of things, but neither was he so naive that he would act without considering the worst possible outcome. He was simply considering how to deal with problems.

If he only cared about surviving, maybe he wouldn't have to do all that—he could just live in the mountains and fields like a beast—but he had too much power and pride to do that.

If he tried to get along with people, things ought to work out one way or another.

In that case, the most important item of discussion was how to increase their war potential. He needed to collect more information about the world, including who the players in it were.

"There has to be some mistake..."

"Is something wrong?"

"Oh no. Things are just a bit different than I thought, so I was momentarily upset. More importantly, could you give me some more information?"

"O-okay, yes." The headman changed topics to discuss monsters.

They had them, just like in *Yggdrasil*. There were dangerous beasts living deep in the woodlands, especially the Wise King of the Forest, and they also had humanlike races like dwarves and elves, as well as subhuman races such as goblins, orcs, and ogres. Apparently some of the subhuman races had even established countries.

People who went around exterminating monsters for rewards were called "adventurers," and there were many casters among them. In big cities, there were adventurer guilds.

Ainz also got some information about the nearest fortress city, E-Rantel. The headman wasn't sure about the population, but he knew it was the biggest city in these parts. It seemed like it would be the best place to gather information.

The information Ainz got from the village headman was useful, but there were still lots of unknowns. Rather than trying to get details here, it would be faster to send a party to E-Rantel.

Then, there was the language. Ainz thought it strange that everyone knew Japanese in this completely other world, so he tried watching the headman's lips and—no big deal—he wasn't speaking Japanese.

The movements of his mouth and what Ainz was hearing were totally different.

From there, Ainz did some experimenting. His conclusion? Everyone here had eaten Translation Gum or something, not that he knew where they'd gotten it. This world's language, or rather the words anyone spoke, would be automatically translated by the time they reached the listener. If a word could be recognized as a word, it would probably work with nonhuman creatures as well, like cats or dogs. He just had no idea how it was possible. The headman, however, didn't seem to think anything of it—it was taken for granted.

So it must just be one of the laws of this world? If I take a step back and think about it, they do *have magic. It wouldn't be strange at all if this world was governed by a whole different set of laws.*

The common sense Ainz had picked up in his life was not the common sense of this world. That was a critical problem. Without common sense, he was in danger of committing a fatal error—nobody ever means anything good when they say, "That guy has no common sense," and he was certainly lacking it now. He had to do something, but no brilliant moves came to mind. *I can't just grab someone and say, "Tell me all your common sense!" That'd be ridiculous!*

Which left him with basically one option.

"...I guess I need to go live in a city, huh?"

To learn common sense would take a large number of models. He also needed to learn about this world's magic. There were too many things he still needed to find out.

As he was going over all of this in his head, he heard the faint sound of footsteps in the dirt outside the thin wooden door. The interval was large, but it didn't sound like stomping—it was a man in a hurry.

The knock came just as Ainz had turned to face that way. The headman looked to Ainz to see how he wished to proceed. *He must feel awkward doing anything of his own volition when he's in the middle of a discussion constituting payment for me saving the village.* "Go ahead, no problem. I was just wanting a break anyhow. I don't mind if you go out."

"My apologies." The headman gave a slight bow and walked toward the door. When he opened it, a villager was standing there with the sun at his back. His eyes went from the headman to Ainz.

"I'm sorry to interrupt, but the preparations for the funeral are complete..."

"I see..." The headman looked Ainz's way as if requesting permission to leave.

"I don't mind. Don't worry about me."

"Thank you. Then, please tell everyone I'll join you presently."

2

The funeral began in the public cemetery on the outskirts of town. The cemetery was surrounded by a shabby fence. Round stones with names carved on them dotted the yard, serving as grave markers.

The village headman appealed to gods Ainz had never heard of in *Yggdrasil,* so that the deceased might rest in peace.

There weren't enough hands to bury all the corpses at once, so they were starting with what they could. Ainz thought it seemed hasty to bury people that very day, but there were no religions he was familiar with here, so all he could do was accept it as different.

Among the villagers present were the sisters he had saved, Enri and Nemu Emmott. Their parents must have been getting buried that day.

Ainz watched a little ways away from the others, running his hands over a wand of about twelve inches under his robe. It was made of elephant ivory and one tip was dipped in gold. The grip was inscribed with runes, giving the whole object a kind of sacred vibe.

It was a wand of resurrection, a magical item that could revive the dead. Of course, he had more than just that one. He had enough to bring back everyone in the village with change left over. But according to the headman, magic that could bring back the dead didn't exist in this world. So there was the potential for a miracle to occur in this village, but as the prayer ended and the funeral entered its last stages, Ainz quietly put the wand back in his item box.

He could bring them back. He just didn't. Not that he was concerned for their souls or had some other religious reason. There just wasn't anything in it for him.

There were casters who could kill and casters who could revive. It wasn't hard to imagine either type getting caught up in some kind of trouble. Even if he did it on the condition they stay quiet about it, the chance of them sticking to that was low.

The power to oppose death—who wouldn't drool over that?

If the situation changed, maybe he could use it, but for now, he didn't have enough information. *Now is not the time.* "I'll have them be satisfied with the fact that I saved the village," he murmured and then turned to take a hard look at the death knight standing behind him.

He had some questions about this guy, too. In *Yggdrasil*, with a few exceptions, summoned monsters expired after a set time, and since he hadn't used any special method to summon this death knight, his time should have been up a long time ago. But he was still here. Ainz had various guesses about what was going on, but without more information, he couldn't reach an answer.

Next to Ainz and his thoughts, two shadows lined up. They were Albedo and a spiderlike monster the size of a human wearing ninja gear. From each of its eight legs grew a sharp blade.

"An eight-edged assassin? Albedo...!" Ainz scanned the area, but there was no sign of any villagers looking their way. Even in the middle of a funeral, the sight of Albedo and especially the bizarre monster should have been enough to draw attention.

Then he remembered: Eight-edged assassins could turn invisible.

"I brought him because he said he wanted to see you, Lord Ainz."

"I do hope you are in good spirits, Lord Momo—"

"Spare me the flattery. More importantly, are you my reinforcements?"

"Yes, sir. There are four hundred minions under me ready to raid the village."

Raid? Why do they think we're raiding? Sebas, this is like a bad game of telephone. "There's no need to attack. The issue is already resolved. And who is commanding you?"

"Mistress Aura and Master Mare. Master Demiurge and Mistress Shalltear are defending the castle, and Master Cocytus is guarding the area."

"I see. If there are too many minions out, they'll just get in the way. Have everyone except Aura and Mare withdraw. How many of you eight-edged assassins came?"

"Fifteen in all."

"Okay, then you guys stand by with Aura and Mare."

After receiving the eight-edged assassin's bow, Ainz turned back to the funeral proceedings. Right as some dirt was being thrown onto a fresh gave, the two sisters collapsed in tears.

Realizing the funeral wouldn't end anytime soon, he headed slowly back to the village. Albedo and the death knight followed behind him.

Although they'd been interrupted by the funeral, by the time Ainz left the headman's house after learning about the area and some amount of common sense, the sun had been sitting low in the sky.

He'd made this dramatic rescue as a favor to an old friend, but it had taken more time than he'd expected. He did feel like the benefits balanced it out, though. Even just realizing that the more he learned about the world, the more questions he had was worth it. Ainz ran his mind over the things he had to do while gazing absentmindedly at the setting sun.

It was extremely dangerous to act without being fully informed. The best thing to do would have been to stay hidden and gather information on the down low, but now that he had saved this village, that was no longer possible.

Even if he had annihilated those knights, their country would have wanted to investigate what had happened to them. In his own world, scientific investigation was advanced, but it was possible that in this world some other way of investigating had advanced.

Even if they weren't advanced, as long as there were villagers alive, there was a high chance they'd be able to find out about him. One way to make sure no information leaked was to take all the villagers to the Great Tomb of Nazarick, but it wouldn't be strange for the kingdom to consider that abduction.

And so he had given his name and let the knights go. He'd had two aims in this. As long as he wasn't hiding out in the Great Tomb of Nazarick, he guessed word of him would spread quickly, so his first aim was to spread word of himself to some extent; he figured it would be good to guide that process. The second aim was to spread the story of how someone called Ainz Ooal Gown saved a village and killed knights. Of course, the ones whom he most wanted to hear the rumor were *Yggdrasil* players.

Ainz wanted to belong to either the kingdom, the empire, or the theocracy. He was sure that if other players were in this world, rumors of them would spread. But if Ainz belonged to an organization called Nazarick, it was bound to be difficult to acquire information, not to mention risky. And if he made the mistake of giving orders to someone with a personality like Albedo, he might inadvertently make unnecessary enemies.

Even just from the standpoint of acquiring information, it seemed like getting under the umbrella of one of the countries would be a good idea. In order to maintain the self-governance of the Great Tomb of Nazarick, as well, it would be good to have the backing of some authority. He couldn't take his situation lightly as long as he was in the dark about the relative strength of the countries. Not knowing what the limit of individual power in this world was also spurred him on. He couldn't assume there was no one stronger than him in any of the three countries.

He could think of plenty of downsides to becoming a member of one of the countries, but he felt the upsides outweighed them. The problem was, in what position would he "join" them?

I'm not about to be somebody's slave, sorry. I'm not interested in being employed at a company with horrible working conditions like HeroHero, either. I'll have to try to impress the various powers and choose the best place once I've seen the differences in how they treat me.

It's just like changing jobs.

So it's just a question of when to start making connections. I might get taken advantage of the way I am now, with barely any information.

Ainz got about that far before shaking his head as if he were a bit tired. He'd used his brain a crazy amount during the past several hours. It was a pain to think anymore.

"Phew…all right. I've done what I came here to do. Albedo, let's withdraw."

"Yes, my lord." Albedo was bristling despite the fact that she had no reason to be on guard; there was no danger in this village.

In that case, Ainz could only think of one explanation. He lowered his voice and asked, "…Do you hate humans?"

"I'm not fond of them. They're such fragile creatures—lower life-forms. I always wonder how pretty they'd be if I squashed them under my feet like bugs. Oh, but…there is one exception, a girl…" Her voice was sweet as honey, but the words she spoke were severe.

Ainz considered the beauty that made her look like a goddess full of love and felt her attitude unbecoming. He replied to admonish her somewhat. "Hm, I understand how you feel, but please keep your composure and treat them kindly. It's important to put on the act."

Albedo deeply bowed her head. Watching her, Ainz worried. Her preferences wouldn't cause problems for the moment, but he wondered about the future. He realized he needed to be aware of his subordinates' likes and dislikes.

With that, he decided to try to find the village headman. He wanted to be polite and say good-bye before leaving.

The headman was easy enough to locate. He was conferring in a corner of the square with some villagers; the looks on their faces were serious, but there was something off—they seemed nervous.

More trouble? Ainz refrained from clicking his tongue and went over to them. *In for a penny, in for a mile.*

"Is something wrong, Mr. Headman?"

It was like a ray of heavenly light beamed across his face. "Oh, Lord Ainz! We have word that there are mounted knights heading toward the village."

"I see."

The headman looked nervously at Ainz. The villagers did the same.

He held up a hand to calm them. "Leave this to me. Gather all the villagers in your house at once, then meet me in the square."

A bell rang, and while the villagers gathered, Ainz positioned the death knight outside the headman's house and Albedo behind himself.

Ainz spoke to the headman in a cheerful voice to assuage his fears. "Don't worry. I'll give you a freebie, just this once."

The headman's trembling lessened somewhat and he smiled wryly. Perhaps he had been prepared for the worst.

It wasn't long before a group of cavalrymen came into view down the main road. They rode in formation and proceeded quietly into the village.

"Their gear doesn't match—they've all got custom setups... Does that mean they're not part of a regular army?"

Watching the cavalrymen, Ainz felt something was off about their equipment.

The knights who had come before with the empire's crest emblazoned on their chests all had matching heavy armor. But these cavalrymen, they were wearing armor, but everyone had arranged their equipment to their own liking. Some wore just leather armor for some parts, while others had taken off iron plates and wore exposed chain mail. Some wore helmets, some didn't. The one thing they had in common in that department was that their faces were visible. They also all wore the same make of sword, but their secondary weapons were all different types—bows, one-handed spears, maces, etc.

From a glass-half-full perspective, they were a veteran order of knights. Otherwise they were just a ragtag bunch of mercenaries.

Eventually the party rode right into the square, about twenty men. While keeping an eye on the death knight, they formed a magnificent row before Ainz and the village headman. One of them, still on his horse, came forward. He appeared to be their leader and was more robust than the others. He practically overlooked the headman, stopped his eyes on the death knight, and then looked at Albedo. His eyes stayed there for a long time, as if he were caught. But when he saw that she was just standing at attention without moving a muscle, he turned his sharp, perceptive gaze on Ainz.

This man had the air of one who made violence his occupation, but Ainz took his gaze and just stood there. One look wasn't enough to disturb him.

Not that he had always been strong against such eyes. It was probably just thanks to his undead body. Or maybe it was due to the confidence he'd gained from being able to use his *Yggdrasil* powers.

Satisfied with his observations, the man addressed them in a dignified manner. "I am captain of the Royal Select of the Kingdom of Re-Estize, Gazef Stronoff. We've come on the king's orders to subdue the imperial knights terrorizing this region." His deep voice carried clearly throughout the square despite being quiet, and Ainz could hear a stir from inside the village headman's house behind them.

"Captain of the Royal Select...," murmured the headman.

Ainz was slightly miffed that there hadn't been anything about this man in the info he'd received. "Who is he?"

"According to the merchants, he was once champion of the royal tournament and is now the leader of a group of elite soldiers who serve the king directly."

"And this is really him?"

"...I don't know. I've only ever heard the rumors."

If Ainz squinted, it turned out they did all have the same crest on their chests. And it did resemble the kingdom's crest the headman had described earlier. But he was still a little too uninformed to believe the story right away.

"You must be the village headman," said Gazef, turning to the headman. "So then, if you would be so kind as to tell me who exactly that is next to you?"

The headman's mouth was half open, but Ainz stopped him and gave a brief self-introduction. "That's not necessary. It's a pleasure to meet you, Captain. I am Ainz Ooal Gown, a caster who saw this village being attacked by knights and came to save it."

In response, Gazef jumped off his horse and landed with a clatter of armor. He solemnly bowed his head. "There are no words to express my thanks that you have saved this village."

A ripple went through the atmosphere.

It must have been a shock in this world, where social standing was so black and white, to see the most likely privileged man who held the position of captain of the Royal Select making a show of respect to Ainz, whose status was unknown. Human rights weren't even properly established in this country—or depending on the case, anywhere. They had probably been buying and selling humans as slaves up until a few years ago.

Despite the fact that they weren't even equals, Gazef had gotten off his horse and bowed to Ainz. That spoke volumes about his character. Ainz decided that the man must actually be who he said he was.

"No, I was doing it for the rewards, anyway. Don't worry about it."

"Oh! A reward? Then, you're an adventurer?"

"Something like that."

"Hmm, I see. You seem quite strong... I'm sorry to say I haven't heard your name before."

"I'm on a journey, just passing through, so my name may not have spread so much."

"On a journey, hm? I feel bad taking an able adventurer's time, but I'd like to hear the details about the nasty bunch who attacked this village."

"Of course. I'd be happy to tell you, Captain. I robbed most of them of their lives. I'd hazard to say they won't be making any trouble around here for a while. Did you need to hear more about that?"

"Robbed them of their lives... You killed them yourself, Sir Gown?" From the way Gazef addressed him, he realized this world's names were Western-style, not Japanese—not surname, name, but name, surname. Now he knew why the headman had looked at him a little funny when he'd asked him to call him Ainz. Certainly if someone Ainz wasn't terribly familiar with asked to be called by their first name, he would have made that face.

He concealed his realization of this faux pas with the mask known as adulthood and continued. "You...could say that or maybe not."

Inferring the delicate nuance, Gazef's eyes flicked to the death knight. He must have sensed the faint smell of blood coming off of him.

"Right now there are two things I want to ask you. One: What is that?"

"A minion I created."

He *hmm*ed his admiration and looked Ainz up and down. "And what's that mask about?"

"I have my reasons as a caster for wearing this mask."

"Could I get you to take it off for me?"

"I'm afraid not. It would be quite troublesome if he"—Ainz indicated the death knight—"were to go on a rampage."

The village headman knew what the death knight was capable of, and the alarm was plain on his face. Voices could also be heard from inside the house. Perhaps sensing the sudden atmosphere change, Gazef nodded gravely. "I see. I suppose you'd better keep it on, then."

"Thank you."

"Well, then—"

"One moment. I beg your pardon, but this village has just been attacked by imperial knights. I think seeing all of you with your weapons will cause them to flash back to that terror. It would probably help everyone relax if you would lay down your weapons at the edge of the square. What do you think?"

"You're right, but these swords were bestowed upon us by our king. We can't disarm without his permission."

"Lord Ainz, we're fine."

"Are you sure, Mr. Headman? Captain, I hope you'll be able to forgive me for my rudeness."

"No problem, Sir Gown. I think your idea was quite correct. If this sword were not a gift from our king, I would have gladly set it aside. Now, then, shall we sit down somewhere and have a more detailed discussion? Also, if you don't mind, we'd like to rest here for the night..."

"Understood. We'll discuss that as well, so please come to my house—" The headman was mid-reply when it happened. A lone cavalryman rode into the square. His rough breathing foreshadowed the seriousness of the news he'd brought.

He loudly announced an emergency. "Captain! Several figures spotted in the area! They're surrounding the village and approaching!"

3

"Your attention, please."

A quiet, level voice sounded so that all present could hear.

"Our prey has entered the cage."

It was a man's voice. There was nothing particular about it. His face, too, was an average one that would get lost in a crowd—if it weren't for his utterly emotionless, almost artificial-seeming black eyes and a scar that ran down his cheek.

"Let us put our faith in the gods."

All those present observed a moment of silence, a condensed prayer to their gods.

Even on a mission in a different country, they took time to pray—not out of confidence, but piety. These agents of the Slane Theocracy in the service of their gods had stronger faith than average citizens. That was how they could perform cold-blooded acts without thinking twice and feel no guilt.

After the prayer, all of their eyes were glazed over, like glass marbles.

"Begin."

One word.

That was all it took for everyone to move in exquisite coordination to surround the village. One could sense it was the result of ceaseless training.

This was the unit that carried out mostly illegal activities. They existed even inside the Slane Theocracy itself only as rumors that followed them like shadows—one of the six scriptures that reported directly to the high priest, the Sunlit Scripture, whose most important duty was the extermination of subhuman villages.

Although the Sunlit Scripture saw the most combat of any of the six special-ops units, they had very few members—not even one hundred, including reserves. Their small size implied how hard it was to be accepted.

First, they each had to be able to use tier-three (the highest level a normal caster could attain) faith magic. Superior mental and physical abilities, as well as a true faith, were also required.

In other words, they were the best of the best.

Watching his elite subordinates scatter, the man breathed out slowly. Deployment was done; it would be hard to monitor their movements now. However, he had no concerns regarding the construction of their cage. Captain of the Sunlit Scripture, Nigun Grid Lewin had the peace of mind of one who knew his mission's success was nearly at hand.

The Sunlit Scripture were not experts at covert or outdoor operations. They'd missed their chance four times. After each failure, they pursued Gazef and his men from the kingdom, careful to not be found. If they missed their chance again now, their days of chasing Gazef would continue.

"Should we…get help from another unit next time? I'd like to let someone else handle this."

Someone was present to respond to Nigun's grumbling. "We really should. Our specialty is extermination!" He was a subordinate who had stayed behind, in part to guard Nigun. "So it's weird that we'd get assigned this mission. It's important, so why didn't they get the Flurry Scripture in on it, too?"

"Exactly. It's unclear why they assigned us alone, but it's been a good learning experience for us. Incorporating covert operations on enemy soil into our training isn't such a bad thing. I mean, it's possible that's why they had us do it." Even as he said that, however, Nigun knew the probability of another mission like this coming their way was low.

Their mission was to remove Gazef Stronoff, a royal warrior so strong that there was no one comparable in any nearby countries. This was more of a job for the Black Scripture, the unit where all members had hero-level power. Normally it would have been given to them, but this time that wasn't possible.

The reason for that was top secret, so Nigun couldn't tell the lower-ranking man, but of course he knew what it was. The Black Scripture was too busy bracing for the resurrection of the Catastrophe Dragonlord—while also guarding the sacred treasure, Ruinous Beauty, and the Flurry Scripture's top priority was chasing down the traitor who had stolen one of the shrine princesses' sacred treasures.

Nigun unconsciously stroked the scar on his cheek. He thought of the one time he'd awkwardly fled from a fight, and the face of the woman who had given him the scar with her black magic sword came to mind…

Magic could have completely healed him, but he had left the scar there on purpose, so he wouldn't forget his defeat.

"Blue Rose…"

That woman was from the kingdom, like Gazef. But what Nigun really couldn't forgive her for was being a priest. Not only did she believe in a different god, but she tried to prevent Nigun and his men from attacking a subhuman village—and she thought she was right! She was a fool who couldn't see the big picture.

"Humans are weak, so we must protect ourselves in all manner of ways. She couldn't understand that, the fool."

The subordinate man, perhaps sharp enough to catch the anger in his captain's glassy eyes, hastily interrupted. "Th-that kingdom, the whole bunch of them are fools."

Nigun didn't answer, but he agreed.

Gazef was strong. That's why they had moved to weaken him by stripping him of his protection.

The kingdom was split into two factions, the king's side and the nobles, who were locked in a continuous power struggle. Gazef was an impossible-to-ignore member of the king's faction, so if the nobles thought they could thwart him, they were liable to act without thinking things through—even if their thought process was being manipulated by an agent from another country.

One of the reasons the nobles hated him was that he had worked his way up out of his commoner background by his prowess with the sword alone.

And the result of all that animosity?

The kingdom was about to lose their trump card.

To Nigun, it was utterly idiotic.

The Slane Theocracy also had factions—six of them, but they mostly worked together. One simple reason they could do that was the fact that they respected one another's gods. Another was that they knew they *had* to stick together in this dangerous world full of nonhuman races and monsters.

"...That's why we have to get them to walk the same path as us, the path based on the correct teachings. Humans are not meant to fight, but to walk together."

And the sacrifice to this ideal would be Gazef.

"Do you think we can get him?"

Nigun took his subordinate's anxiety seriously.

Their prey this time was Gazef Stronoff, the strongest warrior in these parts and captain of the Royal Select. This was harder than wiping out a huge goblin village. So Nigun answered in a quiet voice to dispel his worries. "It shouldn't be a problem. You know those treasures the kingdom permits him to carry? He doesn't have them equipped this time. Without those, it should be a simple matter to kill him... I'd even say that if we miss this chance, it will, on the contrary, be impossible."

Captain Gazef Stronoff's name was known far and wide for his skills, but there was another reason, as well—the kingdom's five treasures. Currently only four were known, but Gazef was allowed to equip them all: the Gauntlets of Vitality that made it so the wearer never got fatigued; the Amulet of Immortality that constantly healed the wearer; Guardian Armor that was said to be able to save the wearer from a fatal critical hit, made from the hardest metal in existence, adamantite; and Razor Edge, a magic sword that was enchanted in the pursuit of sharpness and cut armor like butter.

Even Nigun couldn't win against Gazef Stronoff if his attack and defense were boosted to extraordinary levels via that lineup of gear. Surely there was no human who could. But if he wasn't equipped with the treasures, they had a decent enough chance.

"Plus, we have an ace up our sleeve. There's no way we'll lose this fight." Nigun patted his breast pocket.

In this world there were three types of nonstandard magic items. Relics of the Eight Kings of Avarice who conquered the continent in the blink of an eye more than five hundred years ago were one type. Before the Eight Kings of Avarice ruled, the dragons did. The dragons' hidden treasures, believed to have been created by the most powerful dragonlords' magic, were the second type. Finally, six centuries earlier, the six gods that made up the foundation of the Slane Theocracy descended. The supreme treasures they left behind were the third and final type.

And in Nigun's breast pocket was a supreme treasure—even the Slane Theocracy only had a few of them. It meant guaranteed victory.

He glanced at the steel band wrapped around his wrist. The numbers there indicated the passing of time.

"Okay, let's begin the operation."

Nigun and his subordinate cast their magic—their elite angel-summoning magic.

•

"I see. Yes, indeed…" Gazef confirmed the reported figures from the shadow of a house. He could see three. They were slowly walking toward the village, maintaining a fixed distance among one another. They were unarmed and weren't wearing heavy armor, but that didn't mean they would go down easily. Many casters eschewed heavy armor, preferring lighter materials. In other words, they were probably casters.

What made that completely clear were the glowing, winged figures lined up next to them—angels.

Angels were monsters summoned from another world that many people—especially people from the Slane Theocracy—believed served the gods. It was unclear whether that was true or false, and the priests of the kingdom asserted that they were simply a type of summoned monster.

That religious conflict was one reason the countries disliked each other, but Gazef didn't care who the monsters served. To Gazef, all that mattered was how strong they were.

As far as he knew, compared to other monsters summoned with the same level of magic, angels and demons (which were said to be about equal themselves) were a tad stronger. In addition to having many special abilities, they could use some magic, so Gazef categorized them among the more troublesome enemies. Even so, although it depended on the type of angel, they weren't unbeatable.

These ones wore gleaming breastplates and carried long swords of crimson flame. He'd never seen this type before, so he couldn't guess how strong they were.

Ainz had come with him to take a look and asked, "Who the heck are these guys and what are they after? This village doesn't really seem that valuable..."

"So you don't know them...? If they're not after you, Sir Gown, then there's only one answer."

Their eyes met.

"You've got some enemies, Captain."

"I suppose there's no helping it because of my position, but this is...a rather large problem. If they have this many casters summoning angels, they must be from the Slane Theocracy... And if they're engaged in this kind of mission, it must be one of the rumored six scriptures, their special-ops units. Numbers, strength—they have the advantage." Gazef shrugged his shoulders, all but openly grumbling about what a pain it was. His attitude was relaxed, but inside he was quite anxious. And angry.

"They did a great job using the nobles to take away my gear. If that snake had been sniffing around the court, things would probably have gone even worse, so I suppose we should count ourselves lucky that this was all that happened. Still, I never thought the Slane Theocracy would be after me..."

He snorted.

But they were really outnumbered. They weren't ready. They had no countermeasures to use. They were fresh out of everything. But there was one possibility...

"Are those flame archangels? They sure look like them, but...why would the same monster be here? Is it because the summon magic is the same? If that's the case..."

Gazef looked to the muttering Ainz and said, with a glimmer of hope, "Sir Gown, if it's all right with you, we'd like to hire you."

There was no reply. Gazef just felt an intense stare coming from behind the mask.

"I can promise you any amount in compensation."

"I think I'll refuse."

"If we could even just borrow your summoned knight..."

"I don't think so."

"And if I invoked royal law and forcefully drafted you?"

"That would be a most foolish choice...is...not the kind of violent thing I'd like to say, but if you attempt to use some power against me, including the authority of the kingdom, I'd put up a little bit of resistance."

They glared at each other and the first one to look away was Gazef.

"Huh. We'd be annihilated before we even got into it with the theocracy."

"Ho-ho, 'annihilated,' very funny. But I'm glad you understand."

Gazef watched, eyes squinted, as Ainz bowed. He hadn't been joking. His intuition was screaming at him how dangerous it would be to make an enemy of this caster. Especially when his life was in danger, he tended to go with his intuition over unproductive pondering.

Who is this guy? Gazef thought, gazing at Ainz's mask. *What in the world does his face look like under that mask? Is it one I'd be familiar with, or...?*

"Is something wrong? Is my mask crooked?"

"Ohhh no, I just was thinking what a peculiar mask it is. If you can control that monster with it, it must be an unusually powerful magic item."

"Indeed. It's quite rare and valuable. It's impossible to get one anymore."

If someone possessed valuable magic items, then logically their magic would be powerful. Thinking in that way, Ainz must have been a pretty powerful caster. Gazef suddenly felt hopeless, being unable to win his support. But he still wished that as an adventurer, Ainz would take on this one request...

"Well, it's pointless to stand around here all day. Take care, Sir Gown. I appreciate you saving the village."

Gazef removed his gauntlets and shook Ainz's hand. To be polite, it would be correct for Ainz to remove his gauntlets as well, but he left them on and it didn't faze Gazef. He shook Ainz's hand with both of his bare hands and laid his heart bare to match. "I really, really appreciate it. You did an amazing deed, protecting the innocent from that storm of atrocities. ...And I have to say: I want you to protect them again. I don't have anything I can give you right now, but I do hope you'll consider my request."

"That's—"

"If you ever come to the royal capital, I promise, on my honor as Gazef Stronoff, that I'll give you whatever you desire."

Gazef took his hands away and was about to drop to one knee, but

Ainz stopped him. "You don't have to do that… I understand. I'll protect this village without fail…on my honor as Ainz Ooal Gown."

Hearing this vow, Gazef's heart lightened. "Thank you, Sir Gown! Then, we have nothing to fear. I can go forth boldly into battle."

"Before you do that, please take this."

Ainz must have thought of something as Gazef smiled—he handed him a small object. It was a weird little carving that didn't seem terribly special to Gazef, but— "A memento—I gratefully accept. Well, Sir Gown, it's a shame we must part, but I'm going to go."

"You don't want to wait for the cover of night?"

"There's a spell called Night Vision, so even if darkness is a disadvantage for us, it likely won't be for them. Plus, they have to see that we've fled the village for this to work."

"I see. Your analysis is worthy of your position, Captain. You have my admiration. May you be victorious."

"May your journey continue, Sir Gown."

Ainz watched until Gazef's silhouette grew small. Perhaps sensing something in his mood, Albedo said nothing despite their lack of time.

Ainz sighed. "I feeling nothing more toward a human I'm meeting for the first time than I would for a bug, but…once I try talking to them, I start to get attached as if they were cute little animals."

"Is that why you swore on your honor along with your sacred name?"

"Maybe… No. It was because of the strong will of someone prepared to die…"

He admired that.

Gazef had a strong will, unlike himself.

"Albedo, relay orders to the minions in the area: Check for any ambushing troops. If there are any, knock them out."

"At once. Ah, Lord Ainz, the headman is coming."

Following Albedo's line of sight Ainz saw the headman heading their way with two villagers. Anxiety and unease had spurred them to run, and they were out of breath, but they began to speak as soon as they reached him as if they couldn't even spare the time it would take to recover.

"Lord Ainz, what should we do? Why has the captain refused to protect us and left the village?" The headman's words contained more than fear. The feeling of abandonment was turning to rage.

"The captain did the right thing, Mr. Headman. The enemy is after him. If he stayed, the village would be the battleground and they probably wouldn't pass up the chance to kill the people. Him leaving was the best thing for you."

"So that's...why he left? We should stay here, then...?"

"No. I'm sure they'll come back for the survivors here. We can't run while we're surrounded, but they'll probably attack the captain with all they've got. That's our chance to escape. Let's take that opening."

That was why he'd left the village in such a visible way. He was acting as a decoy to draw the enemy's focus. Comprehending the unspoken nuance that the captain didn't stand much chance of victory, the headman blushed and hung his head. The captain had gone to battle prepared to die in order to create a chance for the villagers to escape... The headman hadn't realized, and his misunderstanding made him angry. He must have been ashamed of himself.

"And here I was thinking... Oh, Lord Ainz, what can I...? What should we do?"

"What do you mean?"

"We live near the forest, but we were never attacked by monsters. We were only lucky, but we mistook luck as safety and forgot how to defend ourselves. The result is that many of our neighbors have been killed and we've been a burden on everyone..." Not only the headman's expression, but those of the villagers behind him, too, were full of regret.

"There was nothing you could have done. Your opponents were veterans. If you had put up a fight, it's possible you'd have all died before I arrived."

He tried to comfort them, but he didn't sense their sorrow letting up at all. Really, this was not something words would fix. All he could do was pray that time would heal them.

"Mr. Headman, we don't have much time. We should get going so the captain's resolve will not be in vain."

"Y-yes, you're right. What are you planning to do, Lord Ainz?"

"I'm going to keep an eye on things and escape with all of you when the time is right."

"We're bothering you again..."

"Please don't worry about it. I promised the captain I would protect you. For now, please gather all the villagers in one of the bigger houses. I'll cast a bit of magic defense."

He could feel the horse's agitation in his legs. Even though the mount was trained to be a warhorse, or perhaps precisely *because* he was so trained, he'd picked up on the fact that they were heading to their doom.

There were only four or five opponents, but they were spread out to surround the village. Because of that, the space between them was wide, but they must have been creating a perfect cage somehow.

In other words, a total trap. Step inside and the jaws of death would open.

Gazef knew that, but he was going to try to break through. That was the only option he had.

He had no chance of winning at range against casters. If he had some archers or someone with the talent and resources to fight at range, it might have been different, but since he didn't, he had to avoid a ranged battle.

Fighting it as a siege would be ridiculous.

Maybe if they'd had a stone fortress with big thick walls, but wooden houses wouldn't do a thing to block magic. One wrong move and the village would be burned down.

There was one last way, but he felt it was definitely the moral low road: Fight inside the village such that Ainz Ooal Gown got caught up in it, forcing him to help.

But if he was going to use a plan like that, his reason for coming to this village in the first place would be lost. That's why he chose the thorny path.

"We'll attack the enemy to draw them out of their circle and then retreat. We can't miss that chance!"

His men gave a spirited reply behind him, and he furrowed his brow.

How many of us will make it out of this alive?

It wasn't as if any of them were talent holders; they were all just what they seemed, but they had come up through Gazef's training and were the product of hard, unceasing work. It would be a shame to lose them.

Gazef knew he was making a stupid move, but his men followed him anyway. He turned to shout an apology for getting them mixed up in this, but when he saw their expressions, he swallowed every word.

They were the faces of warriors. Their expressions showed their determination to see this through despite knowing what lay in store. It wouldn't be right to apologize to these men, who had decided to follow him despite the danger. He felt embarrassed, but his men peppered him with encouragement.

"Don't worry about it, Captain!"

"Yeah, we're here because we want to be! We're with you to the end!"

"Please allow us to protect our country, its people, and our friends!"

Gazef no longer had any words.

He faced forward and howled, "Let's go! We're gonna rip their guts out!"

"Yaaaaaah!"

Gazef spurred his horse and was off and running. His men followed. The horses galloped at full speed, kicking up dirt as they went across the plain straight as an arrow.

As he rode, Gazef took out his bow and nocked an arrow. Rocking with his horse, he drew casually and let go. The arrow flew true and sunk into the head of a caster in front of them—or at least it seemed like it was going to.

"Tch! So these won't do anything… If I had magic arrows, they'd work, but whining about things I don't have won't get me anywhere."

The arrow had bounced off as if the caster were wearing a solid helmet. That bizarre hardness had to be due to some kind of magic spell. As far as Gazef knew, to penetrate magic that protected against projectile weapons, one needed an enchanted weapon. He didn't have one, so he gave up on shooting and put away his bow.

The casters countered with magic. Gazef braced himself mentally to resist, but just then his horse screamed, rearing back and pawing the air with his hooves.

"Whoa! Easy, boy!" Gazef frantically pulled the reins in and leaned forward to grab hold of the horse's neck. That split-second action saved him from falling. The sudden panic sent a chill down his spine, but he managed to suppress it. He had more important things to worry about.

Breathing heavily, irregularly, Gazef spurred his horse, but he wouldn't budge. It was as if he had some other master who was more important than the one on top of him. Psychic magic—they'd put a spell on his horse. Gazef must have resisted it, but his horse was no magical creature; there was no way the animal would've been able to resist.

He dismounted, irritated with himself for failing to foresee such an obvious attack. His men rode carefully around him, parting to either side.

"Captain!" The riders at the tail end of the group slowed down and held out their hands. They meant to pull him up onto one of their horses. But an angel bent on not letting him get away flew over faster. Gazef took aim and whipped out his sword.

A sturdy swing.

The strongest man in the kingdom brandished his sword, and it had the force to cut through anything. Though he cut deeply into the angel's flesh, however, it wasn't enough to kill it.

The blood it coughed up dispersed as a puff of the same magical energy that made up its body.

"I'm fine! Turn around and charge!" After giving the order, he glared sharply at the angel that had gotten away. It was seriously wounded but was still raring for a fight and looking for an opening to attack him.

"I see." Something had felt off when he'd brought his sword down, and he realized now what it had been. Some monsters took very little damage unless a weapon of a specific make was used. Angels had that power. That's why it'd been able to take that blow without falling.

In that case— Gazef gathered the power within him and used the martial art Focus Battle Aura. His blade began to glow faintly. Taking advantage of the opening, the angel brought down its crimson sword, but—

"You're too late!" To the strongest warrior around, it was way too slow. His sword flew. This slice couldn't even be compared to the previous one—he ripped easily through the angel's body.

Its structure collapsed, and the angel melted into the air. The way its feathers glittered as they disappeared was like a captivating illusion. If he weren't in such a hopeless situation, enveloped in the stench of blood, he might have marveled, but his focus was already elsewhere.

Gazef scanned to see where the next attack would come from, and a wry smile played across his face—the number of enemies had increased. In the couple of moments he'd taken his eyes off of the battlefield at large, the enemy had gathered, along with their angels. It was clear that they'd achieved it by no ordinary means.

"Dammit, you can do anything with magic!" He cursed the casters who could perform feats impossible for a warrior like they were trivialities, but calmly counted them and confirmed that it was all the members who had been encircling the village.

So the village was no longer surrounded.

"Okay, Sir Gown, I'm counting on you."

His heart filled with joy for being able to save the lives, which had seemed beyond his grasp, but he remained on guard and stared down the enemy.

The sound of pounding hooves grew louder in Gazef's ears—his men had turned and were charging.

"I thought I told them once the circle started contracting we were going to retreat. Those idiots… I'm so damn proud of them…"

Gazef ran like the wind.

This was perhaps their biggest and only chance. Judging from the speed of the riders, their opponents would probably concentrate their magic on them to prevent them from getting closer. That would give Gazef the opportunity to turn this into a melee battle. That was the only thing he could do.

His men's horses screamed and threw their front legs into the air like his had. Some of the men fell and groaned. Then, the angels attacked.

His men and the angels were evenly matched in terms of strength, but when it came to basic and special abilities, his men were overwhelmingly inferior. As he expected, half of the angels ganged up on them. It wasn't only that—the spells the casters lobbed into the fray created a definite power gap.

One after another, his men fell to the ground.

Gazef ran, not even looking to confirm what he already knew.

His aim was the commanding priest. Not that he thought killing him would make them back down, but it was the only way he and his men would survive. In response to his charge, more than thirty angels moved into his path. That proved what a serious threat they felt he was, but it didn't make him a bit happy.

"You're in my way!" He engaged the ace up his sleeve. The heat from his hand wrapped around his entire body. He flesh went beyond its limits and he achieved hero level. At the same time he simultaneously unleashed multiple martial arts—the equivalent of magic spells for a warrior.

He glared at the six angels leaping for him: "Sixfold Slash of Light!" It was a martial art performed at a godly speed, over in a flash. One swing, six slashes. The six angels around him were cut in two and disintegrated into specks of light.

From the Slane Theocracy's side came alarmed voices—from Gazef's men, cheers.

His arm was prickling after using such a major art, but he could tell the pain was at a level where his muscles hadn't deteriorated.

As if ordered to cut the cheering short, a new group of angels headed for them right away. One of them broke off and came swinging at Gazef.

"Instant Reflex!" The moment the angel's sword came down, the spell activated and Gazef moved in a blur. Before the angel's sword could rip through him, he'd dispatched the angel with his. In one blow, the angel turned into specks of light.

Gazef's offensive didn't end there. "Flow Acceleration!" In fluid motions, he slashed through the angels coming toward him.

He'd taken down another two angels after using a major art. Seeing their captain pull off a feat that would be impossible for a normal person began to give the men hope that they could do it, that they could win.

But the theocracy wasn't about to allow that. Their taunts drowned out the hopeful aura.

"Superb. But that's all. Priests who've lost angels, summon the next! Bombard Stronoff with magic!"

They'd been approaching hope but were plunged back into despair.

"Not good," Gazef spat as he dispatched another angel. There were no more cheers even when he got a kill. His men all swung their swords with fretful looks on their faces.

Manpower, gear, experience, individual strength—on almost all accounts, they came up short, and now they had lost their main weapon, the hope that they'd win.

Gazef dodged the swords that came down around him unconsciously and then hammered back at the enemy. He was definitely making angels disappear with each swing, but there were still so many.

He would have liked to anticipate the help of his men, but magical weapons were necessary to cancel out the angels' defensive ability. Without being able to use Focus Battle Aura, like Gazef, they didn't have magical weapons, and therefore even if they could hurt the angels, they couldn't do fatal damage. That was a problem.

Gazef bit his bottom lip and just kept swinging.

How many times had he made the words *death in one blow* true? He'd used Sixfold Slash of Light so many times he'd surpassed his previous record.

A warrior of Gazef's caliber could normally use six martial arts at once. With his last resort in effect, that went up to seven. He was using one to boost his strength, one to boost his mind, one to boost his magic resistance, one to temporarily enchant his weapon, and one when he attacked for a total of five.

The reason he wasn't reaching the limit was because using a strong art took the focus of multiple normal ones—Sixfold Slash of Light, in particular, took the concentration of three. Even Gazef only had two other major arts, one that used all his focus and one that used the focus of four normal arts.

By making good use of his arts, he was able to easily defeat the angels. But they were only summons, anyway. If he didn't take out the summoner, there would just be more summoned. Biding his time until his opponent ran out of magic was one strategy, but Gazef would probably be out of energy before that happened.

In actuality, his arms were starting to feel heavy and his heartbeat was becoming irregular. Instant Reflex would take his body thrown off-balance by the previous attack and force it to return to attack stance. That made it possible for him to attack immediately, but the forced posture changes were a large burden on his body.

Flow Acceleration temporarily increased the speed at which his nerves worked, so he could attack faster, but extreme exhaustion was mounting in his brain.

And on top of all that, he was using Sixfold Slash of Light. It was too big a burden on his flesh. But if he didn't use it, he'd be overtaken.

"As many as you got, bring 'em on! Your angels are nothing, you bastards!" The roar meant to overwhelm them froze the Slane Theocracy side for just a moment. Almost immediately, however, a composed voice broke the tension.

"Pay him no mind! The beast is just barking, trapped in his cage! Ignore it and keep chipping away at him! Just whatever you do, don't approach—the beast has long claws."

Gazef glared at the man with the scar. If he could take down that commander, the course of this battle would surely change immediately. The problem was the angel at his side, different from the ones with the flame swords. That and the seemingly insurmountable distance and the defenses that were put up again and again.

He was far away. He was so far away.

"The beast is trying to break through the fence. Show him how futile that is!" The man's composed voice bothered him.

Even if he'd entered the hero realm, Gazef had specialized in martial arts for close combat, so he didn't have much of a chance at range. *So what? That's the only path left to me, so I just have to take it.* Strength returned to his eyes, and he set off running. But the path was as difficult as he'd imagined.

The angel's burning swords stabbed and slashed at him. He countered instantly upon evading but was suddenly assailed by a sharp pain, like he'd taken a heavy blow to the gut.

Sensing the direction, he looked up and found a caster casting some kind of spell. "If only you guys used healing magic like priests are suppose—" His words were drowned out by the shock waves that pummeled him to the ground.

He was confident that if there were fewer, even if they were invisible, he'd have been able to dodge them by sensing the atmosphere and watching his opponents' eyes. But when there were more than thirty, he couldn't handle them all. It was all he could do to shield his sword arm and face.

A pain so terrible it seemed like he'd never get up ran through his entire body. There were so many places that hurt that he couldn't tell where, specifically, he was injured. "Gyaghh!" Unable to stand the taste of iron building in his throat, he coughed up fresh blood. The high viscosity caused it to string down his chin.

Gazef was still staggering from the round of invisible shock waves when the angels came at him with their swords. The blows he couldn't dodge hit his armor and were luckily repelled, but the shock that transferred through still hurt. He swiped sideways at one angel, but it easily evaded his unbalanced attack.

His breathing was rough, and his hands shook. The intense fatigue filling his entire body whispered that he should just lie down and rest.

"The hunt is in its final stage. Let's give the beast a rest. Don't let up with your angels—take turns attacking!"

He tried to catch his breath, but the angels surrounding him followed their commander's orders and came at him swinging. He dodged an attack coming from behind and blocked a thrust from the side with his sword. The jabs from flying angels overhead he took with the harder parts of his armor. He couldn't attack enough times to keep up with the ones he had to fend off.

The fatigue and his dwindling muscular strength made killing one angel per swing almost impossible at this point. He barely had enough energy to use martial arts.

His men were all defeated, and the enemy was concentrating their attack on him. He couldn't break through their circle. He could sense that death had sidled right up behind him.

A moment's negligence would find him on his knees, and he tried to put some fight into his body.

The shock waves pummeled him again as he frantically endured. His eyes swam. *No!* He put all his body and soul into his back and legs, but it was as if something somewhere were broken—the energy he could have sworn he was putting in seemed to leak out.

Suddenly he felt the prickle of meadow grass on his skin. That was proof that he had fallen. He panicked and desperately tried to stand, but he couldn't. The encroaching angels' swords chanted *death*.

"Finish him. Gang up so the job gets done beyond doubt."

I'm going to die.

His muscular arms trembled like jelly, and he couldn't even lift his sword. But he couldn't give up. He clenched his teeth so hard they made a horrible grinding sound.

He wasn't afraid to die. He knew that just as he had taken many lives along the way, one day he, too, would die in battle.

As Ainz said, he'd made enemies. Their hatred had turned into a blade that one day had to be thrust into his gut.

But he couldn't accept this, this attacking of multiple villages and killing of innocent people who had no way to fight back. All that just to trap him? That made him sick—he couldn't lose his life to people like that. And he couldn't stand not being able to save himself.

"Grahhhhh! I'm not that easy!" he screamed and gave his body all he had. Drooling a mix of spit and blood, he slowly got to his feet.

The determination of a man who shouldn't have had the power to stand, standing, caused a momentary retreat among the angels who had closed in.

"Ahhhhgh-ahhhgh." Just standing had Gazef out of breath, made his head spin; his body felt like it was made of lead. But he couldn't lie down. It just wouldn't do.

And it wasn't that he sympathized with the pain of the villagers who had died. "I'm captain of the Royal Select! I love and protect this country! I can't lose to bastards like you who would defile it!" *Gown will protect the villagers. So my job is just to take out as many of these guys as possible to reduce, even just a little bit, the chance that more people meet this fate.*

He would protect the future of the country by protecting its people. That was all.

"It's precisely because you spout fantasies like that that you'll die here, Gazef Stronoff," the enemy commander taunted. "If you had just forsaken the people in this borderland, this wouldn't have happened. You life is worth more than several thousand villagers' lives. Surely you must realize that! If you really loved your country, you would have left them to die."

"You and I...will never see eye to eye. Let's do this!"

"What do you plan to 'do' in that state exactly? Quit your futile flailing and die quietly. I'll take pity on you and kill you painlessly."

"If you don't think...I can do anything...then why don't you come over here...and take my head? In this 'state'...it should be pretty easy, no?"

"Hmm. So you can still talk the talk, huh? You seem to want to fight, but do you stand a chance?"

Gazef just stared ahead, clasping his sword in trembling hands, focused on his hateful enemy even as his vision seemed about to blur. He was so focused he couldn't even see the angels surrounding him ready to attack.

"...Such a pointless endeavor. You're just too foolish. After we kill you, we're going to kill the surviving villagers. All you've done is bought them more time to be tormented by fear."

"Heh...heh-heh...," Gazef laughed in response, a grin spreading across his face.

"What's so funny?"

"Gah… The foolish one is you. There's someone in that village who is stronger than me. His power is so unfathomable I'm not sure all of you would be enough to take them… There's…agh…there's no way you'll be able to kill the villagers if he's protecting them."

"Stronger than the kingdom's most powerful warrior? You think a bluff like that will work on me? That's the height of stupidity."

Gazef smiled faintly. *What will Nigun look like when he meets Ainz Ooal Gown?* That thought would be a good souvenir for the next world.

"Angels, kill him." The beating of countless wings sounded over his heartless words.

As Gazef was about to make a run for it, prepared to die in the process, he heard a voice right next to him:

"Seems about time I swap in."

The scenery before Gazef changed. He was no longer on the crimson-dyed plain. He was in the corner of some kind of humble dwelling with perhaps a dirt floor.

His men were scattered around him and villagers were there, looking at him with concern.

"Wh-where am I…?"

"This is a storehouse that Lord Ainz put a magic barrier over."

"The headman…? I don't seem to see Sir Gown…"

"No, he was here up until a moment ago, but you appeared right where he was."

So it was your voice in my head…

The tension he'd been desperately trying to maintain went out of his body. He'd done everything he could do. The villagers rushed over to him as he collapsed to the ground.

The Six Scriptures… Even the kingdom's strongest warrior couldn't beat them. But no one thought Ainz Ooal Gown would lose.

Chapter 5 The Ruler of Death

Chapter 5 | The Ruler of Death

1

No traces remained of the deadly battle that had just occurred on the plain. The blood dampening the grass was hidden by the setting sun, and the scent of it was dispersed on a capricious wind. There were two figures standing there who had seemed to come out of nowhere.

Captain Nigun of the Slane Theocracy's Sunlit Scripture turned to look at them, bewildered. One appeared to be a caster; he concealed his face with a strange mask and wore unrefined gauntlets. As if to prove his high status, he was wrapped in an extremely expensive-looking raven-black robe.

The other was completely covered in raven-black full plate armor. It was a magnificent suit, not one a person could find just anywhere. He could guess from looking that it was a first-class magic item.

The newcomers had appeared in the place of Gazef right as Nigun and his men had had him cornered. And now, Gazef and his men were gone. It must have been some kind of teleportation magic, but Nigun couldn't think what spell it might be. Two unknown individuals using magic he'd never heard of—he couldn't be too careful in this situation.

Nigun had all the angels fall back and form a wall to protect him and the others; they took a bit of distance from their new adversaries. Then, he stayed on his guard to see what they would do. The magic caster took another step forward.

"How do you do, people of the Slane Theocracy? My name is Ainz Ooal Gown. Feel free to call me Ainz." His voice crossed the distance on the wind. When Nigun didn't say anything, the stranger Ainz continued. "And behind me here is Albedo. First of all, I'd like to make a deal with you, so might I trouble you for some time?"

Nigun searched his memory for the name Ainz Ooal Gown, but nothing came up; it was possible it was fake. For the time being, he decided to go along with their story and get some information. Having made that decision, Nigun gestured with his chin to continue the conversation.

"Marvelous... It seems as though you're willing—thank you. Very well, there is one thing I must say up front and that is you cannot win against me."

His tone of voice contained complete certainty. He wasn't bluffing or talking crazy; Ainz believed what he said from the bottom of his heart.

Nigun furrowed his brow slightly.

This wasn't the kind of thing one would say to Slane Theocracy elite.

"Ignorance is a pitiful thing. You'll have to pay for yours."

"Hm, I wonder about that... I've been watching the whole fight. The only reason I came is because I was absolutely certain I'd win. Don't you think I would have forsaken that man if I thought I couldn't beat you?"

He makes sense.

A caster should have other ways to approach the situation. Arcaners, sorcerers, and wizards generally wore only light armor. For that reason, they had a better chance of winning if they avoided close combat and used Fly to shoot Fireball or some other spell from a distance. So for him to come and meet them face-to-face meant he must have some trick up his sleeve.

How did he interpret my silence? Ainz continued speaking. "Now that you understand that, I have some questions. First, a little something I'm curious about: The angels with you appear to be tier-three summons magic flame archangels—is that right?"

Why are you asking if you already know?

Paying no attention to Nigun's bewilderment, Ainz went on. "It seems like you're summoning the same monster as from *Yggdrasil,* but I'm curious if you call it the same name or not. Most of the monsters in *Yggdrasil* have names from mythology; I'm pretty sure many angel and demon names are from myths. The most common source of angel and demon names is Christianity. It feels very unnatural for there to be 'archangels' here when you don't have Christianity. It would seem to indicate that there are others like me in this world."

I have no idea what he's going on about. Annoyed, Nigun countered with a question of his own. "That's enough talking to yourself for now. Time to have you answer a question of mine. What did you do with Stronoff?"

"I teleported him into the village."

"...What?" He hadn't even been expecting a reply and the confusion showed in his voice—he realized why. "You fool. If you lie, all we need to do is search the village an—"

"It most definitely is not a lie. I just answered when you asked, although there is a reason I told the truth."

"To plead for your life? If you don't want to waste my time, I'll consider it."

"No, no, you misunderstand. Actually, I was listening to your conversation with Captain Gazef. You guys have a lot of gall." In reply to Nigun's ridicule, Ainz's tone and vibe changed. "You declared you would kill the villagers that I took the time to save. Does that strike you as a very nice thing to do?"

Ainz's robe flapped dramatically in the wind. The same gust maintained its force and blew through Nigun and his group as well.

The wind blowing over the plain had just happened to come from Ainz's direction, that was all. Feeling the chilly wind all over his body, Nigun cleared away the thoughts that had popped up in his head. *That wind didn't actually smell like death... It was just my imagination.*

"That's some big talk, caster. And what about it?"

Although he was feeling a bit overwhelmed, he maintained his taunting attitude with a sneer. The commander of one of the Slane Theocracy's ace special-ops units, the Sunlit Scripture, Nigun, was not going to be fazed by one guy—no—he couldn't afford to be.

But...

"I mentioned a deal before. How it goes is you surrender your lives without a fuss, and this won't hurt a bit. If you refuse, the penalty for your foolishness is the pain and despair that you'll die in."

Ainz took one step forward.

It was only one step, but he looked huge now. The members of the Sunlit Scripture took a step back, overawed.

"Ahh..." From near Nigun came a handful of hoarse voices—they were scared.

This presence was unbelievably overwhelming. Nigun himself had never been so overawed, so he could understand his men's fear. Even the courageous Nigun, who had made it through many a life-or-death situation and taken countless lives, felt like he was going to be crushed by the pressure exerted by this unknown caster, Ainz. It probably affected his men even more.

Who the heck is this guy?!

What is this caster really? What kind of face is under that mask?

Ignoring Nigun's panic, Ainz's ever coolheaded voice continued. "Here's the reason I told you the truth: I don't care if I tell you because you're going to die anyway." He slowly stretched out both hands and took another step forward. He looked a bit like he wanted a hug, but the sinister curve of his gauntlets gave the impression of a magical beast that was about to strike.

A chill ran from the tips of Nigun's toes to the top of his head. He'd had this feeling before—a premonition of death.

"Angels, charge! Don't let him get any closer!" Nigun shouted orders in what turned out to be more of a hoarse shriek.

He didn't do it to improve morale. He was just scared of Ainz Ooal Gown coming toward him.

Two flame archangels attacked at his command. Flapping their wings, they flew through the sky, slicing through the wind. After making a beeline for Ainz, they thrust their swords without a hint of hesitation.

Albedo will probably step out in front of him. That's what everyone was thinking, but they couldn't believe their eyes. Not because something happened—just the opposite.

They didn't do a thing.

Ainz took both swords without moving a muscle. He didn't use magic, evade, get shielded, or defend; he didn't do a single thing but get stabbed.

Surprise turned to ridicule.

His presence, how strong he was—it had all been just talk. It wasn't that Albedo hadn't tried to protect him—surely the angels had just been too fast. Once their jig was up, these two weren't so tough.

Nigun sighed in relief along with his men in spite of himself. Feeling ashamed for his earlier panic, he looked toward Albedo. "You wretches, trying to fool me with those ridiculous bluffs..." Then, a question formed. *Why hasn't Ainz's corpse fallen to the ground?* "...What are you doing? Pull the angels back! Shouldn't he have fallen by now?"

"W-we're ordering them to pull back, but..."

Hearing his subordinate at such a loss, Nigun snapped his attention back to Ainz.

The angels were flapping their wings hard. They were like butterflies trying to escape a spider's web. Two of them slowly parted to either side. But they were moving unnaturally. They moved away from each other as if someone were forcing them. And then Ainz, who had previously been hidden in their shadow, was clearly visible in the gap.

"I told you, didn't I? You can't win against me. You should take people seriously when they warn you." His quiet voice reached Nigun's ears.

For a moment Nigun couldn't believe what he was seeing.

Ainz was standing there perfectly fine despite swords sticking out of his chest and gut.

"No way..." One of Nigun's men groaned what he himself was thinking. Judging from the position and angle of the swords, Ainz should be fatally wounded, but it didn't even look like he was in pain.

Of course, that wasn't the only surprising thing.

In Ainz's outstretched hands he held the necks of the two angels. They were struggling to escape, but he wasn't letting go.

"This can't be...," someone mumbled. Angels were summoned monsters, and their bodies were made up of the summoner's magical energy, but that didn't mean they were light. They weighed slightly more than an adult human male, plus they were wearing heavy armor. It would be no easy feat to hold that up in one hand. Maybe a muscle-bound warrior who had gone through the most rigorous training would eventually be able to do it, but the man before them was a caster, which meant that rather than muscle, he had poured his efforts into increasing his wisdom and magical energy. Even if he were using magic to increase his strength, if the base number were low, the effect wouldn't be so great.

So why would he do it? And more than that, why is he fine with two swords sticking out of him?

"This has to be some kind of trick."

"O-of course! There's no way he could be unharmed with two swords stuck in him!" Shouts went up in a flustered panic. As a special-ops unit, they'd been to the brink of death many times and survived harsh battles, but they'd never seen anything like this. It would have been impossible even for the angels they summoned.

As Nigun's and his men's confusion deepened, a calm, even voice of someone who must not have been experiencing pain reached their ears. "Greater Physical Damage Immunity—it's a passive skill that makes me immune to damage from low-level monsters and weapons that don't have a ton of data. It can only nullify attacks from up to level 60. In other words, any level above that and it wouldn't have any defensive effect whatsoever; I'd take damage like normal. It's all or nothing...but it seems like it's been pretty useful, huh? Now, then, these angels are in my way."

Ainz took the two angels he was holding and smashed them into the ground with tremendous force. He'd put so much power into it that it felt like the earth shook along with the slamming noise.

The angels died, turned into countless particles of light, and disappeared. Naturally, their swords also disappeared.

"I thought if I could figure out the reason the angels are named the way they are, I could figure out why you can use *Yggdrasil* magic, but I guess I won't worry about that right now."

Nigun's opponent straightened up slowly, still muttering nonsense. That nonsense was part of his mysterious horror. Nigun swallowed hard.

"Okay, have you had your fill of this dull child's play? I take it you refuse to make a deal with me. So now it's my turn."

Ainz the angel killer straightened his posture and stretched out his hands, as if to show he wasn't carrying anything. In the uncomfortable silence, his words felt infinitely loud. "Here I go! This is a massacre!"

Nigun felt like he'd been stabbed in the back with an icicle and wanted to throw up. He felt something that as a veteran slaughterer he'd never felt before.

We should retreat. Fighting with Ainz without knowing for sure we can win is too dangerous.

But he dismissed that gut feeling. They'd had Gazef cornered a moment ago; they couldn't just watch their prey get away now.

Ignoring the warning from deep down, he shouted orders. "All angels, attack! Now!"

All the flame archangels abruptly headed for Ainz.

"You guys really like to play, huh? Albedo, fall back," Nigun heard Ainz's awfully calm and collected voice say in the midst of the angel attack. He didn't seem the least bit anxious about having no way to escape the angels that were bearing down on him from all directions.

It seemed like he was about to be skewered by countless swords, but before that could happen, he cast a spell: "Negative Burst!"

The earth rumbled below them.

All at once, a wave of black like the reverse of light with Ainz at its center swallowed up the area. The pulse took all of a moment, and the results of it were instantly clear.

"This... This can't be!" Somebody's voice was carried on the wind. The scene before them was that unbelievable.

There had been more than forty angels. They were all obliterated by the wave of black light.

It hadn't been counter magic to cancel the summons. The way the angels had been blown away by the black wave meant damage. In other words, he'd wiped out the angels with damage-dealing magic.

A violent chill went through Nigun's entire body. Gazef Stronoff flitted across the back of his mind, along with the words he'd said:

"Gah… The foolish one is you. There's someone in that village who is stronger than me. His power is so unfathomable I'm not sure all of you would be enough to take him… There's…agh…there's no way you'll be able to kill the villagers if he's protecting them."

The words matched the scene before his eyes.

That can't be possible! Nigun dismissed Gazef's words from his head and frantically talked himself down. The strongest group he knew of was the Black Scripture, and their members could wipe out angels. So all he had to do was keep in mind that Ainz was at least as powerful as them. Even if he was Black Scripture–level strong, with their numbers they should be able to take him.

But could a Black Scripture member wipe out an angel with just one spell?

Nigun shook his head and cleared away his questions. He couldn't ask that now. If he realized the answer, he wouldn't have any way to proceed. So he put his hand on his breast pocket and took courage from the magic item inside.

He was convinced that as long as he had that, they'd be all right.

His men, who didn't have that support, were coping in a different way.

"Yea-yearrrrrgh!"

"What the hell?!"

"He's a monster!"

Upon seeing that their angels were useless, they began shooting off any spell they felt they could rely on, shrieking all the while:

"Charm Person!"

"Iron Hammer of Righteousness!"

"Hold!"

"Fire Rain!"

"Emerald Sarcophagus!"

"Shock Wave!"

"Stalagmite Charge!"

"Open Wounds!"

"Poison!"

"Fear!"

"Curse!"

"Blindness!"

They threw all kinds of spells Ainz's way.

Through the hail of magic, he kept his relaxed attitude. "As I thought, these are all spells I know. Who taught them to you? Someone from the Slane Theocracy? Or someone else? There are just more and more things I want to ask."

A being who can kill angels in one shot and can't be harmed with magic...

Nigun felt like he was trapped in a nightmare.

"Eaaagggghhhhhh!" Driven mad by the ineffectiveness of their magic, one of his men took out a slingshot and, emitting a strange scream, launched a pellet. Nigun wondered what effect that could possibly have against a guy who was fine being run through with two angel swords, but he didn't stop him.

The heavy iron pellet flew straight toward Ainz with enough destructive force to easily break a human's bones.

Suddenly there was a sound like an explosion.

One moment.

It only took one moment.

They were in the middle of a battle, so it wasn't as if they'd looked away. Yet there was Albedo, who should have been behind Ainz, standing firmly in front of him. *Did she teleport?* In the place where she had been standing, some dirt was scuffed into a mound where she had kicked off. That strange sound had been the impact...

Moving in a blur, she swung her bardiche in a full arc. It left behind a neat, sickly green afterglow.

A beat later, the man who had launched the pellet crumpled to the ground.

"...Huh?!"

No one could grasp what they had just seen. *Our side attacked, so how come our man got taken out?!*

Another subordinate ran over to confirm the man's status (dead) and cried, "A-an iron pellet cracked his head open!"

"What? An iron pellet? …You mean the one he just launched?!"

He shot it, so how did it kill him? A voice on the wind delivered the answer.

"Sorry about that. My subordinate here used a couple skills, Missile Parry and Counter Arrow, to reverse the attack… It seems like you had some defensive magic up to block projectiles, but if the counterattack is stronger, the barrier would break, right? It's nothing to be surprised about." Having said just that, Ainz ignored Nigun and the others and turned to Albedo. "But Albedo, you know a projectile that puny wouldn't hurt me. You didn't need to—"

"But Lord Ainz! To do battle with you, Supreme One, they must at least meet some minimum threshold of attack. That pellet… It was too great an insult!"

"Ha-ha! If we said that, though, they'd be completely disqualified. Right?!"

"P-principality observation! Engage!"

Responding to Nigun's hoarse voice, an angel that hadn't budged the whole time spread its wings. Principality observation was a fully armored angel. In one hand it carried a mace with a large pommel and its other hand was equipped with an oval shield. Its legs were completely hidden by long skirtlike *hitatare*.

The reason this angel, stronger than an archangel, hadn't moved until now was its special ability. Appropriate to its name "observation," it had the power to raise its teammates' defense just by watching. However, this ability would get canceled if it moved. So having principality observation stand by was the wisest choice.

The fact that Nigun had given it orders showed how shaken he was. It was as if he were grasping at straws, not even caring what could be done as long as something was.

"Albedo, fall back."

The angel took its orders and flew immediately to Ainz. Without losing any momentum, it began beating on him with its sparkling mace. Ainz took it straight on with his gauntleted left hand, seeming put out by the hassle.

These blows should have broken his arm, but they didn't seem to affect Ainz. He remained unperturbed as he took two, three hits.

"Sheesh... I guess it's time for a counterattack now? Hell Flame!"

From the tip of his extended right hand's finger sprang a small black flame, flickering faintly as if one breath could extinguish it. It caught on to principality observation but was laughably tiny compared to the angel's gleaming body.

However...

With a whoosh, principality observation went up in flames. The resulting heat was so intense that Nigun and his men, even at a distance, couldn't keep their eyes open.

Within the roaring blaze that threatened to burn up even the heavens, the angel's form melted and disappeared. It happened all too quickly. Then, having burned up its target, the black flame also faded away.

Nothing was left behind. It was as if both the angel and the black flame had never been there at all.

"Th-that's absurd..."

"In one shot...?"

"Eeeegh!"

"How can that beeee?!"

Nigun's yells mingled with the chorus of confused voices. He didn't even realize he was shouting. He was just saying whatever came to his mind. He had no sense of how loud or shrill he was.

Principality observation was a high-level angel. Furthermore, its ratio of ability points for attack to defense was 3:7. It had the highest defense of all the principalities that could be summoned on the same tier of magic.

Plus, Nigun had a talent that strengthened any monsters he summoned. The effect wasn't huge, but the powers of monsters he summoned were stronger. That meant that there were not many people who could defeat a principality observation summoned by Nigun.

And to do it with just one spell—he'd never seen anyone capable of something like that in his life. That was impossible even for the members of the Black Scripture, who were near the limits of human potential as far as Nigun understood them. In other words, Ainz Ooal Gown's power was superhuman.

"Impossible! That can't be! There's no way you can destroy an elite angel with just one spell! What kind of monster are you?! Ainz Ooal Gown—how could I not have heard of you before? What the hell is your real name, you bastard?" He'd lost all semblance of composure. All he could do was scream his inability to acknowledge what had just happened.

Ainz spread his hands apart. The gleam of the setting sun made them look stained with blood. "Why didn't you think it was possible? It seems to me that maybe you're just ignorant. Or maybe it's just how things are in this world? Allow me to answer one of your questions." Everyone quieted down in anticipation, which caused Ainz's voice to sound extra loud. "My name is Ainz Ooal Gown. It's not a pseudonym."

This wasn't the answer they'd wanted, but Nigun could sense the pride and joy coming through in every word. It all left him speechless. A mysterious answer from a mysterious stranger—it made sense in this messed-up situation.

Nigun felt like his shallow breathing was obnoxiously loud.

The wind blowing over the plain was obnoxiously loud, too. His heartbeat felt abnormally loud. Someone's heavy, irregular breathing sounded like they'd been doing sprints.

He thought of various ways to console himself, but the sight of Ainz taking both of those swords, the sight of him wiping out all of those angels with one spell, etc., drowned it out with, *He's more of a monster than I ever could have expected. I can't win.*

"C-Captain, wh-what should we do?"

"Figure it out yourself! I'm not your mother, dammit!"

The frightened look on his subordinate's face after being yelled at brought Nigun back to reality. He couldn't lose composure in the face of this unknown monster.

As the sun set, darkness swallowed the world bit by bit. And along with it, the jaws of death seemed to open, ready to swallow everything up. Frantically suppressing his fear, Nigun gave orders.

"Defense! Anyone who wants to live, buy me time!" With trembling hands, he took a crystal from his breast pocket. The chains of fear bound his normally quick subordinates and their movements became sluggish. Even a soldier who wasn't afraid of death would hesitate when asked to act as a shield against such a monster, but he had to get them to buy him some time nevertheless.

Two hundred years ago, when an evil spirit had been terrorizing the continent, a single angel was said to have destroyed it. Sealed in this crystal was magic to summon that most powerful angel. It had the capacity to take out an entire city with ease.

Nigun had no idea what it cost or how much effort was needed to summon this angel, but if he could kill this unfathomable foe, Ainz Ooal Gown, then it would be worth it. More than anything, they'd all be doomed if he didn't use the crystal and then Ainz stole it. Those were the excuses he used in his head. In reality, he was just scared to become a lump of meat like the many beings he'd slayed.

"I'm going to summon the highest-level angel! Buy me time!" Dangling that carrot perked his men right up.

Their flame of hope blazed, and Ainz must have noticed, but he didn't do anything to stop it. He was just muttering things Nigun couldn't understand. "So he has a crystal with magic sealed inside…? From the sparkle, it doesn't seem to be super tier. And it's probably an item we had in *Yggdrasil,* so…the highest-level angel would be…seraph class? Albedo, use some skills to guard me. I highly doubt it would be a seraph a sphere, but even if it were a seraph the empyrean, we'd have to fight with all we've got. Or…I wonder if it could be a monster specific to this world?"

While Ainz stood, unmoving, the crystal glittered in Nigun's hands as it broke down as crystals did when used. Then, it was as if a sun that had been trying to hide suddenly appeared at ground level. The plain was filled with an explosive white light and a faint scent tickled everyone's nostrils.

The legendary angel of whom tales had been told throughout the ages arrived before him and Nigun reacted joyously. "Behold, the noble dominion authority!"

The angel was a cluster of sparkling wings. Inside, a hand was holding the symbol of sovereignty, a scepter, but besides that there were no legs or a head or anything else. Its appearance was certainly strange, but no one could doubt that it was holy—from the moment it showed itself, the air was purified.

Before this supremely good being, Nigun's subordinates' emotions exploded and they burst into applause.

This will be able to kill Ainz Ooal Gown.

It's his turn to be scared.

Know your folly before the power of the gods.

Faced with the object of their delight, it was all Ainz could do to string a few words together. "That's it?! This is you getting serious? This angel…is the ace up your sleeve?"

Ainz's astonishment banished Nigun's insecurity from earlier; he started to even feel pretty good. "Yes, that's right! This is the highest-level angel—I know you can't help but be frightened. Normally it'd be a waste to use something like this, but I took the liberty of deciding you were a worthy adversary."

"What the heck…?" Ainz slowly raised a hand and put it over his mask. Nigun could see the gesture only as stemming from despair.

"Ainz Ooal Gown. I summoned the highest-level angel against you—I respect you as an opponent. Take pride in that! You are a tremendously powerful caster!" He solemnly shook his head. "Honestly, I'd like to welcome you as a brother. It would be great to have someone as powerful as you for an ally…but forgive me. My orders this time don't allow for that. But we will remember you, the caster who forced us to summon the highest-level angel."

In response to Nigun's admiration came a cold voice. "This is truly… ridiculous."

"What?" Nigun couldn't comprehend what had just been said. From his point of view, Ainz was nothing more than an offering to this angel. But he seemed far too relaxed…

"Albedo, I'm sorry...for actually taking precautions against this kids' stuff. You even used some skills for me..."

"It was nothing, Lord Ainz. If you consider the possibility that something more than we were expecting could have been summoned, it makes sense that we should try to lower the chance you would be injured as much as possible."

"Hm? Well, you're right, of course. Even so, I can't believe that this is all they could muster. I'm stunned."

The two of them were giving off the strong indication that even bothering with Nigun and his men any longer was absurd. Nigun began to get hot under the collar. "How can you act this way before the highest-level angel?" he bellowed at them as they chatted in a leisurely manner, ignoring it. His delight was canceled out by their overwhelmingly superior attitude and his previous insecurity and fear returned. *Ainz Ooal Gown couldn't possibly surpass even the highest-level angel, could he?* "No! It can't be! It can't be! It cannot be! No one should be able to beat this angel! It even beat an evil spirit! No human can win against this angel—you must be bluffing! This has to be a bluff!" Nigun no longer had the means to control his emotions.

He couldn't accept that there could be an enemy of the Slane Theocracy who was stronger than their strongest angel. Nor could he accept the fact that that enemy was standing in front of him. "Use Holy Smite!"

There was a realm of magic humans could never reach: tier seven and above. In the Slane Theocracy they were able to use some of those spells by performing large-scale ceremonies, but a dominion authority could use them on its own. It wasn't the highest-level angel for nothing.

The spell Nigun asked for, Holy Smite, was a tier-seven spell. In other words, it was a spell of ultimate power.

"Okay, okay. I won't budge, so bring it on. Will you be satisfied, then?" Ainz's response was totally easygoing, as if he were yielding at a stop sign.

That attitude frightened Nigun.

This angel was the strongest being on the continent, possessing ultimate power—it had even defeated an evil spirit. *There shouldn't be any way to take it out.*

But what if there were?

What if the mysterious caster before me right now could do it?

That would mean that this man is far stronger than an evil spirit.

How could such a powerful overlord exist?!

In response to its summoner's wish for an all-out attack, the dominion authority's scepter shattered. The shards began slowly revolving around the angel.

"Aha. A once-per-summons special ability that amplifies spell power? It seems dominion abilities are also the same as in *Yggdrasil*..."

"Holy Smite!"

The spell was cast and a column of light shone down—at least, that's what it looked like. With a roar, the pale, pure light enveloped Ainz as he held a hand up like a visor.

The seventh tier—this was a spell impossible for a human to cast.

Beings of evil would be "cleansed" by absolute purity. Even if they were good, they would meet the same fate. It was just a difference of whether a little bit of them would be left over or they would be completely expunged. That's what a spell that transcended human potential could do. It would be strange if it *couldn't* do something like that.

...But Ainz was fine.

The monster had neither been expunged, nor fallen to the ground, nor burned to a crisp, nor anything else—he was standing there on his two feet. He was even cackling.

"Ha-ha-ha-ha-ha! Just what I'd expect from a spell cast by a being strong against evil... So this is what it's like to take damage? This is pain, then. I see, I see. But even in pain I can think clearly and my movements are not inhibited." The column of light faded despite not having done much of anything. "Marvelous. Yet another experiment completed." His voice was unconcerned—no, it actually sounded content somehow.

Realizing that, all Nigun and his men could do was twitchily grin.

There was, however, one person who was furious.

"You lower...you base scuuum!!!" A shriek cut through the air. Its source, Albedo. "You lower life-form bastaaards! How dare you cause our loved and respected master, Lord Ainz—the man I love, the man I suuuuper love—to be in paaain?! Know your place as garbaaage! Death is a fate too merciful for youuu! I'm going to give you the maximum pain that exists in this world and mess with you till you go insaaane! I'm going to burn your limbs off with acid, make minced meat of your man bits, and force-feed it to youuu! When you recover, use magic to heal him! Aaaah, I hate you! I hate you, I hate you, I hate you so much my heart feels like it's going to explode!" Her armored arms flailed.

It felt like the world was warping around that spot. The sign of something twisted by an evil faith in death battered them like a bomb blast. It was wriggling violently beneath that full suit of armor. Something big was trying to burst through. Even though Nigun could see that was the case, there was nothing he could do but stand there stock-still and watch as a monster that would surely sully the world was born.

There was only one person in the universe who could stop Albedo. He quietly raised a hand and said, "Albedo, it's fine."

Even just that was enough to stop her short.

"B-but Lord Ainz! The lower life-forms, they—"

"It's fine, Albedo. Aside from the unexpected fragility of their angels, everything has been going pretty much according to my plan. So why get angry?"

Hearing those words, Albedo put a hand over her heart and bowed her head. "You're always right, Lord Ainz. It's so fitting that you would have such a carefully laid plan. I am deeply impressed."

"No, I mean, I'm glad you were anxious for me and got mad, but... Albedo, you're more charming when you smile."

"Tee-heeeee! Ch-cha-charming! Ahem. Thank you, Lord Ainz."

"Well, then, sorry to keep you waiting."

Nigun, who'd been going numb watching how carefree they were, came back to himself at this address. "I know what you really are! Evil spirits! You're evil spirits!"

Nigun had practically no knowledge of beings who could do battle with high-level angels. There were the six gods, which included the one he believed in; the kings of dragons—the most powerful race—dragonlords; the legendary monsters who were supposedly so strong that one could take out a country, nation breakers; and evil spirits.

It was said that the Thirteen Heroes defeated the evil spirits and sealed them away. It made the most sense to Nigun to consider that blast just a moment ago the seal on an evil spirit being broken.

And if they were evil spirits, Nigun still had a slight hope that it would be possible to defeat them, as long as he had his angel.

"Again! Beat him down with Holy Smite!" *Ainz said he'd felt pain last time. So maybe he took damage? He's standing, but maybe that's all he can manage.* Innumerable *maybes* occupied his mind. If they didn't, it would surely break.

But Ainz wasn't about to let him attack twice.

"It's my turn, isn't it? Know despair: Black Hole!"

A tiny dot appeared on the dominion authority's glimmering body. Before everyone's eyes, it grew bigger and bigger—a vacuum.

It sucked everything in.

Soon nothing was left and it had gone so laughably, stunningly easily.

With the brilliant dominion authority lost, the light in the area dimmed all at once. The wind rushing over the plains, rustling the grass, seemed to echo. In the midst of the silence, a hoarse voice spoke. "What *are* you...?!" Nigun asked the impossible being again. "I've never heard of a caster by the name of Ainz Ooal Gown. But then, there can't be someone who can take out the highest-level angel in one shot. It would be wrong for such a person to exist." He shook his head weakly. "All I know is you're vastly stronger than evil spirits. It doesn't make sense... What ar—?"

"I'm Ainz Ooal Gown. Once this name was known by all. But I think that's enough chatting, don't you? Any more than this and it'd be a waste of time for both of us. To prevent further time wasting I'm going to let you know ahead of time that I've cast anti-teleportation magic around here and

I have men waiting to ambush you throughout the area, so know that escape is impossible."

The sun had sunk completely below the horizon and the land was wrapped in darkness. Nigun felt like this was the end, and it was obvious that that was the case.

Suddenly space broke over his crouching men—like a clay pot shattered. But it was back to normal in an instant, leaving no trace of the abnormal view.

As Nigun floundered for an explanation, Ainz gave him one. "Sheesh, you should be grateful. It looks like someone was trying to monitor you with intelligence magic! Luckily, I was within range and my attack wall activated, so I don't think they managed to get more than a peek. Sheesh, if I'd have known this would happen, I would have linked it with a higher-level attack spell..."

Those words were a revelation for Nigun. His home country must have been checking in on him periodically.

"If I only use Explosion boosted to have an increased area of effect, they might not learn their lesson... Anyhow, that's enough fooling around, I think."

Realizing what he meant, a chill went down Nigun's spine. The taker of lives' life was about to be taken. And he was so scared he couldn't stand it. Just like everyone whose life he had taken so far, he was terrified to have his life stolen away. The eyes of his subordinates gathering on him was bothersome.

He felt like he might start to cry.

He *wanted* to cry and scream and beg to be spared, but Ainz didn't look like he was big on mercy. So he held back his tears and groped frantically for a plan. But no matter how much he thought, there was no one to support them. In that case, all he could do really was depend on Ainz's mercy.

"W-wait! I'd like you to wait a moment, sir— Lord! Lord Ainz Ooal Gown. Please wait! I want to make a deal! I swear you'll come out ahead! I'll pay you whatever you want if you'll spare our lives—no, even just my life!" In his peripheral vision he could see his subordinates staring agape at him, but they were no longer his concern. What was important now was his own life, nothing else.

Besides, his subordinates were replaceable, whereas he was not. He ignored their resentful voices and continued. "It must be hard to satisfy such a great caster as yourself, but I will match your desired amount as closely as possible. I may not look it, but I'm quite a valuable asset to my country. I'm sure they would pay an exceptional sum. Of course, if there is something you would prefer besides money, I could arrange that as well! So please, I beg you, spare my life!" Having said all that in one breath, Nigun gasped a few times. "S-so, how about it, Lord Ainz Ooal Gown?"

In response to Nigun's desperate supplication came a soft, friendly woman's voice. "Did you not refuse Supreme Being Lord Ainz's most merciful offer earlier?"

"But—"

"I get what you're saying. 'Even if I took that deal, I would've been killed! I want to live!' right?" The suit of armor's helmet moved in a way that all but said, *Good grief.* "That attitude is plain mistaken. Lord Ainz wields the power of life and death in Nazarick, so when he says you will die, you lower life-form humans bow your heads and wait for the end, full of gratitude." She spoke in a tone that said she believed every word from the bottom of her heart.

She's insane. This woman has no means of rational thought—she's completely bonkers. Fully realizing this, Nigun turned to Ainz with a glimmer of hope.

Ainz had been silently listening to their conversation up to that point, and when he realized they were waiting for his decision, he shook his head with a "sheesh." "Let's see, I think it went something like... 'Quit your futile flailing and die quietly. I'll take pity on you and kill you painlessly.'"

2

Night had fallen on the plain. Walking along, Ainz looked up and noticed again how full of pretty stars the sky was.

Maybe I went a tad overboard.

As long as Albedo was watching, he couldn't do anything clumsy. As master, he had to carry himself properly in front of his servant. Partly due to that, he might have gotten a little too carried away, but still, he'd been playing his part as if his life depended on it.

So did I pass or not? As long as she's not disappointed in me...

Ainz didn't know she was thinking, *Holy cow, you were so cool, Lord Ainz! Tee-hee-hee-hee-hee!* beneath her close helmet, so he ran over again in his head how he had acted that day.

"But Lord Ainz, why did you save Gazef?"

I wonder... He didn't feel like he could accurately explain the workings of his heart at that moment, so he said something else instead. "It was a problem we brought on them, so I figured we should be the ones to solve it if we could."

"Then, why did you give him that item?"

"That was strategic planning. Him having that was handy for me, too."

The item he'd given Gazef was a cash store item from *Yggdrasil*—one Ainz had quite a few of. He didn't think he'd be able to acquire any more, but giving one away this time was not a major loss. On the contrary, Ainz was happy for their number to decrease.

Those items were consolation prizes for the five hundred–yen gacha, so having so many just reminded him how he'd wasted all his money and ended up poor. But that wasn't all. After pouring so much cash into it and finally getting the super-rare item he'd been after, his former guildmate Yamaiko got it on her first try. The shock from that still remained in his mind as a hairline crack.

He'd thought to throw them away many a time, but when he remembered that each one had cost five hundred yen, he couldn't just chuck them.

"Well, I could have used that item or not, but either way was no loss for me, so..."

"Wouldn't it have been better for me to wipe them out? There was no need for you to go save that lower life-form... I didn't sense any truly formidable signals in the area. I don't think there was any reason you needed to go personally."

"I see..." Ainz didn't have this signal detector built in, so that was all he could say.

In *Yggdrasil*, he could tell roughly how strong an enemy was compared to him by the color its name was displayed in. He could also get information from walk-through sites or his guildmates' intelligence magic.

It was a little bit nostalgic.

I should have learned some intelligence magic. Ainz regretted not having those abilities. Of course, he wasn't sure if it would function the same here, but he probably wouldn't have had to take risks like he had that day.

Well, it's no use crying for the moon. Ainz decided to think about something else.

"Albedo, I know how strong you are and I trust you, but you shouldn't take things so lightly. Consider the possibility that someday an enemy could defeat me. That's especially important now when we don't have much info about this world. That's why I had Gazef do some work for me out there."

"Aha, so you sacrificed a pawn to test the strength of your enemy. Truly, that is the proper use for the inferior human race." He couldn't see her expression under her close helmet, but the tone of her voice was cheery as a flower garden.

He'd been wondering for a while, but as a former human, current undead, Ainz wanted to know if she really hated humans that much.

Not that he felt sad or lonely because of it. On the contrary, as the captain of the floor guardians in the Great Tomb of Nazarick, the headquarters of a guild made up of grotesques, it was probably the correct attitude. It seemed that way to him anyhow.

"That's right, but of course, that's not all. If you reach out to help someone when they're on the verge of death, they'll be extra grateful. Also, since the enemy we were up against was a special-ops unit, even if they were to go missing, their country probably wouldn't be able to launch a high-profile search for them, so I felt like if I had the chance I wanted to intervene."

"Ahh, I'm impressed as always, Lord Ainz. Such deep thoughts… I suppose that's why you captured the commander and his men alive? Brilliant."

Hearing Albedo's praise, Ainz felt like bragging. He *was* making quick decisions and engineering plans with no inconsistencies or impossibilities. *Maybe I'm executive material after all?* he was thinking, all self-congratulatory, until he heard Albedo's concerned voice.

"But Lord Ainz… I wonder if perhaps taking both of those angels' swords was not the best course of action…"

"Oh? I figured I had confirmed that Greater Physical Damage Immunity was working using those knights outside the village when we first arrived in Carne."

"Yes, that is as you say. I witnessed it with my own eyes. However, it is unforgivable that you should have been stabbed with their vulgar blades while I was standing by right next to you."

"Ah, you're right. I acted without thinking of you, even though I was having you protect me. Sor—"

"And what woman could approve of her love being stabbed, even if he were unharmed in the end?"

"Um, indeed." Never knowing what to say in these situations, Ainz gave a short reply and headed back toward the village. Albedo didn't particularly seem to want a reply and followed him without saying anything else.

When they entered the village, everyone came out to greet them, led by the death knight. In the midst of their countless praises and thanks, Gazef Stronoff appeared.

"Oh, Captain. Glad to see you up and about. I would have liked to save you sooner, but that item I gave you takes a little while to warm up. I apologize things got so down to the wire."

"Not at all, Sir Gown. I am grateful. After all, you did save me. By the way, what happened to…?"

Sensing a change in his tone of voice, Ainz took an inconspicuous look at him. He had already taken off his armor and was dressed lightly in regular clothes, completely unarmed. His face was covered in bruises and one of his eyelids had swollen up—his head seemed just like a misshapen soccer ball—but his eyes twinkled.

When Ainz looked away slightly, as if it were too bright, he spotted a ring on Gazef's left ring finger.

He's married… I'm glad we didn't make his wife cry! Ainz thought as he continued his act. "Oh, I drove them off. I figured it would be impossible to take them all out, and I was right."

That was a lie, of course. He'd sent them all to the Great Tomb of Nazarick. Gazef squinted for just a moment, but neither of them said anything. The atmosphere was tense.

Gazef was the one to end it. "Wonderful. You've saved us from danger so many times now, Sir Gown. However can we thank you? You must stop by my manor if you are ever in the capital. I would like to give you a proper welcome."

"Oh? Well, then, I may take you up on that, thank you."

"You won't come with us now, then, I take it? What are your plans, Sir Gown? My men and I will rest here."

"I see. As for me, I intend to head out, although I haven't decided where I'll go yet."

"It's already night. Traveling in the dark is..." Gazef trailed off. "Please excuse me, Sir Gown. You're strong enough that you don't need me to worry about you. I hope you'll remember me if you come to the capital. My gates will always be open for you. And I don't have words enough to thank you for allowing me to have one of the suits of armor from the knights who initially attacked Carne."

Ainz nodded and judged that everything he had come here to do was finished. Somehow or another, a lot of unexpected things had happened and he had stayed longer than he meant to.

"Let's go home," he said in a voice only Albedo could hear. She nodded happily in response, although she was still wearing her armor, of course.

Epilogue

Ainz's luxurious private chamber was ornately furnished and had a crimson rug. Normally it was covered with a veil of silence, but on this particular day, it was so quiet the silence could be heard as its own sound. The maid who normally stood by was gone, leaving only Ainz, Albedo, and a death knight standing at attention in the corner holding a sword.

Albedo's voice sounded sweet like honey, so it didn't spoil the atmosphere. "Allow me to report: The commander of the Slane Theocracy's Sunlit Scripture that we captured near that village has been sent to the ice prison. The plan is to have an officer of intelligence gathering get information out of him."

"If you're getting Neuronist to do it, that's no problem. But you know I want to experiment on the corpse, right?"

"Yes, my lord. Then, we are currently appraising the gear we stripped off the knight-looking things, but I have heard none of the items are very enchanted. I imagine we'll put everything in the treasury when we're done."

"Sure, that seems appropriate."

"Lastly, as a precaution, we've sent two shadow demons to that village. How should we handle Gazef Stronoff?"

"Leave the captain alone for now. More importantly, Carne is our only outside foothold and the only place we've managed to build friendly relations. We may rely on them for cooperation in the future. Do your utmost to avoid ruining that connection."

"Understood. I'll make sure we do. Well, then, it was brief, but that was my report."

Ainz thanked her and took a closer look. She always wore a gentle smile, but today's was different—she seemed to be in a nearly uncontainable good mood. The reason was on her left ring finger being stroked by her right hand—a Ring of Ainz Ooal Gown. Where she wore it was up to her, but it wasn't hard to guess why she put it on that finger.

If those were her genuine feelings, as a man, Ainz might have been glad, but her feelings were the result of his fiddling. Guilt smoldered in his heart.

"Albedo, the love you have for me is something I warped. It's not how you really feel. So..." *What else should I say? Would manipulating her memories with magic be the right way to handle this?* Ainz faltered and couldn't say anything more.

Albedo, still smiling, asked, "How was I before you changed me?"

A bitch.

Not that he could say that, though, so he wasn't sure how to explain things. He looked calm on the outside, but inside he was frantically searching for a solution. Albedo, watching him, was again the first to speak: "In that case, I prefer my current self, so you don't have to fret about it."

"But..."

"But?"

Ainz was silent. He was getting some kind of unfathomable sign from her, as she continued to smile.

Since he wasn't speaking, she continued. "There's only one thing that's important." Ainz was waiting for her to continue, and she spoke in a sad voice. "I'm not a bother to you, am I?"

He opened his mouth and gazed at her face. Her words gradually sank into his brain—not that he thought he had one—and finally understood what she was trying to say. He hurried to her defense. "N-no, not at all." He wasn't upset about being loved by such a beauty. For now.

"So then, it's fine, isn't it?"

"Um..." It didn't seem to be, but he couldn't come up with a way to convince her.

"It's fine, isn't it?" she repeated.

Ainz definitely sensed something strange but asked as his last resort, "I distorted the backstory that Tabula gave you! Don't you want to get the real you back?"

"I'm sure Tabula Smaragdina would forgive you as a father forgives his daughter for becoming someone's bride."

"Y-you think so?"

Is that really what he was like?

As Ainz was pondering that, there came a clatter of metal. When he looked in the direction it came from, there was a long sword on the ground. The death knight who was supposed to have been holding it was nowhere to be found. It had just been summoned a little while ago.

"Monsters summoned in the usual way return after their time limit is up... From the way the sword from this world fell to the floor, their gear was not a bond that would allow them to remain in this world. In that case, when using a corpse as a base for the summons, it doesn't return because the tie to this world is stronger? If we had a pile of corpses we could use them to fortify Nazarick."

"Then shall I gather a pile of corpses?"

"Let's not go digging up Carne's graveyard or anything."

"Understood. But we should come up with an idea how to gather a large amount of corpses. Now, then, if the death knight has vanished, it must be almost time for the meeting. Please come with Sebas. I'll go on ahead."

"Oh? All right, Albedo. See you later."

Having left Ainz's chamber, Albedo saw Sebas walking her way. "Sebas! Perfect timing."

"Oh, Albedo. Is Lord Momonga in his chamber?"

"Yes, he is." She felt slightly superior because Sebas was still calling him Lord Momonga.

Sebas raised an eyebrow. "You seem to be in a good mood. Did something nice happen?"

"Kind of." Knowing about the name wasn't the only reason she was happy. She was remembering her previous conversation with Ainz. She'd said "bride" and he hadn't refused her or evaded. In other words… Her gentle expression twisted to become impure even for how evil she was. She would never wear that sort of smile in front of Ainz.

"Tee-hee-hee-hee-hee! I can get him. I'll show her. I will be the one seated at his side! Shalltear can have a place to stand." She whispered her aims not as captain of the floor guardians, but as a woman, and clenched her fists. "My succubus blood is boiling!"

Sebas looked on, a bit disgusted.

Ainz arrived in the Throne Room accompanied by Albedo. A great many beings were there, down on one knee to express their loyalty. No one moved; it was so still not even the sound of breathing could be heard. The noises were Ainz's and Sebas's footsteps and the clacking of the Staff of Ainz Ooal Gown on the floor.

Ainz climbed the stairs and sat on the throne. Sebas, of course, stopped at the foot of the stairs and kneeled behind Albedo.

Having seated himself, Ainz silently surveyed the scene stretching out before the stairs. Almost all of the NPCs had gathered. The best part of this was seeing everyone all together; there were so many different beings it was like a parade of demons. He wanted to applaud once more the imaginative power of his guildmates who had brought all this forth.

Looking over everyone, he noticed a few people missing, but that was unavoidable. The ultra-giant golem Gargantua and Guardian of the Eighth Level Victim couldn't get away. Not that it was to make up for their absence, but there were more than just NPCs gathered. There were many high-level minions, no doubt painstakingly selected by the floor guardians.

Even so, the Throne Room was so spacious it felt a little empty. The Throne Room was the heart of the Great Tomb of Nazarick and its most important area, so he understood why people would hesitate to admit minions, but he thought the rule could be relaxed a bit more.

But that's a matter for another time. Ainz decided to address it at a later date and opened his mouth to speak: "First, I'm sorry I acted on my own," he apologized in a voice that didn't sound like he felt sorry at all. This was just for appearances; what was important was that he apologized. He'd acted at his own discretion, but he didn't want those beneath him to think he didn't trust them. "Ask Albedo what happened while we were gone, but there is one thing I want to tell all of you here right away. Greater Break Item!" Ainz cast a spell that could destroy magic items of up to a certain level. One of the big flags hanging down from the ceiling fell to the floor. The crest on it was Momonga's.

"I changed my name. From now on, call me…" Ainz pointed his finger and gathered everyone's eyes. "Call me Ainz Ooal Gown, Ainz for short." His finger was pointing to the tapestry behind the throne with the guild's crest. He struck the floor hard with his staff to get everyone's attention. "Anyone with objections, stand and say so."

No one had anything to say in response. Albedo spoke, beaming. "We have heard your honorable name. Hail, Lord Ainz Ooal Gown! To you, most noble one, Ainz Ooal Gown, we of the Great Tomb of Nazarick pledge our absolute loyalty!"

Then the guardians joined in. "Hail, Lord Ainz Ooal Gown! The one who brought the Supreme Beings together was you. To you we devote everything.

"Hail, Lord Ainz Ooal Gown! You are a king who wields horrific power. All beings must know your greatness!"

The NPCs' and minions' cheers echoed across the Throne Room.

Bathing in the praise, Ainz thought, *Mates. What would you think of me monopolizing our proud name for myself? Would you be happy? Or would you furrow your brows? If you have an opinion, come and tell me. Tell me it's not my name alone. When that time comes, I'll gladly return to being Momonga.*

He looked out at everyone below him. "I'm going to give a strict order now, a guideline for our policy going forward." Ainz paused for a few moments. Everyone's expressions had tensed. "Make Ainz Ooal Gown an enduring legend!" He thrust the Staff of Ainz Ooal Gown into the floor with his right hand. The second he did, the colors from each of the jewels began to come out and shimmer in the air. "Where there are many heroes, crush them! Because Ainz Ooal Gown is the greatest hero. Make it known to all living creatures. If we come up against someone stronger than us, then make it known by something besides strength. If we come up against a mage who has a large number of men with him, then choose some other method. We're still in the preparatory stages, but we must work toward the great day that will surely come. We must make it known that Ainz Ooal Gown is the greatest!"

He wanted to spread his name and get it into every ear in this world. His old friends, the guild members of Ainz Ooal Gown, were supposed to have quit, but there was still a possibility they might be here. That's why he wanted to get to the legendary point where everyone knew his name.

On the earth, in the sky, and over the sea—all sentient beings must know. Then, it just might reach a former guild member. Ainz's voice, brimming with ambition, was powerful enough so that everyone in the room could hear. Everyone bowed their heads, so in sync that the motion was audible. Their attitude could be called *prayer* or *worship*.

The throne looked a little lonely once Ainz had left, but excitement was still high in the Throne Room. Receiving orders from their absolute ruler and getting started on their tasks all together lit a flame of passion in each of their hearts. Especially zealous were the ones who had received a direct order.

"Everyone, raise your heads." As if tugged by Albedo's soft voice, everyone whose head had stayed bowed looked up. "Each one of you who has received a direct order, follow it humbly. Now, we have something important to discuss." Her eyes never left the Ainz Ooal Gown tapestry behind the throne. The NPCs and minions behind her looked at it, too. "Demiurge, please tell everyone what Lord Ainz told you."

"Understood." He was still kneeling like everyone else, but his voice carried so all present could hear. "This is what Lord Ainz said to me while gazing at the night sky: 'Perhaps the reason I came to this land was to acquire this untouched box of jewels,' and then he continued. 'No, I shouldn't monopolize it. The Great Tomb of Nazarick, my friends in Ainz Ooal Gown, should be adorned as well.' The 'box of jewels' here is this world. So here we see his true intention." Demiurge smiled, but not warmly. "The last thing he said was, 'Taking over the world does sound kind of fun.' Which means…"

Something glinted in all of their eyes—the color of their determination.

Albedo slowly got to her feet and surveyed everyone's faces, and they all gazed back at her, keeping an eye on the Ainz Ooal Gown tapestry behind her as well. "Comprehending Lord Ainz's true intention and preparing to fulfill it is proof of our loyalty and the mark of able subjects. Know that our ultimate goal is to give this world, this box of jewels, to Lord Ainz."

Albedo grinned ear to ear, turned around, and smiled at the tapestry. "Lord Ainz, we will make this world yours without fail." Her voice echoed as she continued. "We will give all this world has to offer to its true ruler, Lord Ainz!"

OVERLORD
Character Profiles

Character 1

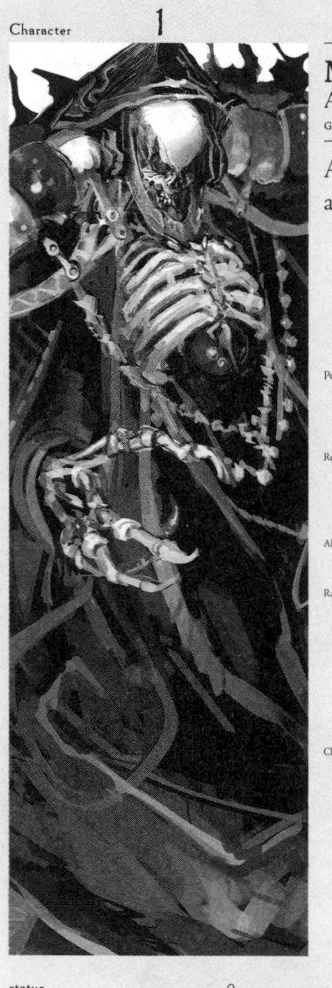

Momonga

Ainz Ooal Gown

GROTESQUE

A caster with ultimate power who appears as a skeleton

Position — One of the 41 Supreme Beings; Ruler of the Great Tomb of Nazarick

Residence — His chamber in the Great Tomb of Nazarick's ninth level

Alignment — Extreme-Evil (Karma Points: -500)

Race Levels — Skeleton Mage — lv 15
Elder Lich — lv 10
Overlord — lv 5
Etc.

Class Levels — Necromancer — lv 10
Chosen Undead — lv 10
Etc.

[Race levels] + [Class levels] — 100 levels
● Race levels Class levels ●
40 acquired total 60 acquired total

status 0 50 100

Status
Comparative ratio on a scale of 100

HP (Hit Points)
MP (Magic Points)
Physical Attack
Physical Defense
Dexterity
Magic Attack
Magic Defense
Total Resistance
Special

Character 2

Albedo

GROTESQUE

A merciful, snow-white demon

Position — Captain of the Floor Guardians in the Great Tomb of Nazarick; primary wife of Momonga/Ainz (self-styled)

Residence — Throne Room; a room on the ninth level

Alignment — Extreme-Evil (Karma Points: -500)

Race Levels — Imp — lv10

Etc.

Class Levels — Guardian — lv10

Blackguard — lv5

Unholy Knight — lv10

Shield Lord — lv5

Etc.

[Race levels] + [Class levels] — 100 levels

● Race levels — Class levels ●

30 acquired total — 70 acquired total

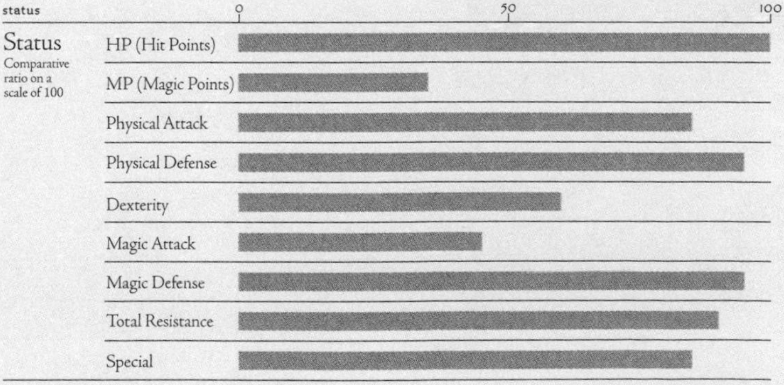

status

0 — 50 — 100

Status
Comparative ratio on a scale of 100

HP (Hit Points)

MP (Magic Points)

Physical Attack

Physical Defense

Dexterity

Magic Attack

Magic Defense

Total Resistance

Special

Character 3

Aura Bella Fiora

HUMANOID

An expert tamer with an unyielding spirit

Position — Guardian of the Sixth Level in the Great Tomb of Nazarick

Residence — A giant tree on the sixth level

Alignment — Neutral-Evil (Karma Points: -100)

Race Levels — None, because she's humanoid

Class Levels — Ranger — lv 5

Beast Tamer — lv 5

Shooter — lv 5

Sniper — lv 5

High Tamer — lv 10

Etc.

● Class Levels

100 acquired total

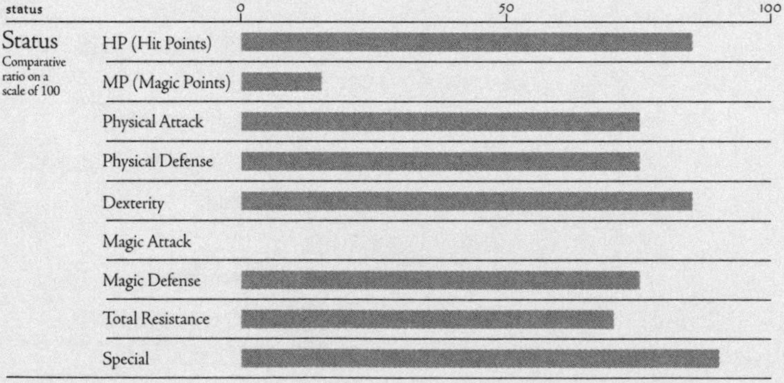
status
0
50
100
Status
Comparative ratio on a scale of 100
HP (Hit Points)
MP (Magic Points)
Physical Attack
Physical Defense
Dexterity
Magic Attack
Magic Defense
Total Resistance
Special

Character 4

Mare Bello Fiore

HUMANOID

Wimpy ambassador of the forest

Position — Guardian of the Sixth Level in the Great Tomb of Nazarick

Residence — A giant tree on the sixth level

Alignment — Neutral-Evil (Karma Points: -100)

Race Levels — None, because he's humanoid

Class Levels — Druid — lv 10

High Druid — lv 10

Nature's Herald — lv 10

Disciple of Disaster — lv 5

Forest Mage — lv 10

Etc.

● Class Levels

100 acquired total

status

Status
Comparative ratio on a scale of 100

0 — 50 — 100

HP (Hit Points)

MP (Magic Points)

Physical Attack

Physical Defense

Dexterity

Magic Attack

Magic Defense

Total Resistance

Special

Afterword

To you who are reading this afterword, nice to meet you. I'm the author, Kugane Maruyama.

This book is a version of the *Overlord* I first released on the Web, revamped with new characters, deleted scenes, and other edits. Thank you very much for buying it. If you are just flipping through, I'm sending vibes so you'll take it to the check-out counter. *Hrmmm.*

The protagonist of this story is a great caster skeleton and the leader of a large evil organization—no matter how you look at him, he's pretty much a final boss. So this is a great book for people who can't believe that the heroes in books and movies save people for free, never put their own interests first, etc. Maybe! It's pretty nasty.

This work has been out for quite a while on the Web, but I added some pretty major new characters for the book version. I really hope you like them.

Anyhow, this is the afterword, but to be honest, I don't have much to write here. So please allow me to say some thank-yous:

To the editor I gave so much trouble to, F-ta, and to so-bin, who provided the fascinatingly beautiful illustrations: I'd like to give a special thanks.

And to Code Design Studio, who made the amazingly cool cover, and to Osako for correcting so many proofs: thank you so much.

Then, a thank-you to the people who sent me their impressions of the Web version and to all those who read it. If you hadn't thought it was interesting, it probably would never have gotten turned into a book.

Also to my friend from college Honey, who checked the manuscript for inconsistencies and unclear spots: I'll bother you again, so thanks in advance.

Finally, a thank-you to everyone who bought this book. I really hope you think it's a fun read.

By the way, I'm planning even more edits, added text, and new scenes for Volume 2. It's practically going to be a whole new book, so I'm already sobbing about how little time I have to finish it. Please stick around!

Okay, I think I'll leave off here. Thank you so much, again! I hope you'll continue reading.

Well then, see you.

KUGANE MARUYAMA
July 2012

Profile

Author Profile ——————— Kugane Maruyama

Having given up his dream to be a writer, he worked as a normal company employee, but when his tabletop RPG group declined when the members got too busy, the frustration of those stymied ambitions combined with his desire to write the best story he could, which led to him posting *Overlord* online in 2010. It became popular with some kindhearted people and got made into a book. In other words, he's a modern-day Cinderella (although he looks like a pig wearing a suit).

Illustrator Profile ——————— so-bin

An illustrator. Switched jobs and got too busy to make any time for hobbies. Then started illustrating and ended up even busier. A pet rabbit provides comfort during the pursuit of various endeavors.

A MYSTERIOUS WARRIOR ARRIVES WITH A CASTER IN THE FORTRESS CITY OF E-RANTEL. WHAT IS THEIR OBJECTIVE? WHO ARE THEY REALLY? AND ALL THE WHILE, THE SHADOW OF AN EVIL ORDER ENCROACHES...

Who will survive
the vortex of death
in Volume 2?

I'll revise the Web version a bunch!
...is what I said, so there's no
turning back. I'll do my best!
—KUGANE MARUYAMA

OVERLORD

Volume 2: The Dark Warrior

Kugane Maruyama | Illustration by so-bin

Coming soon from YEN ON!